Marcus Bird

NAKED AS THE DAY

Copyright © 2013 by Marcus Bird

Cover design © 2013 by Marcus Bird

Author photo by Marco Vasquez

ISBN 978-0-9913239-0-6

"Fall down seven times, get up eight."

-Japanese proverb

NAKED AS THE DAY

Chapter 1

Tokyo was never a final word. It had always been a pit stop, an in-between point, a destination. It was a consideration if you will, of the panoply of excursions one can make in the fair land of the rising Sun. It was never a place to rest one's hat and call home. Tucked safely in the distance is where it always lay, safely over 'there' somewhere past Fuji, somewhere before the north got really cold. In fact, Tokyo was always an escape from the dreariness of where I am now, an ejaculation into a weekend of debauchery that usually left me winded yet still ready for work on Monday morning. I'm presently in a sleepy town somewhere in Shizuoka, spending my days walking idly through the hallways of a reasonably conservative high school, waving at my charges and counting down the hours until the workday is over. It isn't difficult work, and by all rights difficult work should never be bothersome, but the slow crawl of time during the days and the repeated actions of my daily motions started to make it all an agonizing experience.

I don't sleep very well, and often I find myself up at four or five in the morning. At that time, I slip on a pair of fuzzy slippers and slide into the kitchen. Well, if you want to call it that. My kitchen is actually a passageway from the front door to the other side of my efficiency, which serves as the bedroom, living room and entertainment room. Either way, when I'm in the "kitchen", fixing myself a steamy cup of green tea, possibly entertaining the idea of watching some derelict pornography, I usually end up staring out at the cold blackness of the early morning, listening to the neighbourhood shout silently at me. In fact this absolute silence initially frightened me. I wondered, *don't people around here get laid?* I understand the idea that people can be reasonably quiet and relaxed, but there must be a time that Mr. Kurosawa wants to give Mrs. Kurosawa a good rogering. Alas, nothing greets me in the morning, neither the frantic squeaks of who I would assume to be a reasonably sexy woman in her mid-thirties doing the dirty with her husband fresh from a sixteen hour workday. So, I ponder things like these while staring out at the sky, lying in bed and looking at the ceiling above me, thinking about new and more interesting ways to pass the time at school. Then I take a shower, slip on my work uniform and ride my bicycle to the train station. This is actually one of the more enjoyable parts of my day; the sensation of the wind of my face as the buildings fly by, that morning air crisp on my lips like cold beer, and the stark emptiness that streets have when everyone isn't up yet. Then I coast into the parking garage, lock my bike and head on the train. There I stare forward at no one really, since the same people are on the 6:30 a.m train with me everyday. There is one girl in particular I wish I could speak to. She is young, probably early twenties, with striking eyes and a face chiseled by the gods themselves. She's normally seated across from me, staring directly ahead, as am I. No one speaks, and no one interacts, save a few students who happily chat about whatever it is they talk about. For all I know they could be talking about somebody rogering someone else. But I stand there adrift in the sparse sea of morning bodies, taking an occasional peek at my goddess sitting across from me, whom I'll never speak to.

Eventually, the train comes to a stop and I get off, taking a flight of two stairs down through a turnstile that leads onto a broad road with a light outcropping of trees that follows it into the horizon. My shoes crush gravel for the twenty-minute walk to the school during which time, I pass by small houses, farm plots and occasionally, an ancient man or woman sweeping dust passionately off their porch. There is a relative truth to the westernized belief about Japanese landscaping (at least in this town) because it is humbling to walk each day on streets devoid of anything even remotely resembling garbage. As I walk, probably listening to some old mix tape on my iPod, an increasing sense of dread begins to cloak me as I near the school gates. Then I see the same thing I always see, a set of teachers outside, telling each student a hearty good morning. I walk up myself, saying the same in my most resolute voice, smiling at whoever is in the vicinity, then immediately begin grumbling upon my entry into the teacher's changing room. I am greeted with more silence in here, even worse that my neighborhood's.

At least in the neighborhood I'm lost in thoughts of an imaginary frolic between an equally imaginary and frisky couple called the Kurosawas. But here, in the dark of a changing room that smells like old, sweaty clothes, is the real silence. It is the statement made to me everyday, that the sum total of my life is this place where I put my things in the morning. A sweaty locker, thousands of miles from anything I know.

So the routine goes on. I watch the clock tick and feel my heart palpitate, waiting for four o' clock to come around so I can shout *shitsureishimasu* and run to the nearest convenience store and grab a drink. As I said before, the work is easy, and easy work shouldn't be stressful, but something is happening. The casual days, the quiet teachers and the empty voice I use to read English sentences causes my hand to tremble after a few hours. I'm roaming through dangerous territory; only it is populated by cute schoolgirls with incredibly short skirts and boys who often compensate for a lack of height by talking in a low growl. Here I am, in a 'dangerous' place slowly being driven crazy by seemingly nothing. This was fine for the first few months until I started feeling a strange nausea. The meals I brought to school were often rapidly cooked bits of chicken with loads of soy sauce and black pepper, which could be the perfect recipe for feeling a little green. But this sensation would come at ill opportune moments; on the walk to school, if I took a break and snuck up to the roof to get a little alone time, or on the way home.

My doctor told me that the blood tests they ran didn't show any abnormalities. My nausea was a ghost, fluttering invisibly around me. As time passed it worsened and naturally, I became worried. A reasonably strapping twenty-something year old man shouldn't be having these issues. I was probably sick of my environment I thought, the 'dangerous' territory of cute schoolgirls and days predicated by reading sentences aloud while fighting to stay awake. I was often regaled with stories of young men like me being accosted sexually in their schools by their female counterparts. This was always a point of interest for me. I never had an inkling of attention from any of the female teachers I worked with, particularly a very attractive one my age with a large well-proportioned pair of you know whats. So there were no sexual trysts to keep me teetering on the edge of daily excitement, just the nausea. This general malaise translated into more sleeplessness and unrest, which led to high levels of weariness. I became relatively famous at one convenience store near school, (if by fame I mean simply going there each day) because I would buy a "Big Black" coffee daily to prevent myself from falling headfirst into a sea of desks.

So the routine continues. Today I'm walking to school listening to *FutureSex/LoveSounds* and looking at the same farms, plots and old people sweep stuff as I walk to school. I say hello to the teachers and go into the locker room again, choking at the musty smell of sweat. The principal nods at me and I nod back, then I sit down at my station. Today I don't have any lessons until 9 a.m, but I need to be at school at 7.30 a.m, so I sit idly. School policy dictates there is no recreational use of computers during school time, so there's no way I can peruse interesting internet forums, troll people or checkout what's happening in the world on CNN. I bring a book with me occasionally, but if the cover is too bright or loud, it undergoes scrutiny from my assigned head teacher, who may or may not report me to my company, who may or may not request that I come in for an "evaluation", which is essentially a short reprimand that states I shouldn't read "brightly coloured books" because they might distract students visiting the staff room that may see it on my desk.

So often times I can't read, and if I do read there is a high chance the book cover of what I'm reading may potentially and forever corrupt the mind of a young child. So I tap my fingers on the desk, stare at the clock and then talk a walk through the hallways. I go past the student entrance and where the collection of the students' white outdoor shoes are arranged neatly into dozens of pairs. I walk some more, past a small recording room to my left where one industrious student comes to school almost as early as I do to broadcast the daily announcements. I trot up a few flights of stairs and stroll past some classrooms, hearing a giggle or two as a few students see me roaming. Then I walk up another flight of stairs on the third floor, which leads to a door that exits on the roof. Up there, in the distance is an unrepentant panorama of dark grey rooftops. The long white snake of a bullet train in the distance was also visible, and other than the low hum of an occasionally passing vehicle, I could hear nothing in all that space. Something in me wanted to be out there, doing something else, away from all this. The feeling boiled inside me more strongly than usual. I stepped forward, watching the train disappear into the horizon, wishing I could go wherever it was going. Then the school bell rang, signaling the start of the day. A teacher told me there was some gathering in the gymnasium, another one of those mandatory assemblies, but my blood was still boiling, the need to be elsewhere as strong as it was before. I couldn't move. Nothing in me wanted to go back down those steps and into that building. My legs were encased in steel clamps, and I reached out, seeing my hand touch the horizon, a horizon I would never fully experience once I remained here.

Then, my chest hurt. It began slightly at first, but I could feel the sensation moving across the breadth of my pectorals in a wave of knotted pain, like being pressed inwards at both sides by two vehicles. This of course freaked me out, and after enduring the needles in my chest for the rest of the day, I went to a cardiologist. He was a dashingly handsome man who spoke fluent English, to the surprise of the nurses in his employ the first time he spoke to me. My presence was somewhat of a blip in the puddle of their reality, as I saw one of the nurses give me a lingering eye as I took off my shirt, and the doctor explained my situation.

"These numbers reflect the average levels of heart activity for someone your age, and the numbers are fine," he said, shifting a perfect lock of hair away from one eye.

"The scans of your lungs from the chest scan we did also show no abnormalities, and your heart rhythm sounds normal as well," he said, pulling an x-ray out of an envelope.

"So I'm fine?" I asked.

"Yes, there is nothing wrong with you. You are probably stressed or depressed, and you need to do something about it," he said.

I paused, momentarily glancing at his overly handsome face, curious about where he learned fluent English, but more importantly how many women he had squired during his time there.

The lady who accompanied me to the doctor, a misses Yamada was part of a team of women who lived in the area who spoke fluent Japanese and English that helped us teachers out with potentially difficult stuff like going to city hall, opening new bank accounts or getting cell phones. I'd been to the doctor with her several times.

"I'm sorry you are sad," she said, looking at me through a pair of rimless glasses.

She was small, with a very slime frame, and long hair that stopped below her shoulder blades. About forty or fifty, a few delicate wrinkles around her eyes hinted that she was shifting into a more mature look, but a youthful sensuality remained in her eyes, and her voice was calm and soothing.

"When people are unhappy, maybe they should be doing something else," she suggested. "Are you unhappy here?" she asked.

We were standing outside the medical facility now, under the orange-red sky of the late evening. In the distance, I saw the silhouette of several office buildings set up on an open plot of land, making them look like toy houses.

"I don't think so," I admitted, rubbing my chest. "I was always told that if your body is under stress, it can create the most bizarre reactions. You can imagine for me, a twenty-something year old, chest pains are pretty scary."

"Yes, I can imagine," she said with her velvety voice. "Maybe you need to do something else."

I nodded at this statement and we headed into her car, a small white Subaru, and drove off. On the way back, layers of my life peeled away. The school came to me in a series of repetitive images: me sitting at the desk, walking into the locker room, reading sentences aloud in classes and saying good morning to the teachers. It was a photo carousel of memories. No longer was I in the front seat of miss Yamada's car, I was sitting in a private theater watching everything flash rapidly on a large screen synched to the backdrop of creepy calliope music. Another sharp jolt of pain ran across my chest, and I cursed slightly.

I went inside my apartment after she dropped me off, slipping between the passageway and "the kitchen", and flopped onto the bed. As usual, the neighborhood greeted me loudly with its silence. After a while I slid open the large, opaque door that led to a tiny outcropping of concrete that served as my porch. I stood there, looking out at the rooftops in the distance, seeing the last of the day's light vanish in a murky ripple on the horizon.

I tossed my clothes in a heap on the floor and put on a pair of jeans. A convenience store was a stone's throw from where I lived, and I purchased my usual poison; a cashew nut snack and a few Chu-His. I loved the taste of these wine cooler style drinks. With a few in my satchel and nothing to do, I roamed a bit, as I usually did after work. There was one main street in town with enough lights on it to warrant it being called "the strip". People were milling about; handsome boy band types inviting people into alternating eateries, rogue students, indistinguishable salary men and other residents. Three of my Chu-His were now empty, and my vision was a thin-mish mash of noise and vibrations. Glancing downward, I saw a streak of orange slide across the surface of the can as I stepped past another streetlight. I had been on this street countless times in the same manner, cans in my hand, walking nowhere and talking to no one. I looked at the sky, remembering the bloody orange sunset from earlier, and I saw miss Yamada again, her eyes lower from a furrowed brow of genuine concern, mouthing her statement about me being happy. I tossed the can into the trash. The next days visuals hit me in a torrent; me waking up at four in the morning fantasizing about the Kurosawas, me making green tea, my train ride with the beautiful mute girl, then my pit stop at the convenience store, my chugging of the Big Black coffee before I reached school, the smiling faces of the teachers, the locker room, my desk, the classes, the clock and then the walk back home. My chest surged with pain again, and I froze in mid-walk, grasping it tightly. After a few deep breaths it began to subside. I finished my last drink and tossed the can away. This town, with its one street with the lights, the one bar where the foreigners hung out and a main attraction which was a large statue of some huge fish, started to ripple and fade. The pain in my chest and miss Yamada's question made things spin and turn, and I closed my eyes for a moment. The call of something far away cawed like a crow I saw the first day I walked into the school. It was much larger than average, perched atop a light post. It had delicately confident body language, as if it was a bird that could stand akimbo. It cawed in a series of disturbing shrieks. "Yes!" it declared, "This is my world! Welcome to it!' I had held eyes with the creature as it looked on me without pity and concern from its avian throne. Sometimes I would see it in the evening when I went home, the large wings spread out as it monitored everything below; a master of its domain.

Now I heard the crow's voice again, but far away, slightly muted. Something distant was pulling me forward, shattering the mirrors of this town around me. That sometimes was Tokyo. Yes, I could feel it calling. I knew I only went there on weekends to escape the drudge of where I was, but maybe now it wouldn't just be an in-between place, it could become a *place*, a place for me. Tokyo was calling, and like the crow, I could hear it. The entire time this spiel ran through my head, I had my eyes closed, leaning on some wall near a 7-11. When I reopened them I knew what the plan was. Nothing was keeping me here. Well nothing except Yumi.

Chapter 2

Yumi would never come inside.

It was a habit of hers I found interesting, especially if she was early to pick me up to go on an excursion and I wasn't fully ready. I'd always ask if she'd like to come inside, but she would always respond a friendly "that's okay," on her cell phone and sit in her car, a gray cube-shaped Toyota, until I came out. I met her through a mutual friend at the company during training.

She was a calm individual, but her personality had an undercurrent of raging energy that came out in her eyes. If we chatted about movies or current events, her eyes maintained a flat, casual energy, keeping their soft brown hue. But should we speak about anything related to her life, they would become bright and flickering with an internal flame. She wanted to be a pianist, and had studied for many years. Then she wanted to do psychology, but gave up after deciding she didn't want to go back to school. Now she spent her days as an office lady at a small accounting firm in town. She was tall in the way I like tall women, but brutally quiet. She was my guide of sorts, a tempered segue between this new world and me.

We went to movies and parks, firework shows and to dinner with her friends. All the while, she kept a calm veneer in the face of whatever her life was, never raising her voice, always laughing with a twinkle.

Her face was slender, and fit the hairstyle she always wore, long at the sides past her ears, with the hair at the back flowing down past her shoulders. Our conversations ran the gamut, and each time we sat and spoke, I could feel a gulf between us. Real or imagined, I wasn't certain, simply because I was still steeped in the naiveté of Japanese sexual relations. We laughed, and chatted, went to salsa lessons and sat under moonlit ceremonies doing yoga, but not once did I sense a hint of sexual interest. I couldn't find it in her eyes, but more than anything, her unwillingness to come into my abode was probably what gave me that deciding assertion. I had no idea I was wrong.

There was one moment, when we went to see some fireworks in a neighbouring town. It was a thirty-minute drive to get there, in the midst of an expensive Japanese suburb, with flat, two story houses; shadowy surroundings populated with trees and slick asphalt streets. That night, as little children ran up to me and exclaimed *He's so cool!* I had some beers and noticed something with Yumi. I was sitting with a guy from England and his enviously hot girlfriend. Apart from us, Yumi sat chatting in a group of people, the overhead light of the verandah accentuating her features, turning her smiles into continuous, showy exposés. The English guy made a joke that made me laugh long and hard. While doing this I turned my head slightly to see Yumi looking at me, quietly. It was the first time I had seen something else in her eyes. Her forehead was tilted forward slightly, as she gently clasped a small can of beer in her hands. There was no smile on her face but a smirk, one which contained a message more direct than any of her smiles had ever given me. In a blink, she turned back to the people she was chatting with, while I remained staring at her, holding on to the moment.

"Yumi is very beautiful," the patron of the house said.

She was in her late thirties, with clear polished skin, and a casually attractive face. She wore a juicy couture shirt and dress shorts. Her hair was dyed brown and I could see her eyebrows weren't real. It was however, her eyes that stood out the most. They were a cloudy green, giving her the appearance of a goblin. We were standing in the kitchen, when she spoke to me, while pouring me a glass of wine.

"Do you like her?" she asked me.

"We are friends," I replied cautiously.

She paused as she poured the wine, and emitted a little sound I didn't quite understand, before chuckling.

"Why are your eyes that colour?" I asked, changing the topic.

"It is funny to me," she began. "I'm not sure why my eyes are this colour. People say to me that possibly a few generations ago, I had an ancestor who was white, and had green eyes, but how can I figure that out? I mean maybe there were Japanese people who had green eyes and they were a dying breed and I got the last of the eye genes."

"You think so? Really?" I asked.

"Well, it isn't necessarily about how true it is. It's like that Winston Churchill quote about truth, where he says 'truth is incontrovertible'. Who say there weren't a dying breed of Japanese people with green eyes?"

"I guess there isn't any way to prove it," I said, taking a sip of my wine.

"Exactly, so just like my eyes have a hidden truth in them, I can see a hidden truth in you as well."

She kept her stare at me for a second, and I immediately felt lost in her eyes, treading in dark water. She chuckled again.

"All I'm saying, Yumi is a good girl, and you are very handsome, you would have beautiful kids."

I laughed, nearly spilling my wine.

"I'm glad you are having fun," she said. "Even if nothing happens."

She walked outside and started playing with her son. Soon afterwards, everyone went upstairs to watch the fireworks from the rooftop of the house. About twenty people sat in different places, the sky dark and brooding above us. Then, hot streaks of color in the sky accompanied by resounding booms were everywhere, a million hot feathers in the night. I was sitting near Yumi, who kept remarking at how beautiful the fireworks were. She got up to go and use the bathroom. As she walked away, I followed her long sloping legs as she walked gracefully to a doorway that led downstairs. She opened the door, and through some magic of physics, the blend of the light on the roof and the light emitting from the doorway made her light yellow dress almost transparent for a brief instant. In that split second, I could see how the delicate slope of her legs continued upwards to her waist, banded by lightly coloured underwear. Her ass looked supple and smooth, and as she turned slightly to go down the hallway, I could see the faintest shadow of pubic hair through her panties. Blood rushed to my loins and I caught my breath. Then the light changed and her dress was yellow again, the door closed and she was gone. I sat there on the roof, slightly uncomfortable and surprised by the intensity of my erection. Fireworks boomed all around me, and all I saw were Yumi's thighs, sloping upwards almost forever, and her little sacred patch, which for that brief moment, was exposed to the world. Gone was my calm feeling around her. I turned back to the fireworks, seeing the sky echo in a shower of orange before turning black again. I felt a hand on my shoulder, and saw the lady from downstairs with the green eyes.

"Having fun?" she asked.

I nodded in a flush, feeling my manhood aching against my leg. She walked to another side of the roof where she sat with her husband and son. That glimpse at Yumi's body invaded my consciousness. Soon she returned and sat down. She touched my knee, sending a jolt of pleasure through my system and I stiffened once more, now genuinely worried I'd be requested to stand up.

"I find these things so beautiful," she said. "Human beings and their magnificent work, the things they create to give us little moments of pleasure."

At the time it seemed she was saying this to herself, but that slight gesture of touching my knee felt to me as if she had torn open my shirt and begun ravenously sucking my nipples. Then her hand slipped off my knee and the fantasy faded into the cavernous display of the last firework.

Unbeknownst to her, the pains in my chest had been continuing through the end of the semester, including the nausea. School and my nightly walks were a drill in the side of my head, as something invisible hammered at my chest. But I had to finish my time at the school. I couldn't see myself just vanishing at the end of that journey. I made a deal, I had signed a contract, and that had some significance. Time passed and I found myself at the end of the semester, at a mandatory government-sanctioned meeting. We had these every few months. At the last one, for some reason I was called up to speak. The details aren't clear now, but as I stood there commenting on some non-specific issue, I coughed slightly into my palm, looking at the bored, slothful eyes of the other teachers in attendance and somehow it came out of my mouth that I was leaving. The resulting response—mostly protracted coughs and a sharper sense of the noise a massive air conditioning unit behind us made—revealed the reality of my world. The sleepy town periphery had come full frontal, showing it's holiest of holies on the cover of the town's most distinguished magazine.

I wanted to slip away from it all with no goodbyes and acknowledgements, but shortly before leaving I told Yumi. The surprise in her voice was obvious. She immediately made dinner plans.

The restaurant Yumi and I went to was Italian, and we sat there, eating chicken pasta with eggplant, while Tina Turner's "Simply the Best" played over the airwaves. She had cut her hair slightly shorter, and I realized it had been sometime since I had last seen her. Her outfit was a tad more provocative than usual, as she wore a slim black sweater and a black skirt with matching leggings.

"I can't believe you are leaving," she said softly. "I—I wish you had mentioned something. I thought you would be teaching here for another year perhaps."

"Something happened," I said.

I went into the diatribes of my chest pain issues, the boredom and the nausea. After I finished, I realized how strange it was that despite many of our long conversations, it had never come up how isolated and off I had been feeling. She looked at me intensely as I spoke, and I saw that fire in her eyes again, but this time it wasn't for her. The flames flickered and danced across her irises, and as I spoke, I felt her passion reach across the table. The image of her lower body from the night with the fireworks popped into my mind again and I could feel it, another concrete erection, straining against my thigh.

"I'm sorry about that. It all sounds painful," Yumi said distractedly. She looked away, humming along to the Tina Turner song and ate some more of her pasta. It was two days to my departure, and I felt like kicking myself.

The dinner ended as it began, calm and uneventful. Before she left, Yumi gave me a kiss full on the lips. She broke it quickly, and I was surprised more than aroused by this open display of affection.

"Maybe I will see you in Tokyo," she said.

"Maybe," I replied.

She went to her car and waved at me as she drove off, signaling the true goodbye to my sleepy town.

Chapter 3

"Welcome to Tokyo motherfucker," came his voice.

I turned and smiled, seeing the tall, solid build of my friend, Zeus, whom I'd be staying with in Tokyo until I found my own place. We'd connected through a mutual friend in the best kind of way; in the dying embers of a raging bender that ended up with my friend lost, Zeus back at home unaware of where we were, and myself, curled up on a sidewalk with a plastic garbage bag as a pillow. We were at the bus station terminal, my arms sore from lugging the suitcases through the labyrinthine maze of Tokyo station. Zeus waved for a cab.

"Isn't that going to be a little expensive?" I asked.

"Please," Zeus replied, as if what I said made absolutely no sense at all. We went into the cab. Hours earlier, I'd been sitting at a bus stop, with both my suitcases beside me, looking out on the blue sky with its familiar backdrop of distant mountains. All I could see now was the tightly stacked blur of differently hued buildings, as we drove by.

"Did I leave anything behind?" I said, mostly to myself.

"Your silly job," Zeus replied flatly.

Fifteen minutes and five thousand yen later, we were at his apartment building, a sprawling erection of glass and steel. To my left I could see the Mori building, with its jagged exterior. Each time I looked on it, I imagined it to be one of those Transformers from the 80's, popping out legs and accessories, a laser gun and giant feet.

"Tokyo will be good for you," Zeus said. "It took balls for you to just come here, brass fucking balls. People like you make it here."

"I sure hope so," I replied, a little afraid I'd feel a jolt of pain in my chest. So far, I felt nothing. The lobby of his apartment building was decorated with large plants set on a long chair less stretch of black carpet. We stepped through the lobby towards a bank of elevators. As the elevator shot up, an outer section of the building with transparent glass brought the city into view, creating the illusion of flight. As the elevator stopped a voiced droned "Twentieth Floor" in sleepy Japanese. We rolled out, Zeus pulling my larger suitcase as if he had owned it his entire life. He pressed a black piece of plastic onto a small panel beside his apartment door. A clicking noise came from the wall and with a hiss, the door opened, revealing the sprawl of his apartment. The décor was supremely relaxing and functional, the walls lined with expensive furniture.

Tokyo isn't a word anymore, I thought.

"First order of business," Zeus said, after propping up my suitcase near an open closet. He stepped to an enormous black fridge and threw me a can of Asahi dry. He downed his quickly and opened another, taking another beer for me as well, even though I'd barely started my first one. He flopped on the couch.

"So what's the plan? You have any prospects lined up yet?" Zeus asked.

I felt a little twinge of fear. Not even a full hour in Tokyo, and reality was already creeping up on me. I took a sip of my beer. "Not exactly. English teaching drives me a bit crazy, I'd love to find something else."

This answer seemed to satisfy Zeus, whose eyes looked directly ahead, his brow slightly furrowed. I sensed he was in computer mode, processing some new and top-secret data. He snapped out of his trance and stood up.

"In an hour or so I'm going to go and play poker with some friends," he said.

He turned and smiled. "Don't worry, you aren't invited, I can't do that to you. You just got here and you don't live anywhere yet! The buy-in for each game is forty thousand yen."

I did the math in my head. Playing a few hands would have made a serious dent in my savings. I don't play poker, and I was happy for the non-invitation. He tossed me his spare apartment key and went to the bathroom to take a shower. I sat on the couch, or rather, my new bed, and let out a sigh. My sleepy little town in Shizuoka felt far away, a black fly in a wide sky.

It has always been said that a city can make you or break you, and guys like Zeus are the makers. The guys who get it done, ignoring the tick tock of the life clock and saying fuck it all to whoever will stop them. Once, when I snuck away from teaching to do an interview in Tokyo for a magazine job, I stayed with him for the night. When I told him what I was going to wear to the interview the next day, black slacks and a well-worn suit jacket, he shook his head to say no. Then he had walked to his closet and slid a door open noiselessly, revealing a legion of suits. He plucked one out and held it in front of me.

"Wear this."

I had slipped the jacket on, feeling a sense of power because of how well it fit my body. Despite his slightly bigger build, the suit looked tailored for me. In it I felt like a maker, ready to grab my share of the sexy *femmes* running around Shibuya with too much makeup on. That was then however, before I left an apartment and job for … whatever this is. I lay down on the couch; my head mired in thought, and slowly, everything drifted away into nothing.

When I awoke, Zeus was gone and the apartment was dark. The silhouette of nighttime Tokyo stung me in a stream of symmetry. A soft glow filled the room, yet I couldn't hear any of the melee outside. Yawning, I felt restless. I took another Asahi from the fridge. There was a note on the door, written in bold letters.

F-BAR.

It was near where we were, near Roppongi, in the neighbouring borough of Azabu-juban. At the foot of Zeus' building, I took a stroll that carried me past the Mori building, glistening in the night. I navigated through a maze of tunnels and tiny parks, following directions on my phone. Unlike the silent yell of my old neighborhood, I was regularly greeted with the hum of engines, the clicking of women's heels on the sidewalk, and the din of the rising night. Down every street and path I took there was a person, or groups of people. Coincidentally, I was wearing the jacket Zeus had given to me, with skinny jeans and black boots. After a little wrangling with the phone's map under a small overpass, I found the establishment and approached the door. A short man in a sharp suit smiled at me and waved me in. *Strange*, I thought. I was about to ask him how much to pay to get in. Inside had a cool temperature. The floor and the bar were made of what appeared to be slick marble, and a long, wide walkway stretched past a series of tables on slightly elevated platforms parallel to the bar. The place was filled with very tall, thin people. Assailed by the sea of cheek-bones, eye shadow and nervously confident energy I realized these people were all models.

I stood for a few minutes by the bar, thinking of a social strategy. The bartender waved at me and handed me a beer. Puzzled again, I thanked him, and sipped on it, watching the crowd. This environment felt vaguely familiar in the way that places that require one to schmooze always feel. The first person I spoke to was a young woman named Anastasia. Dressed in full black with a nonexistent body, 'Anastasia' had mocha coloured skin and the features of a space alien. Beside her, a girl wearing what looked like a tin foil dress with sides of her head shaved smile at me.

"I'm Mari," she said.

I wanted to ask her about her dress, but she had already trotted into the distance, running to hug a guy with David Bowie looks.

"Are you new?" a voice came from behind me.

I turned to see a short man in a lime green suit.

"Yes," I replied.

"I'm Tako," he said, shaking my hand firmly. "Nice to meet you."

He walked away into the crowd, seemingly satisfied. This must be some sort of open event, I reasoned. Why else would people give you free beer in Japan? I took a gander at the models, and mulled over the reality of the industry. To me, the modeling scene was a scene of degrees. If everyone was attractive, they were separated by degrees of attractiveness. If they were famous, they were separated by degrees of fame. It was the superficiality conundrum at work. At my spot by the bar, I met girls from Russia, Sweden, the United States and Brazil. The Brazilian girl struck me the most, as I'd never seen a Brazilian like her, with pale white skin and platinum blonde hair. When she spoke, she tilted her neck a lot, and cast her gaze at me through eyes that glowed like gem stones. Everyone kept saying, "Do you have Facebook?" immediately after saying hello. This happened with no less than ten people, which made me figure it must be a model thing because everyone said it with the same rapid inflection, regardless of what country they were from. Half the models in attendance were in town for a month or less, living at a variety of model houses in the city. The bartender had given me six beers now with no sign of stopping. The world became soft and nice again, crisp like the beer on my lips. I was also offered coke, which I politely declined.

The girl with the foil dress came over to me. "We are going somewhere else. Want to come?" she asked.

"Sure," I replied.

Outside, the first symbols of dawn were stretching their arms and yawning. The clouds were a dark purple, sending a thin film of light on the street. In front of the club, two black cabs of the same make sat idly. The girl held a large flat silver phone to her ear, chatting quickly, with concern on her face. Still speaking, she pointed at me and motioned for me to follow her with an assertive curl of her index finger. She went into the backseat and I slid into the middle, with David Bowie lookalike beside me.

"The Ana hotel," she said to the driver.

I sat there, a thin sheet of lethargy slowly covering me as I watched the streets stream by. The driver, nonchalantly looking forward with a lifeless expression on his face barely moved. I felt a hand on my thigh and looked at Mari. She looked like the other women I'd seen before, with the usual high cheekbones and a prominent, somewhat Victorian nose, but it was her eyes; they held a powerful substance to them I couldn't exactly label.

"So what's your agency?" she said to me.

"My agency?"

"Yeah who do you model for?" she said with the same intensity.

"Actually I don't model. I never have," I replied.

Her confident look vanished, replaced by a childish expression of wonder.

"What do you mean? I saw you getting drinks at the bar."

"Oh? That has something to do with models?"

"You walked in free right?"

"Uh, yeah."

She reached across my lap and tapped the David Bowie lookalike.

"Frank, he's not a model!" Mari said excitedly.

"What?" Frank replied. "Could have fooled me." Then he smiled, and I could see why he was in the industry.

"So you really didn't know?" Mari said, looking at me. She held my gaze for a while, probing. "Models get in free silly, and they also drink free at the bar."

"Oh," I said. It all made sense now.

"You have a gift, and I think gifts should be exploited," Mari said. "My grandfather told me that." She said this while looking at her phone and typing rapidly on its large touch screen.

"He was a farmer in Kyushu and he worked every day on his farm, right up until the land got hard during the wintertime. He grew all sorts of things, but he was an expert at growing onions. I tell you, they were the tastiest onions you could ever eat. If I ever had the chance to go there for a visit, I didn't want cake or cookies, I'd be sitting in his kitchen, snacking on onions. Can you imagine that? A little girl, sitting there eating onions.

"He always laughed and had a twinkle in his eye when I did this, and he told me that his gift was putting his love into the onions. Onions are bitter things, and bitter things are usually disliked, but if you can love an onion, then things are a bit brighter, he had said to me. I believed him, I could feel his love and taste it as well with each bite of every onion."

I nodded as the cab idled at a red traffic light, my eye wandering to a woman crossing the road in an incredibly short skirt. It was five a.m.

Mari continued. "So I always wondered what my gift was, and I even thought of doing farm work, but I was a real city girl in Osaka, so that wasn't for me. I grew older, and then people started looking at me *funny* you know? I didn't get it. In my mind, I'm this normal person. But people were saying, 'It's your eyes, Mari. There is something about them'."

"I didn't notice," I said with a weak smile, as sleep pinched my ribs.

"You are nice, but I know you noticed. *Everyone* notices. So for a while I felt a little insecure about it, but then I realized, this was my gift. Something about my eyes did something to people without me speaking; it was as if I had a superpower. Then I grew older and taller, and I decided to be a model.

"I didn't choose to look the way I look, with my funny eyes. But now the right people call them interesting, captivating, pertinent, intimidating, lustrous, sensual, loud, sexy, and fiery. These are words in the industry. These things *matter*, and I accepted it."

"Okay miss 'eyes', what does this little spiel have to do with me?" I asked.

She took a quick glance at her phone and giggled as she snapped a picture of herself pouting her lips into a kiss.

"It's obvious you haven't accepted things about yourself. There is something inside you, mucking up the works, like the crap that blocks old pipes."

"I can't see why you'd say that," I retorted slightly.

"Last week Leonardo DiCaprio was at F-bar. Of course, he strolled in with little to no entourage. Before that, I heard Watanabe Ken had passed through. At that place it's a stream of 'it' people and music people, then of course the models. You just strolled in. That means you have something, but you are completely clueless about it, so you haven't accepted what you have."

My neck throbbed in a pang of annoyance. Mari spoke in torrents of words that hit my forehead like water blasting from a showerhead set on high.

"Do you know Kaoru Tetsuya?" she asked.

The name didn't ring a bell. At my admission of this Mari nearly had apoplexy. Apparently the man was the new god of underground fashion design. She spoke a little longer, tell me the names of other movers and shakers, other people I'd never heard of. A full, proper day hadn't passed yet, and Tokyo already felt insistent and urgent. I could hear the crow again, cawing somewhere in the distance. The cab pulled up in front of the Ana Hotel. Mari look through the car's rear windscreen. The other cab hadn't arrived yet.

"No matter, let's go up," Mari said.

Frank had said nothing this entire time, focused mostly on his phone, smirking at it seductively. Mari mentioned to me that the person staying at the Ana was a designer, in town for the week. On the fifth floor, the room was large, with twin beds and a huge LCD TV set atop an exquisite table. She introduced me to the designer, a gay European named Boris, and then I sat in a chair facing one of two spacious windows in the room. Boris chatted to Mari and two other young men while Frank lay on the bed, still on his phone, typing to whomever. My tiredness had morphed into a little slimy monster, clutching my neck in a leaden grip.

With the exception of Frank's generally subdued state, Mari was as hyper and energetic as she was five hours before. The young men with Boris also were exceptionally upbeat despite sipping on glasses of Belvedere chased with ice at five thirty a.m. The door opened and the people from cab number two spilled into the room in a wave of frantic energy and pretty faces impervious to the effects of fatigue and time. In minutes people did more shots and someone connected an iPhone to a speaker system. Mari was dancing with Boris near the window. Frank and a girl were passionately kissing near the doorway. I assumed this must have been the girl he'd been communicating with. Everyone else was talking loudly, sitting on the floor or the bed. The guy that offered me coke earlier was there too, his eyes wide and bright, his teeth like perfectly cut white squares of cartridge paper. Frank and the girl went into the bathroom. Soon after, the sounds of their passion leaked clearly into the room. A few people laughed at this, but the mood of the gathering barely changed.

"Isn't that Anna?" one of the guys at the bed nearest to the bathroom said.

"Anna is fucking Fraaaank," a boyish looking girl in a trucker hat sang with a smile.

"Wait, didn't Anna hookup with Brian at F-Bar earlier?" the second guy said.

The group laughed, their youthful bliss echoing in my increasingly dark field of vision. Sunlight soaked the room with light, but my eyes were almost closed. Mari walked over, with a shot glass in her hand. "You need some of this," she said. I took the drink, feeling the quick burn down my throat as I swallowed it. My senses reawakened slightly, but I still felt like two thousand pounds of soggy newspaper.

"I have to go," I said, getting up slowly.

I told her I'd call her sometime and hugged her goodbye, feeling her small breasts press against my chest, my forearms feeling much bigger grabbing the frail vessel that was her body.

All the while, the echo of Frank and his girl floated over the airwaves, intermingling with the wailing sounds of progressive house coming from the speakers. Outside, the sky sneered at me indignantly, the morning light stabbing at my eyes as I looked around. I remembered the area from one of my previous Tokyo sojourns, and started the long slow walk back to Zeus' place in Roppongi.

Chapter 4

Early morning light leaked in through the slit blinds of Zeus' apartment. I walked to the couch, lay down, tossed my shirt on the ground and closed my eyes.

"Looks like you had a good first night," came Zeus' voice.
I turned to see him in the Kitchen hallway, impeccably dressed in a white striped shirt with a tie knotted so tightly on his neck I wondered how he was breathing. He stood up straight as a rod, sipping on a power shake with the gleam of ambient morning light shimmering on his designer pants.

"Yeah, welcome to Tokyo," I muttered.

"Don't worry man, I'd probably be raging my first night if I had been living in the country myself."

He glanced at his watch.

"Gods, I'm going to be fucking late. There's some Chinese in the fridge if you are hungry. Laters."

With a few clicks of his shoes, he was gone, and the apartment was quiet. I pulled the blinds open, revealing the breadth of Mid-town Tokyo. The scene was again, a revelation, in its contiguous jigsaw puzzle of differently sized buildings, highways and angry-looking electric poles spread out in a blissful sweep. Standing shirtless at the window on the twentieth floor of an upscale building, I almost felt as if I had made it.

I took a glance at my temporary new bed, the surly looking purple couch, remembering my old apartment. Images came back to mind; the flat quiet of the early mornings when I would walk into the 'kitchen', the deep exhale I would make when flopping onto my firm little futon after work, and the large plastic door that led to my 'porch'. That was all gone now, locked away in the decision to leave I had made a few weeks earlier. The airtight window gave the bustle of the world below the look of a silent film. In my mind was a brief flash of my first and only love hotel experience. Her name was Noriko, and she was an attractive hip-hop dancer. That night I had lucked out, and ended up with her in a seedy love hotel in Shinjuku. It was also an inadvertent lesson about the supposed sexual hygiene of Japanese women. I found this out sometime soon afterwards, on a slow night back home in the local foreign bar.

"Listen man, I can't stand that hairy pussy shit," a guy named Rick had said.

"Is it really like that with every Japanese woman?" another person replied.

"What are you new to Japan?" Rick said.

"Yeah, just been in town for a month now," said a young man, with a crow's nest of Sandy blonde hair on his head, wearing a work shirt one size too large, with mismatched brown Dockers.

"It's pretty true," Rick replied.

At the time I had stood in the shadows, sipping on a beer while listening to the conversation. The new guy, whose name was Dave, was from Oregon. His eyes were beaming with intrigue as he processed this information, visibly awed by the seasoned teachers in town. Dave was most definitely inexperienced, and most likely a virgin.

"There isn't so much sexual activity going on with a lot of these women," Rick said, puffing his chest slightly. "Which is where we come in!"

"As long as I'm getting it, I don't give a damn," another guy said.

"Well try not to get burned, you can call Japan *Clapan* if you like," Rick said with a short laugh.

"*Clapan?*" Dave asked.

"Most girls you hookup here won't even ask you for a condom. Unless you're black."

"Oh fuck off," a guy named Gary replied with a grin. Gary was an African-American from Indiana.

"No, but seriously, it's true," Rick insisted.
The new guy let out a *hmmm* and sipped on his beer.

"But trust me man, if you ever meet a Japanese woman that's shaved like a bald eagle down there, run for the hills," Rick said to Dave.

"Why?"

"Because she's probably fucked every foreign guy in town a few times. Especially the ugly ones."

The group laughed at this and then the conversation had shifted to something else. I had laughed as well, until I remembered Noriko at the love hotel. As Rick put it, she was 'Bald as a Bald Eagle' down there. Well, I didn't phrase it that way, but a woman being shaved never usually raised red flags for me. Maybe it was just her personal preference. I had read somewhere that Japanese men had a predilection for the fuzz, but at no point had I officially tried to confirm it. Regardless, I never saw Noriko again.

Within reason, I had tried to get my Tokyo fixes in whenever I could afford it, being drawn into the city's seductive arms with its milieu of random nights. The happy go-lucky salary men that sometimes bought me drinks, serially frisky JET program girls looking for one-night stands and me completely drunk, arguing with taxi drivers who often tried to overcharge me on the way back to my hotel. The city was an alcohol-laced dream that left me trembling with regret on Monday morning when I'd be back in front of little kids, reading sentences in a baby voice from a horribly written English textbook. I'd walk back to my desk in the staff room and see a portal appear. In it, the women I'd met that weekend would wave back at me with their stiletto heeled personas and expensive jackets. They would keep waving as the portal gradually became smaller in radius until it disappeared.

But now I was here, in a high-rise apartment looking out at my destiny, or my destruction. I went over to the closet my large suitcase leaned on and took out a large, yellow pouch. In there, was my entire life savings. In total it was almost one million yen. Another glance outside made my heart tingle.

Zeus had done pretty well for himself, finding a niche in the financial market as a banker. I'd met his types before, arrogant, wealthy and justifiably so. For these guys, Tokyo was a playground filled with spread-eagled chess pieces. I'd gotten a solid glimpse into that world, on a night we'd hung out previously. There were eight of us in the group, and for the entire night his friend had bought everyone whatever they wanted to drink. With drinks costing a thousand yen a pop, the night must have run him into the thousands of dollars. But it was all in a day's work for whoever he was, happily paying the bill then leaving with his girlfriend, a gorgeous bombshell I heard was from Malaysia.

These thoughts faded as I bathed and put on fresh clothes, preparing to visit a building with an available room for rent. The first thing I saw as I exited the station was a garish neon sign with red lights propped dangerously on the narrow second story ledge of a building across the street. It read, in old English block letters "BUZZ", seeming to signify nothing and everything about Kabukicho, Tokyo's derelict sprawl of sex shops, love hotels and gangster bars. The light was on in the middle of the day.

The image I saw of the room on the real estate website showed paneled floors, a desk and enough ground room to signify reasonable space. The skill that came with trying to determine relative physics through viewing such pictures was a skill I didn't possess. I looked at the small printout in my hand.

60,000 per month, large bedroom, utilities.

The price was okay for my budget, but I didn't like that ugly neon sign by the station. Soon, a short fellow with long, scraggly hair stepped out of the apartment building I had been waiting in front of. He introduced himself as Jeff. His left eyebrow ticked as he spoke, and in between words his eyes would dart rapidly right to left. I shook his hand, which was mysteriously wet.

"Hey man, how are you?" he asked.

"I'm fine. Let's see this place yeah," I replied.

We walked up a dark, narrow flight of stairs to the third floor. A faded, slightly ajar door labeled '121' was our destination. An ancient carpet sprinkled with brown stains was the first thing to greet me. The second was the barely intelligible statement a giant fellow with a red beard said as he stepped out of his room, which was directly facing the door. I couldn't make out anything behind him, not because of his sheer size, but because the room was a dark hole. He mumbled something to Jeff and went back in. The door wasn't fully closed and try as I might, I still couldn't see anything in there. By my feet, an armada of shoes filled most of the tiny entryway space. To my right was a stove with only one burner, small and blackened from overuse. This was adjacent to a small sink, filled with dishes and cups. In my estimation the entire area was no more than three feet square.

"Yeah, so as you can see we have a kitchen, this is just like, the area you drop your stuff y'know."

Jeff said it as if it was information he had recently discovered, gleaned from years of research. He pointed to the stove. "So yeah, y'know if you want to cook or whatever, it's cool because we have that here."

I took another look at the black stove, covered in a film of tar. Not taking off his shoes, he walked forward and we went into the room I had seen online. It was actually pretty spacious, about six feet by six feet with a twin sized bed and a small white desk near a series of small yellow power outlets on the wall. There was a window, but the only view it gave was of the outer wall of the building next door. It was a pretty bright day outside but the room was quite dark. *Night must be like the other fellow's room*, I thought, imagining myself being sucked into the room's black hole night after night.

"Where's the bathroom?" I asked.

Jeff's eyes brightened up.

"Oh yes, follow me," he said.

We walked outside the apartment, and down a short flight of metal stairs. I saw what appeared to be a communal bathroom, with thin, semi-transparent sheets that served as the arbiters of all things private.

"So yeah, this is where we take our showers, which is okay because it's, y'know, nice and refreshing."

I nodded absentmindedly, not seeing myself there in this moment, but in the future, cursing and pissed off as I went to the shower in a bathrobe, as the winter's cold nipped at my balls and made my toes freeze. I imagined myself, with a new job or career, trying to get dressed in the damp of that little area, oddly trying to hide my junk from my neighbours behind the pathetic shower curtains.

"This area doesn't seem very private," I noted.

"Oh it's no problem," Jeff said with another big smile. "We have a gate for the private entrance at the side, and no one can really come through there. Only we use this bathroom on this floor, so it's pretty private. I bathe here all the time and I've had no problems."

Jeff sounded a tad too proud to bathe in such circumstances. I thought about my apartment back in Shizuoka. It was small but cozy, and my bathroom was definitely indoors.

"So when do you think you'll move in?" Jeff said.

"Pretty soon," I lied. "I'll e-mail you later."

The next place was in Ikebukuro, on a quiet street lined with older buildings. The man renting the room was an extremely tall Australian, whose hand dwarfed my hand when he gripped in a handshake that could pulverize bone. His first statement was about the garden, which had been advertised on the property.

"These are my Azaleas," he said confidently. "Took me a while to get them sorted, but after a minute or so they started cooperating."

In front of me were three wilted flowers that seemed ready to die.

"For me it's important a household have some harmony both outside and inside. One of our guys here plays music, and sometimes we have barbeques. You should have moved to Tokyo earlier mate, you would have loved it. Jim—one of the roommates—used to be a chef back home."

"He's also Australian?"

"Coincidentally, yeah. So he cooked up these great steaks and it was a beautiful day, I mean clear blue skies with a light breeze and we just had some beers and kicked back. I dropped some water on the Azaleas and it was just a good vibe mate."

Try as I might, I couldn't see his vision. The yard was quite small, sprinkled with sparse patches of angry grass near a broken old gate. We walked inside to a pretty standard abode. There were a few semi-forgotten tatami mats lying around, placed haphazardly on a tiled floor. The furniture was heavily accessorized with random paraphernalia. On the couch alone, the Aussie pointed out a Brazilian quilt, two Malaysian throw pillows and a towel from a hostel in Greece. We passed through a hallway, walked past a few doors, and stopped at a red door. Stepping in the room, I almost hit my foot on a desk wedged into the corner, with only a foot of space between it and the bed, an old, well-worn futon scrunched into the corner. This wasn't a room; it was a flamboyant closet.

"You can see it is a *little* bit on the smaller side which is why it's fifty thousand yen a month. Also, if you really don't like it, we have people come in and out of the house pretty regularly, so there's always the option to switch to a bigger room."

I didn't feel like asking why people left the house regularly. We went outside where I took a look into the kitchen, which unlike the room, was reasonably sized. A small flyer near a large silver microwave caught my eye.

"You'll love that mate, really opens the eyes," he said.

The flyer was for the Kanamara matsuri, festival of the "Steel Phallus" that happened each spring.

"You can meet a lot of girls at the Penis Festival!" he boomed with a laugh.

I laughed as well, knowing I wouldn't be living there. As I exited the premises, I let him know I'd be e-mailing him later on, which of course, I wouldn't. So far it seemed these residences were all cramped, a bit dirty and way too expensive. Another hint of nervousness ran through my arms and legs, tingling the tips of my fingers. A sleepy eyed kid with huge headphones glanced at me sideways as I boarded my train back to Roppongi. *Sixty thousand and fifty thousand yen for dirty rooms and glorified closets!* My face felt hot, despite the cool air blasting through thin vents above the handrails. As I went back into Zeus' building and into his opulent apartment, I looked around. A huge LCD TV sat on a marble cube adjacent to the window. My bed, the couch, was a velvety purple number that felt far more comfortable than any futon I'd slept on. The bathroom was spacious and tiled, with the option of turning the bath into a Jacuzzi. The kitchen had loads of breathing room, and Zeus, not to be even considered a man without culture, had it stocked with a small store's worth of spices, expensive gingers and dried vegetables. The cost of this place must be astronomical, I reasoned. Zeus told me I could stay as long as I needed to while I looked for a spot. This wasn't entirely comforting as I imagined Tokyo as a craftsman, slowly whittling away at my savings. I thought about teaching English again, and probably applying to the branch in Tokyo. Immediately, a searing pain hit my chest. I clutched it tightly, taking in deep breaths as I looked out at the silent vista of Tokyo in front of me.

Chapter 5

The biggest penis I had ever seen was directly in front of me. It was painted a loud pink colour, supported on a dual set of planks wrapped with white rope. Roughly twelve people bore its load. One of the frontrunners was a large man with his hair in red pigtails. His face was covered in makeup, and even from here, I could see his fake eyelashes, heavy eye shadow and red lipstick. Behind him there was another man, with a builder's shoulders and chest. They were both holding position at the left plank. His hair was also done in a childish set of braids. Several similarly built men held the other plank, all of them wearing pink silk outfits that looked like bathrobes, as they took heavy steps forward, chanting *Yo Issho*. As they did this, the penis bobbed up and down like an apple in the ocean. Cameras flashed constantly as they moved by in a surge, and I was pressed uncomfortably against a small fence as the crowd swelled to watch them. This was an excursion I took based on events from the day before.

Feeling nonplussed about my apartment prospects, I had a few beers at a nearby convenience store, and went back to Zeus' apartment. As I stepped inside, I saw an extremely attractive girl standing in the kitchen wearing nothing but a black silk robe. She gave me a weak smile. The smell of food cooking filled the apartment.

"Ah, he's here!" came the voice of Zeus.

He stepped out of his room in a white V-neck t-shirt, his large chest threatening to tear it open.

"This is your friend?" the girl said.

She spoke in heavily accented English with an inflection that definitely wasn't Japanese.

"What are you stupid? You think anyone can just stroll into my place?" Zeus asked in playful voice. The girl smirked mischievously and put the spatula down on the counter and walked over to me. She opened the robe, revealing a pair of immaculate breasts.

"So?" she said.

"So?" I replied.

I turned to Zeus, wondering what this all meant, but he was watching the television. Without looking at me, he responded. "Give her an opinion, I already have... multiple times."

The way he said the word *multiple* made my skin crawl. I felt my face flush and turned back to the girl, who had closed the robe.

"Very nice," I replied, trying not to make direct eye contact. She stared at me in a long, probing way. Virtual hands were streaming from her eyes, and I could feel them tugging at my clothes.

"Just nice? Tell me, 'friend', how often do women show you a pair like mine and ask you for an opinion?"

"Uh, not often," I replied.

"Would you fuck me?"

"What? Zeus, I'm not sure what's happening here, is she your—"

"She isn't," he replied.

He turned away from watching the television and smirked at me. "Are you saying you wouldn't fuck her?"

I felt my arms getting cold and the light buzz from the few beers I had earlier slowly drifted away. If this was some sort of bizarre test, I wasn't ready for it. In that moment I saw myself through the eyes of the crow, flying outside the building. Everything was sharper and clearer through those bird eyes, and I could see the crow zero in to the windowsill outside Zeus' apartment. I saw myself inside with the woman beside me in her black robe. Then, things shifted back to normal, and the crow was gone, but I could hear it laughing at me, high above. I sat with my hands on my knees, looking forward.

"I'm sure you are a very nice lady," I said in a stutter. "B-but, I'm not very comfortable you know, making that statement. I'm sure you and Zeus are, well, *close* and it would be a bit weird for me to... in fact this conversation is weird, I think maybe I'll come back later."

I tried to stand up, but the woman walked forward and stood directly in front of me, which forced me to sit down. The smell of her perfume glided into my nostrils. It was a familiar scent, like a brand of sweet tea I had a day shortly after coming to Japan.

"I know you want me," she said, standing closer.

Beside me, Zeus laughed. He laughed until tears were in his eyes. He patted a heavy hand on my shoulder.

"Sorry dog, sorry, I can't let her keep doing that to you!" he said.

My teeth were chattering and I felt a cold annoyance build within me. I stood up, and walked away, going back outside. "My name is Miko!" the girl said, also laughing as I left the apartment. Standing by the elevator, I heard the door of the apartment open with its usual hiss. Zeus came out, still chuckling and wiping tears from his eyes.

"Hey man, it was a joke, sorry. I didn't realize you'd get so upset."

I sighed.

"It's not so much upset, just uncomfortable. Your sense of humour is a bit odd," I said.

"It's not me, it's her. Trust me, if four guys came through that door right now she'd ask them the same thing. I think it's some weird thing of hers to release stress."

"Stress? What does she do?"

"She's a banker," Zeus replied.

"No way," I said.

"Dude, she is a beast. You think I earn money? Hah!"

As he said this, he slapped me on the shoulder. The strange energy from before shifted into something else, and a fresh image of the woman's picture perfect breasts came to mind, blanketed by her steely, probing expression.

"Does she do that all the time?" I asked.

"No man, on a whim she likes to fuck with my friends. Well I don't mean she *fucks* them, but knowing her, who knows? But you get what I'm saying!"

He laughed again, and this time I joined in, as our voices spiraled in a whoop through the stretch of the large hallway.

"Let's grab a beer," he said.

Back in the apartment, I found out her name was Ayumi, and it was she who told me about going to the Kanamara matsuri. A plate of food rested on the table directly in front of where I was previously seated. She stood with a plate in her hand, leaning on a column in the kitchen. She smiled as I came inside.

"Sorry about busting your balls earlier," she said, putting down the plate and extending her arm. "I'm Ayumi."

I paused before shaking her hand, because her voice had changed. Now, she spoke with a crystal clear American accent.

"Wait, so you were—"

"Just busting your balls man," she said with a confident smile. "I'm from New York by way of Hawaii."

Nodding at nothing in particular, I went to the fridge, grabbed a beer and sat beside Zeus on the couch. I took a bite of whatever was on my plate. It was warm, and left the flavour of honey in my mouth. A talk show was on TV, where the host was pranking innocent bystanders walking through a dark alleyway, by pretending to be a giant, speaking robot. Ayumi sat on Zeus' lap, and I could see a hint of nipple from my current angle. We were three, watching the show, but it felt like four. Myself, Ayumi, her nipple peeking at me, and Zeus.

"Zee tells me you are new to Tokyo," she said. "You should see the Kanamara matsuri, it is a good experience."

"You'd never catch me alive at a Penis Festival," Zeus remarked.

"You aren't locked to any type of schedule right now I assume?" Ayumi said, ignoring Zeus.

"Not at the moment," I replied.

"Then go, what do you have to lose?"

She was right. The only thing I remember about any such Japanese festival was a documentary I had watched a few years prior, about the Honen fertility festival in Nagoya. I saw images of the temple with a giant wooden phallus, and for quite some time after that I thought Japanese life must be bizarre. A place where people worshipped penises and carved twenty-foot replicas of them? Madness, no? But sitting with Zeus, Ayumi and her nipple, it seemed to make sense.

I made the trip to Kawasaki the next day, listening to *The Power Of Intention* on my way there. Mike, a guy I knew who was in my training group before we got assigned to our respective prefectures to teach, lived in Tokyo and would also be at the festival. We agreed to meet in the afternoon. My train arrived sometime earlier than we were slated to meet, and I went for a

stroll. A few streets up, I saw a bald man with a gold stud ear-
rings sitting on a blanket carving giant phalluses from fresh
turnips. His hands were quick and precise as he did his work,
whittling away at the turnips until a massive sexual organ was
in his hands. With his quiet eyes and a permanent smirk on his
face, no doubt people would be asking themselves what he was
packing below his *happi*. He sat there with his legs folded under
a tree, the smirk constant as he made phallus after phallus. Two
girls in light petticoats came by. They both had brown hair,
bright eyes and round faces.

"It's so big!" one of them exclaimed.

She reached her arms forward, tentatively, as if it was a true
flesh and blood behemoth, pulsing with distended veins, attached to some alien creature licking its lips lecherously.

"It's okay," the monk said in a deep voice, his eyes bristling
with sexual intensity. The girl picked up the phallus with both
hands, moving it up and down slowly to weigh it. She passed it
to her friend, who remarked excitedly at its size and weight as
well. Behind them, I could see fantasies blazing in the monk's
eyes, despite his rigid stance. Well who could blame him? This
was after all, a penis festival. Why shouldn't he be thinking of
what everyone else came here to see? They were the gatekeep-
ers of all things phallic in this part of Japan. Kawasaki, the
place that helped countless men to buy loud, aggressive bikes
to compensate for possibly other shortcomings, was now
flooded with loud aggressive versions of what they were com-
pensating for.

The girls took a picture with the monk and walked away to
join the throng. I followed them for a little while, since there
was no easy way to figure out where the shrine was. A few
times they stopped to take pictures with people carrying phalluses, or with any of the myriad street vendors selling penis and
vagina candy. I stifled a laugh seeing a yellow and red vagina
candy molded in exquisite detail. Not only were the clitoris and
labia well done, but the brilliant use of what looked like Tic
Tacs created the illusion of a slight outcropping of pubic hair. I
bought one.

Around this time, I saw the parade with the pink penis, and
another procession with men carrying a significantly smaller
black penis under a more elaborate wooden carriage. I walked

away from the crowd for a few moments. My phone vibrated in my pants. It was Mike. We met under a tree about twenty feet away from the train station. Beside him, was a short girl with dark hair wearing large, dark eyeglasses?

"Mike," I said.

"Dude, it's been too long," he replied.

I said hello to the girl he was with, who replied only with a nod. Mike was tall, with a smoothly shaved face and high arching eyebrows that kept him frozen in a constant look of surprise. He also shaved his head, which meant for most people (I assumed) the first thing they would see were his eyebrows, always in a state of shock.

"I've been here three times, and each time I'm more fascinated by this display. I mean look at that," he said, pointing to a Japanese family walking by. They had three little boys with them, all sucking penis lollipops.

I admit, such things would be frowned upon in the west. The idea of taking your son to a penis festival and buying him a penis lollipop wasn't your regular day at the picnic. Vagina candy would probably be just as bad, but a savvy father would hide this from the kid's mother of course.

"So this is some sort of phallic worship?" I asked.

"Not really," Mike replied. "You saw the dudes with the giant pink penis earlier yeah? Those guys dressed in drag represent the transvestites or prostitutes who used to come to the shrine to pray for protection against sexually transmitted diseases. But the really interesting story relates to that black steel cock.

"Apparently, a demon was hiding in some chick's vagina, and not one but two dudes got their junk bitten off on their wedding nights nonetheless. So what did the lady do? She went to the shrine for help, and some brilliant monk made a steel penis. The demon, still in the lady's vagina, bit the penis and his teeth broke, releasing him from her special place."

"And thus, it became a holy relic," I said.

"Exactly!" Mike replied, his eyebrows arching even higher. The girl behind us, who I still didn't know because Mike never mentioned her name, was quietly walking with her camera pointed at us. To me it seemed like she was taking video, but her eyes, completely hidden under her huge glasses, hid her intentions.

We followed the crowd towards the shrine. The noise of the parade was still clear, about three streets away. There were hundreds of people at the shrine by the entrance. A large crowd encircled something I couldn't see clearly. When it came into view I saw that it was a pair of wooden phalluses, no less that six feet in length. They were parallel and raised upwards at an angle. At a glance they looked like cannons, which I'm sure, gave the monks who made these a good chuckle when they were originally fashioning them. More interesting than the 'cannons' were the legions of men and women constantly mounting the devices, posing for pictures, licking the wood and pretending it was a horse. The men in the crowd; husbands, boyfriends and single men shouted, "Lick it!" or "Suck it! Suck it so hard!" Many women became red faced as the men around them said this, many of them slim and short, their arms barely able to fit around the giant wooden shafts. One particularly adventurous woman, started deepthroating a bottle of Smirnoff ice while straddling the phallus, which lead to a resounding chorus of cheers from both men and women in the crowd.

Something was odd about it all. Despite the overt displays of sexual behaviour, something dark was present. The people were too into the whole affair, a bit too voracious with their appetite for cock candy and gargantuan penis cannons. Idly, I left the circle. Nearby, three Americans, two white and one African-American were doing the rounds, each decked out in a plastic outfit with a large penis attached to their hips. They hooted and hollered, doing fake shows of fellatio, masturbation and occasionally humping random girls. I walked past the guys and looked at one of the little stalls. There I saw boxes of "Fun Loving Couple" wind-up sex toys, and a Gorilla Key chain accessory. The Gorilla naturally, had an arm-sized member which it gripped at the base with one hand. The eyes on the toy were inverted, looking inwards, as if the throes of its onanism were pushing it towards a climax. Ever more funny, it was labeled: "Interesting Gorilla Keychain". I bought a beer from the vendor and walked back over to Mike.

"I have some Jamaican friends here man, you should meet them," he said.

It had been some time since I'd interacted regularly with any Jamaicans. They were with a mixed group of people from other islands, local Japanese folks and a smattering of Americans and Canadians. As I shook hands and did cheers with a few of them, my mind went back to my one street in my formerly sleepy town, the road I had walked on so often looking for someone to chat with. In just a few days I'd met more people than I had in months. The sense of relative diversity I was experiencing felt pleasant, yet tugging at the nape of my neck was that inkling of worry; knowing that my nest egg was be getting smaller day by day. The DJ played a Michael Jackson song, and a foreign guy with a shock of long blonde hair, wearing a plaid mini skirt and psychedelic tights began dancing to the music. The group, and particularly the Jamaicans, made a lot of noise at the spectacle, laughing at the young man, who was tall and extremely broad-shouldered with forearms covered in a black pelt of hair.

"This is some crazy business eh?" came a heavy voice beside me.

I turned to see a fellow a few inches shorter than myself. He was handsome, with a mid-sized Afro and slightly beady eyes.

"Yeah, this is definitely an interesting phenomenon," I replied.

"Dem foreign boys crazy!" he said in patois.

Then he laughed, a laugh that swept over everything in the immediate vicinity, ricocheting off everything and then out into the world. I laughed too. He extended his hand.

"Dubz," he said.

"That's your name?" I asked.

"Just cool man," he said with a smile. "Everybody calls me Dubz."

In that moment I turned to see Mike. He gave me his normal expression as he motioned with his hand to me at the bizarre dance off, and again, I couldn't tell if he was surprised or just having his regular facial expression. We chatted for a little while about the scene, with Dubz casually informing me about who was hooking up in our group, dropping tidbits about Reggae parties and clubs around town and how to hustle teaching private lessons. I told him I'd only been in town for a few days, and his eyes opened wide.

"You have somewhere to live?" he asked.

"Looking for that now," I replied.

"Yo, yo! Where I live, a room just opened up man, trust me you'll like the place."

For a second, I saw the faces of the previous tenants hawking their tiny and dirty rooms. They had the same expression on their faces; a mix of barely tempered intensity soaked in a belief that where they were was the best place ever. Then I thought of Zeus and his friend Ayumi. Was there more to his nightly menagerie of strange girls? I didn't want to find out. The crowd starting making noise again, and Dubz and I turned to see a man holding a large red dildo by his crotch in a moonwalk dance off with the guy wearing the miniskirt. It was hilarious because the man strikingly resembled a fat Japanese Austin powers. Dubz and I laughed and raised our drinks in a cheer, to this wild, uncertain future.

Chapter 6

It was another morning. I made some chamomile tea and listened to music playing through a Bose box Zeus pointed out to me the night before. The last few days had been rather expensive. Already, I'd spent twenty thousand yen in under a week. Relatively speaking it wasn't *that* much, and when I took a peek into my yellow pouch filled with ten thousand dollar notes, it hardly made a dent. Where I lived before, I wouldn't spend more than five thousand yen a week, if so much. All I needed were my two hundred yen Chu-His, an occasional snack and the solitude of the town streets. Here it was high priced beer, expensive lunches and many late dinners. For Zeus this life was normal. The constant outings and meetings, expensive train rides, high stakes poker games, and interesting women. Being here still had the touch of an illusion, particularly as I looked down at the highways in the distance, seeing the slow crawl of traffic like ants in my vision.

Dubz had arranged to meet me in the mid-afternoon, and I spent the remainder of the time thinking about the near future. I'd noticed more women than an average number of women looking at me here, and I wondered if what Mari had said was right. Possibly I had something I wasn't aware of, hidden under the folds of my blurry self-perception. I set another pot of water on the stove to boil.

In high school, I wasn't the 'it' guy nor was I an outcast. My younger life was a predictable montage of walking a reasonably conservative line all the way to college. One smiles when he has to, engages in activities like clubs and goes to the occasional party, maybe has a few hookups or finds a girlfriend. There was a girlfriend or two in college, maybe I loved them, maybe I didn't. I had always existed in the periphery, where I felt most comfortable; away from things and people, perched atop my light post like the crow, seeing the world below me with my dark, coal eyes. The sum total of it all had lead me here, standing over a couch looking into a pouch of cash. High school, College, relationships, failures and victories were contained in that pouch, and little by little, like how I had felt in my small town months before, it would begin to empty. My life would begin to empty, and some day the pouch would be as sparse as the streets I always saw in the morning. What then? The pot was boiling now, and I turned the stove off, and made my tea.

The apartment I was meeting Dubz to see was located somewhere in Yotsuya, a part of town I'd never been in. I walked past a few convenience stores and upscale restaurants to a 7-11, where Dubz was waiting on me. He gave me a hearty handshake.

"Nice area yeah?" he said.

Many of the buildings looked relatively new. Few had the faded appearance of the kind I tended to see in Shinjuku and some of the older boroughs. More than that, the area had a sense of space, where other parts of town were choked with the smell that came from the daily presence of a large number of individuals. I liked this aspect of things, as one of my fears was living in a place like Shibuya, where at all hours thousands of people wandered about like zombies after an apocalypse.

"Looks like it," I replied.

"Trust me, you'll like it man," Dubz said with the same gusto as the day before. "Everything happens for a reason you know? I mean you just reach to Tokyo and this room opens up, and you meet me at that thing, the Penis place? Hah! But yeah, we meet, we link up, and now you are coming through."

I agreed with the serendipitous observation. That afternoon as I had traveled to Kawasaki, I'd focused on Wayne Dyer's voice. *Intend it,* he had said. Maybe I had unconsciously intended this all, pulling Dubz out of a hat the size of a small car as my audience *oohed* and *aahed.* In my magician's suit and top hat, I would then step back, and say "Voila! That, my beautiful audience, is the *intention trick!"*

We turned onto a narrow street filled with cobblestones. It was quiet. After two more turns we came to a building with a large gate. Dubz pressed a small card onto a dark panel about shoulder height on the gate. It whirred to life, and opened slowly. When Dubz turned to walk in there, I paused. From the outside, the building looked like something out of the wizard of Oz. Its exterior was covered in some kind of semitransparent plastic, accentuated on the edges as it stretched upwards for several stories. Betwixt a set of more traditionally aesthetic apartment buildings, it looked like a diamond, hidden on this random back street. There was also a spacious garden out front, with two large trees spread out over a walkway with two iron benches on either side. The trees were grown to bend slightly towards the doorway, as if to say "Welcome." Dubz was smiling at me at the top of the walkway. *I told you so,* his eyes whispered. I walked forward through the pathway, following a row of small, well manicured bushes about five feet tall that led to a large glass door. I followed Dubz to the glass door, which slid open noiselessly.

"Welcome to GreenLeaf," he said beaming his smile.

We were in a large lobby with a darkly tiled floor. In front of me the lobby stretched forward for about twenty feet, illuminated by a series of soft lights in a star formation on the ceiling. The light from these bulbs shone down on an exquisite carpet that covered most of the lobby floor. To my left, was another room, the kitchen. It had a large transparent window, and inside I could see a young woman, stirring a small pot with a large spoon. To my right, a door made of glass gave a clear view into a large room filled with small couches and throw pillows. A saw a few people in there, watching something on a giant flat screen television.

"This way," Dubz said, walking forward.

Going through the lobby took us through another glass door, which slid open as we walked through it as well. The dark tiles were now hidden under a dark carpet, which stretched forward for fifty feet.

"These are some of the ground floor rooms," he said, pointing to the doors. Unlike the time Jeff excitedly told me the obvious about a disgusting one-burner stove, I found myself nodding along as If he was giving me scintillating new information.

"As you can see," Dubz continued. "The hallway at the end splits off a little further down. Down there you have some more rooms and a bathroom at each end."

I followed him to the end of the hallway. We were standing in front of a large white door with a silver handle. "This is one of the bathrooms we all use," he said, pulling the handle. It didn't open.

"I guess somebody is in there," he said with a smile. Turning to me, he winked mischievously. "One time I walked in there and a girl was bathing because she didn't lock the door properly."

"What happened?" I asked.

"Well, we looked at each other for a little bit, then I said I was sorry and stepped out," Dubz said.

"That's all?"

"Well, a little later she started talking to me still, but more on that later."

I could predict the outcome of this little anecdote, but if I was going to live there, I was sure I'd eventually hear how the story actually ended. We took a left down the first hall, where we saw two more doors on each side, and another bathroom with a similar white door and silver handle.

"We live in suites here," he said, looking over his shoulder, as if forgetting something. "I'll show you mine, because Mr. Oba would have to give you your room key to see your spot."

The first suite at the top of the hallway beside the bathroom was his. Stepping inside, there was a very small dark space with two doors. He opened a door to his right, revealing a reasonably sized room, with the same brown tiles on the floor as there were outside. A small bed was in the back, along with a desk, a small sink and a micro fridge. His room was filled with clothes and random junk, but the walls were clean and white. Gone were the feelings of trepidation I had at the previous apartments. The opulent sprawl of this place and its potentiality seemed linked to the *intention* I was throwing out there.

"Looks good," I replied with a smile.

"Good, good, because somebody was going to come look at the room tomorrow, but Mr. Oba will give it to you today."

"How so?"

"Money him defend," Dubz said in patois, laughing. "Okay, since you like the place, let me call Mr. Oba so you can get your key and look at your room."

Dubz walked into the main lobby, his phone on his ear. For a few moments I soaked up the environment, first taking a closer look at a black and white photo of a man in a clown car dressed in a tweed business suit. There were several photos like this along the length of the hallway, including one of Marilyn Monroe in a taxi. I went back into the main lobby where Dubz was sitting in a large, blood red chair. I heard a loud *ping* and turned to see doors sliding open to the far right of where I had entered into the lobby. It was an elevator.

A man stepped out of the elevator in what I am sure was a cape. Not a superhero length cape, but definitely the kind of cape a man no more than five feet five inches tall could wear comfortably without looking ridiculous. This was in addition to a sharkskin coloured blazer, a brown v-necked undershirt and dark slacks. His eyes were bright but his expression bland, giving me the impression he was looking at a computer screen at something shocking. The man stepped lightly, walking on the ground as if it were a moving conveyer belt. His skin was unusually tan, and a thin white scarf was wrapped around his neck.

"Soon come back," Dubz said, walking to the direction of his room.

The man motioned for me to sit on a black chair I hadn't noticed before, directly facing the red one Dubz had been sitting in. I sat down, and then he did, effortlessly slipping into the chair with his legs crossed. His shoes were an unusual pair of low top black boots. I could tell the leather was expensive.

"So, are you a teacher?" he said in a crisp accent.

"Yes," I replied.

"Ah, and you come to Tokyo to teach perhaps?"

"In a few weeks possibly, but I plan to stay in town for a while," I replied.

Mr. Oba strummed his fingers on either armrest rapidly for a few seconds, holding me in a quiet stare.

"You are Jamaican, like Mr. Dubz?"

"Yes I am."

What could be described as a smile came across his face. He opened his mouth slightly, jutting out his lower jaw and smacking his lips.

"I saw Harry Belafonte, at one time," he said, squeezing his shoulders together slightly. "He is a great musician."

I nodded in agreement.

"Do you like electric boogaloo?"

I paused, not sure what to answer. Somewhere in the recesses of my mind, was a memory of what exactly it was, but I couldn't pinpoint it. As if reading my mind, Mr. Oba let out a chuckle that sounded like a dry cough.

"I like Calypso and electric boogaloo," he said. "Good music. Very stimulating."

The lobby seemed larger now, and deathly quiet. I couldn't hear anything. Not the girl in the kitchen making something to eat, or the voices of the people in the entertainment room only feet away. It was just myself and Mr. Oba, on the expensive carpet, floating in the sky. He strummed his fingers a few more times while looking directly at me, occasionally shaking the ankle of the leg resting on his knee. I tried not to keep looking directly at him. His hair was black, but I couldn't tell how old he was. The skin on his hands and face looked smooth and supple, but even so, I could tell there was age there. Significant age.

"The room we have for you is seventy thousand yen a month," Mr. Oba said.

He held me in a stare.

"Price okay?" he said, still strumming his fingers.

I felt as if I was being hypnotized. That delicate strumming of his fingers, the way he sat bone straight without breaking his gaze, and the sudden quiet that fell around us when he started speaking.

"Y-yes, that's fine," I said.

"Okay."

He stood up and adjusted his sport jacket. A gripping presence immediately lifted from around me. I sighed inwardly; glad to feel Mr. Oba and I come back to reality, away from the other plane of existence we had traveled into.

"I just need your identification for the office. Here is your room key, your room is 114. Also, to move in, I just need a ten thousand yen deposit. Price okay?" he said.

Afraid he would sit down once more and start strumming his fingers, I almost gasped, "Yes."

"Okay, I be back in, maybe five minutes."

He walked in sharp steps across the carpet and to the tiles in front of the elevator, and went inside once it opened. The entire time I could see his head looking slightly down, as he scrutinized my I.D card. The red chair was remarkably comfortable, and I took the moment to take a deep breath, still a little perturbed by Mr. Oba's unusual aura. I heard a door latch open to my right, and I saw a girl come out of the kitchen. She had dark hair that flowed down to her shoulders, lightly covering a pretty face. She rubbed her forehead as she came into the lobby, giving attention to her sensuous eyes and full lips. Something told me she was European, and I was correct. She smiled and I smiled back, but not before she began speaking rapidly in another language to someone I couldn't see. Behind me, someone had emerged from the entertainment room. Another girl who looked strikingly like the one from the kitchen. They gestured with their hands often, and their loud accents flooded the previously quiet lobby. Even though I wasn't a linguist, it sounded like they were speaking Italian. Ignoring me, they both went into the kitchen, and the door shut behind them, throwing the lobby into silence again. I sat there for a little while longer, taking in more details. One of the large pots near the front doorway had an elaborate image of a dragon painted in gold across its surface. Near to my feet, I could see that the carpet had tiny fringes on the edges from relative wear, but its thickness indicated it was very durable. Over to the right, the elevator doors were under a small archway made of a dark wood, and on either side at the foot of the doors, were small black marble columns. What purpose they served was a mystery to me. I heard the *ping* again, and Mr. Oba came out.

"Thank you for your patience," he said with no emotion.

He handed me a set of keys. There were two room keys, a mailbox key, and the gate access card on a small plastic key ring with the room number on it. Mr. Oba told me if I lost the key, the replacement fee was five thousand yen. I nodded and thanked him. He nodded back with his head tilted and his eyes looking upwards slightly, as if he was agreeing more to a negotiation, than a simple statement. He turned without saying anything else, and went to the elevator.

I walked through the hallway and into my new room. Unlike the dark entryway in Dubz' room, this one was dimly lit by a tiny light recessed into the leftmost wall. I opened the door to see an exact replica of Dubz' room, but spotlessly clean. The room was small but not claustrophobic and there was a thin carpet over the brown tiles. There was also a window, blocked by an air conditioning unit similar to the one in my old Shizuoka apartment. I sat on the bed, feeling it softly grip my buttocks, and let out a relaxed sigh. I walked out of the room and closed the door. Dubz was in the hallway.

"Yo, yo, it's going to be good having you here man, I can tell. We don't get too many yardies coming through you know?"

"About how many people live here?" I asked.

"A good number, but people here have plenty kinds of different jobs, so you don't see everyone all the time. But don't worry man! It won't get noisy or anything like that."

I wasn't worried. This was the Ritz compared to the Kabuki hole I'd visited a few days prior. I thanked Dubz, and left the apartment building. The train ride back to Zeus' place was quick and uneventful. In a text message I let him know I'd found a spot. I read his reply.

Congrats dude. Dinner and drinks to ring it in.

My two suitcases were a bit of trouble on the journey back, as going down the winding streets and the cobblestone road seriously tested my arms by the time I reached back to the house. Both suitcases fit comfortably in the entryway and the room remained for the moment, reasonably spacious. A sudden tiredness came over me, and I turned on the air conditioner and fell asleep. Before waking up to go and meet Zeus, I had a nightmare about Mr. Oba. In the dream, he was a man-sized bat with wings, biting my neck. As he licked his lips smeared with my blood and did that smile where the jutted his lower jaw, he whispered, "Price okay?"

Chapter 7

Despite my good fortune in finding this bizarre place in the middle of a wealthy Tokyo district, proper sleep still eluded me. Whatever pressure cooker I had been sitting in back in my sleepy town had followed me here. I tossed and turned in my new room, even though it was remarkably quiet. As such, my usual nocturnal roaming became a different sort of beast, complete with partners in crime that helped me seize the night.

The partners had different faces and were from a myriad places. I'd only been at the house for a week or so, and I was beginning to understand the hierarchical structure of things. My level was the ground floor, which served as the social nucleus of the house. Since this floor had a large kitchen, a lobby and the entertainment room, people went throughout this area quite often. Dubz mentioned there were also people who lived downstairs, and shortly after I had moved in, I visited the basement floor. The area was a mirror of the first floor, albeit with a smaller kitchen, but kept the same long, Y-shaped hallway with multiple suites and bathrooms. Down there I noticed, was also an office, complete with a printer and several workstations for residential use.

The more upscale dwellings were upstairs. It didn't really matter to me that Mr. Oba never mentioned these when I met him, because I couldn't have afforded any of them. But upstairs on the second floor, were similar suites to those on the bottom floor, with the exception that those apartments also came with private kitchens. On the third floor, were the top tier apartments with a single room, personal bathroom and balcony. I didn't ask Dubz how much they cost, but sometime later he mentioned a person had just left one, and Mr. Oba was looking for a new tenant to pay the one hundred and twenty thousand yen per month to stay there. The top two floors were for Mr. Oba, and there was no way to access those levels without an elevator security key, which only he had. One night I took a look up at the top two floors, but I couldn't see much except the soft glow of light emitting from the windows.

Standing at the foot of the estate, one could only wonder what he was doing up there.

One block away were not one, but two convenience stores, and already I'd perused them both, happy to find my Chu-Hi brand heavily stocked, but sadly, not the cashew snack I'd come to enjoy with them. Nonetheless the convenience of these places was compounded by the presence of a supermarket in close proximity. Along with a few bars and decent restaurants, anything a person needed was within a five-minute radius. I'd deposited a good portion of my money in the bank, leaving two hundred thousand yen in my yellow money pouch for emergency purposes. Sometimes in the room I would count and recount the money, as if trying to create more through thought alone. A part of me was worried. This house could be an illusion like Zeus' apartment. I could be standing at another large window staring outside at the city before me, pretending that I was solidly rooted into everything, including the city's pulse, but it possibly wasn't true. What direction was I heading in specifically? I didn't think about this for the next few weeks, for a few of reasons.

The first reason was the array of characters I met on my floor alone. There was Briggs, a semi-famous English teacher who did some videos called *Tokyo Roving*. I searched for him online after we met, seeing his face in a bright video thumbnail raging with bold kanji characters labeled "Storming Shinjuku". The video had over seven hundred thousand views. Akiko was a quiet actress type who lived in the basement. She had an unusually curvy body and a penchant for giggling. Fortunately, it wasn't an annoying sort of giggle. She wanted to eventually have her own *Pikura* brand, her face emblazoned on thousands of photo strip print machines. She also said she sang a little, but became embarrassed when I asked to listen to some of her work. There was Mick, a busy bodied teacher who spent a lot of his free time running. Apparently, he was training to be a world-class runner. In this year alone he had done three five-kilometer runs and one ten-kilometer run. There was something very serious about his voice when he spoke about running, and I asked him why he was in Tokyo.

"I just ended up here," Mick had said while doing a light warm up in the hallway. He was a tall slender Canadian with a short head of curly brown hair. "Originally I just wanted to make some money, and I came here. The money's good, so I stayed. Then I picked up the language and so on, all the while doing my training. Time passed and I just never left, but I keep training."

"Are you trying to be an Olympian?" I asked.

"God no," he replied, doing an over arm stretch. "Exercise fuels me, and when I challenge myself to be strong and fast, I keep focused on other things. My running is a parallel to other things and ideas, stuff I'm formulating and putting together. I map it out in the same way I map out the maze of these streets when I'm pushing past sixty minutes of running, when my body is screaming for liquid and I'm saying no, no, one more kilometer."

He did another light ground stretch before turning to me. "You'll like it here man, the women are frisky."

With that statement, he had bounded towards the entrance and through the front door, disappearing quickly down the walkway. Then I met Barbara, who didn't live on the first floor, but was often down in the entertainment room, or making tea in the kitchen. She worked as a software programmer for a Google subsidiary. She was short and chubby, favouring mostly black clothes and shirts that alternated from 80's anime images to screen-prints of old, difficult to read Japanese Kanji characters.

"Japanese futurism is totally underestimated man," she said to me during our first encounter. "I mean, if you go back to the seventies, the *seventies* man, they have these cartoons that are just leagues beyond anything in the States, or anywhere for that matter. But not just the detail, the concepts. Epic levels of creativity blossoming in so many ways man.

"Did you ever watch Golgo thirteen? You should man, you should. I was sold on anime being superior when I saw this scene from the movie where the main dude assassinates someone by shooting at him *through a few other buildings!* That's forward thinking complexity. Manifesting the real from the imagined."

Barbara spoke at a normal pace, but waved her arms and gestured quickly.

"Maybe it is a reflection of superior cultural mores," she said afterward.

"Superior culture? How so?" I had asked.

"Well in programming you always have this extra data, called junk data that does meaningless stuff. You take a picture with your camera, there is Metadata. You write a document in Microsoft word and there are all these tags and XML thingies that reference little things that ninety percent of people don't give a damn about.

"But say you take a Papaya fruit and call that big data. All that little junk is the stuff in the middle, the black seeds you scoop out. So let's say big data is kind of like superior culture, where you scoop out the unnecessary stuff and leave the juiciest bit behind."

I had sort of understood what she was saying. We were sitting on the carpet in the lobby.

"So in Japanese culture you think they scooped out what they don't need and left the core stuff in society," I said.
Barbara sighed in agreement.

"Exactly, exactly. Sometimes a lack of emotion can create structure in a way that produces stuff like Anime, or the bullet train."

"But what about the notoriously inefficient way management works here? Despite certain cool creations, companies are often pretty slow to adopt new ways of thinking," I added.

"I knew you'd say that, but it doesn't matter because, even though that is a function of the society now, it won't always be. Comparatively, when you think of the 'junk' that happens in Japanese company management, yet look at the way the general layout of society falls into a certain level of superior functionality, I say it works."

"So the ends justify the means," I said.

"Exactly, exactly," Barbara replied.

I didn't really know what we were talking about. Some of what she said seemed to make sense, but I rarely thought about society. For me it was something to absorb and swallow in pieces, as I lived moment to moment. Also this conversation had begun after the consumption of a good bit of alcohol.

There were a few more persons I met, including Hans, a German student doing a language course at a nearby university.

More than once he asked Dubz and me if we knew a popular reggae song. If we said yes, he would smile and say "Bless up!" then walk away. If we said no, we didn't know the song, he would smile and say "Bless up!" and then walk away.

On the second night I was at the house, mulling around the entertainment room. A girl walked in. She was tall and slender, with dark, brooding eyes and short hair. With her hands on her hips and a cigarette in her mouth, she took a quick glance at all in attendance, then did an about face and went outside. Something fluttered in my chest with that motion, particularly her dismissive nonchalance. I saw her size up the crowd, decide it wasn't worth her time and go to find other things to do. The striking eyes left a mark on me, and I immediately decided I wouldn't like her, whoever she was. Dubz, sitting beside me as we watched a rerun of *Independence Day* on the TV, nudged me in my shoulder.

"You noticed her right? She's a model," he said.

"Hrmph," I said in response. "I can't see the big deal with modeling anyway."

This was the truth. Despite what Mari had said to me the night I met her at F-bar about "having something", I didn't really understand it. This girl, whoever she was, understood *it*. I could see it in her face and body language as if she typed *it* and pasted *it* all over the building. She knew she had it, and that others didn't. With her sexy cigarette and her perfect little breasts, I was already annoyed with her attractiveness, and her world. Whatever encounters we would have in the future, I was determined not to like her.

"Make it a big deal," Dubz said. "She's your roommate."

That was my first introduction to Melodie.

Chapter 8

The second time I saw Melodie was outside the house, after a late night with some of the boys. She was standing quietly under one of the large trees, smoking a cigarette, eyes locked on the street behind us. She held the cigarette with the two forefingers of her right hand, her elbow resting in the nook of her left hand, which lay flat on her stomach. Standing up, she looked as if she was sitting down contemplating something. I glanced at her on my way in, but she didn't pay me or anyone I was with any attention. Possibly, she didn't even know if we were roommates. This made sense, because she was rarely ever home.

Whatever mystery lingered behind her perfect eyes wasn't important to me. Tokyo had welcomed me with open arms, and for the first month at least, it was exciting. I am a gradual person, and I like to take things in doses. However, it seemed that every day was another party or club, restaurant outing or excursion to Shibuya. There was always someone visiting the premises, people taking runs to the convenience store, or someone doing something in the kitchen. Used to a previous life of slow days in my efficiency apartment with my laptop as my primary companion, this was an explosion to the senses. Today, as I lay in my room idly, I heard a knock on my door. It was Mick.

"Hey man, an Izakaya nearby is having a ninety yen beer special," he said.

My ears perked up. This was the perfect occasion for a man like me with no foreseeable steady income. I told him I'd be there soon, and took a quick shower. In the lobby, were Dubz, Mick, Hans and a few other students from Hans' language school. We walked in a boisterous group to the restaurant. A short man wearing a black apron seated us. Mick scanned the menu.

"We just need to buy something to eat to qualify for the price of the beers," he said, slapping the large menu shut.

Everyone quickly ordered food and began to swallow beer after beer. Beside us, a group of college students were at the very end of enjoying their discount beers. They were a dense collection of girls and guys with rosy faces. Somehow, Dubz found himself in the middle of this group, giving guys high fives and telling everyone he was from Jamaica. I chuckled at the spectacle as I sipped on another beer, while Hans and the guys from his language school spoke in rapid German to one another. Sometime afterward Dubz returned to our table, with a wide grin on his face.

"If that bitch wasn't so drunk, I would have steal her from her man," he said, echoing one of his loud laughs.

"Don't you mean 'stolen her' from her man?" Mick said.

"Mick don't be messin' with my Jamaican accent now!" Dubz said, effortlessly switching into a perfect American accent. Their exchange was funny to watch, but more so for the young German students, who saw Dubz' quick dive into the massive group of college kids as an act of courageous wonder. The beers kept flowing, and at number twelve or thirteen, it was decided that we were all going to club Camelot, in Shibuya.

"Dubz, you are good with the ladies," Hans said in a heavy voice.

"Wait till we go to Shibuya," Dubz replied.

This was my first time out with a group of young men for a long as I could remember. It was thrilling, but I maintained my usual role, somewhere on the periphery, trodding carefully on the margins I'd always kept to. Dubz and Mick however, were on fire. From the moment we exited train by the Hachiko exit, they were chatting to girls with the gusto of the men who tout for sleazy establishments in Kabukicho. If Dubz wasn't waving excitedly and saying hello to a group of girls, Mick was. In no time they spoke to most of the girls in the area and secured a few phone numbers.

"Oh snap!" Dubz said, pointing to his left.

Standing there was an attractive girl in a short pink skirt, wearing a thin silver jacket and a shiny blue halter-top complimented by green spray painted Chuck Taylors.

"Get it," Mick said, nudging Hans.

Hans went over to her, clearly motivated by the liquid confidence we had consumed earlier. He bombed terribly, succeeding more in scaring her than anything within the realm of what anyone would consider constructive. Mick and Dubz rescued him from further embarrassment by pulling him out of reach, but not before laughing until tears came to their eyes. We walked for a little while, stopping by a Family Mart to get some more drinks. As we stood outside, sipping our fresh drinks, Mick gestured towards a set of girls, standing beside a bench down the road from us, causing liquid to fly from his can and splash on the ground.

"There isn't any religion in Japan really see, so the way you hookup with women is different here," Mick said.

"Really?" came the voice of Hans.

For Hans, the night had been more pleasurable than it was for everyone else. He had been laughing, hugging and high fiving both Dubz and Mick for the last twenty minutes, roaring with laughter each time either of them got a new phone number, or made an irreverent joke. The fact that he was put into a position to be ridiculed by them hadn't fazed him either.

"Yes," Mick said with a slight slur. "Where you have religion, like most countries in the west, you have loads of religious guilt. Here, there isn't much real religion, so there isn't any religious guilt. A girl could come home with me tonight and not care, because she hasn't been drilled her entire life about premarital sex or whatever."

Mick continued his little sermon as we started walking again, talking about the various things you could say to pickup girls, rude expressions in Japanese, and going 'caveman' which was just doing whatever worked in that situation. He talked about exit strategies to perform at clubs if things were getting heated, and talked about love hotel time policies. Here Dubz interjected, disagreeing with the idea of a love hotel, because he felt having a room meant you should bring a girl back home.

"Not if she might be F-ing crazy," Mick said.

He stopped walking and poked an assertive finger into Hans' chest. "Be very careful you don't get stalked either. Remember that lack of religious guilt I spoke about? Well there's a lack of other stuff going on with tons of these women, and sometimes you step into their life, and you become *all of it,* even if you met while you were both blazing drunk and had a quick smash in some dirty bathroom."

Hans nodded in a toothy smile. Mick's rambling went on for another block or so, shifting into an erudite spiel about the Japanese economy, until he stopped and looked quizzically around. The psychedelic mish mash of endless neon lights that bounced off the shoulders of contiguous metal buildings had been replaced by quieter streets with significantly less people. We had walked in some direction away from the popular Shibuya Hachiko exit, but no one knew exactly where we were. After asking three bouncers, two policemen and a cute girl for directions, we were still lost. A shaggy guy with a sign hung over his shoulders advertising cheap ramen on his chest told me vaguely, "Go north of here". The group followed this instruction.

"To the north!" Dubz shouted.

"North!" Hans and his two friends shouted.

We walked 'North' for a block or so, until we saw a group of foreigners walking in the opposite direction across the street. "Hey man do you know where Camelot is?" I said to one of them.

"Hell yeah," he replied in a heavy California accent.

The guy was wearing aviator glasses, his long hair mostly hidden underneath a pilot's hat. The fellow mysteriously handed us all discount passes to the club, and told us to follow him. Muscular bouncers with faces used to the night greeted us with quiet smirks and we were ushered in.

I was immediately hit with waves of light and noise, the smell of people and perfume, my toes throbbing from the vibration of nearby speakers. On the first floor to my left was a room dense with the fog of body heat, where I saw ten girls in strange white hats dancing with their eyes closed. In front of me a small bouncer with a black suit held a rope in the middle of the main passageway to control the movement of human traffic. I stood there for a few moments, occupied mentally by three dancers gyrating on a platform a few feet away from the rope. As I watched the display, I noticed another bouncer hovering by my shoulder. He would step in front of me with each move I made, and seemed to be singling me out. He was a large African fellow, much taller than me, with shoulders like a barn door. After stepping in front of me for the sixth time, I patted him gently on the shoulder and told him I wasn't going to touch the girls. He didn't respond, standing more resolutely and closer in proximity to me. I sighed and turned around, chatting to a girl whose name I wouldn't remember.

As I moved around I saw Hans at some point, in the corner with a fat girl who looked fresh from the country, kissing her as if his life depended on it. In the far corner near the bar I saw Dubz and Mick drunkenly eyeing a girl near them. Despite the flashing lights and movements of people around me, I could see her sensuous lips, delicate eyes and curvy body. On the second floor, they were playing reggae music, and there I danced with a girl or two, but didn't get any numbers. The music droned on as I coasted on my buzz, feeling the sensations around me ripple like water in a bucket.

When I returned downstairs, the crowd had thinned and the bouncer and the rope were gone. I stood in the hallway and a girl walked past me. She was a foreigner, with her hair pulled tightly back in a long ponytail. I said hello. She took a step forward then stopped and turned to face me. The next day I would have no idea what I said to her, but whatever it was had made her laugh and give me a slight hug. She told me she was going to find her friends, and I didn't see her again, though I did receive a text message an hour later from her that read:

Hey Jamaica. Let's do that "thing" we spoke about. Cheers.

I didn't know what the "thing" was, and I didn't care. The claws of sleep were pulling at me now, the world around me swimming dreamily in beer goggle Technicolour. A hand touched me on my shoulder and I turned to see Mick, smiling sheepishly. Dubz, Hans and his friends had disappeared. We rode the train back to Yotsuya together, barely speaking as we drifted in and out of consciousness.

The walk back to the house from the train station woke me up completely, but Mick remained in a state of semi-sleep. He patted me heavily on the back as we went up the walkway and into the house. That's when I saw Melodie under the tree, smoking and looking pensive. Even at a glance I was temporarily drawn in by her strong facial features, hidden half in shadow from the branches above. I went to my room and threw the jacket I had been wearing on the bed. It smelled strongly of beer and women's perfume. The lobby was quiet and bright, and the entertainment room was empty. The eye-shutting feeling that had been hugging me like a hefty schoolboy only minutes ago was gone. I decided to get a drink. Stepping out onto the walkway, I expected to see Melodie still there, but she wasn't. This surprised me, because I didn't hear her come into the suite behind me. *Maybe she isn't real,* I wondered to myself. As I walked to the convenience store, I thought of everything around me. Dubz, Mick and Hans probably weren't real either, just figments of my imagination in this illusory Tokyo world, standing by the same window I had a week earlier in Zeus' apartment, looking at the same vista. Melodie and the people in the house could all just be phantoms with nowhere to go, forever trapped in the dimly lit cobblestone back streets of Yotsuya.

I grabbed another Chu-Hi and relished the loud hiss it made as I opened it. The cool, orange flavoured liquid doused in sake kicked my tongue, and I took a step back to reality, away from thoughts of phantoms or disappearing roommates. The walk back to the house was nothing more than a quick breath, and again I was in my room, listening to the quiet whir of the air conditioner. The drink made me slip into a semiconscious state, and a few times I saw Yumi in my mind, in the same yellow dress she wore the night of the fireworks. This time, she lifted the skirt, revealing her pubic hair, and visibly moist genitals. She leaned forward I could literally see the fire in her eyes, little flames dancing and spinning in her irises. She licked her lips, and I felt the blood rush to my loins, creating an aching erection. She said something I couldn't hear, as she slid backwards into the distance, pulled by an unseen force; the yellow dress flailing in the dreamlike breeze as she floated to the far side of the gulf that had always been there between us, further and further until she was a speck on the horizon. Then I reopened my eyes, back in the real world again.

Chapter 9

The psychiatrist's office was somewhere in Omotesando, quite a long walk from the closest train station. I'd never been to a psychiatrist or any sort of counselor before, but I'd also never had a severe panic attack. The idea that something invisible could be a controlling force, literally holding you down and crippling you was foreign to me.

My first rent check was due a day or two ago. When had I opened my pouch to pay the seventy thousand yen, I was shocked to see how little was left in there. Sitting on the carpet in front of the bed, I counted the remainder of the money. In all, after taking out my rent, I had thirty thousand yen left. This meant in the month I had spent gallivanting at clubs and bars with nameless people, my first month at that, I had spent exactly one month's rent. *On nothing!* I hadn't bought any snazzy new pairs of shoes, no slick jeans, or even a discounted Mr. Children album. All I remembered was going occasionally to the convenience stores, a few restaurants and clubs here and there. One month's rent, on nothing. Poof.

I decided to go to the head office of my former company and see if they had any available jobs for people wanting to teach English in the area. At the very least, that would supplement me until I could find something else. The trip to the office was uneventful, until I walked near to the main building. My arms were trembling and it was very hard to breathe, as if I'd walked into a pocket of hot air. Then, when I stopped to catch my breath, I couldn't. The air around me had morphed into a billowing, asphyxiating blanket. Then the searing pain shot across my chest, and down I went, sitting flat on the sidewalk, huffing and wheezing. To my left, nothing but the empty street greeted me. A minute earlier, in the distance I had seen a young man who could have been me. He wore a crisp black suit, and walked with the fresh steps of someone ready to take on the world. But unlike me, he was invulnerable to this invisible force pressing me to the ground. The choking sensation increased and everything darkened, as I lay flat on the ground.

I woke up to the feel of water on my face, staring at a man no less than sixty years old. His head was wrapped in a towel, indicating to me he was some kind of outdoor vendor or cook. I eased myself up, feeling the beginnings of a pounding headache.

"Are you all right?" he asked.

"I think so," I replied.

"A person like you should be able to handle the sun I would think," he said to me without smiling.

I didn't know how to respond. In a way he was right. People like me are supposed to be the antithesis of the norm here. Me, tall and resolute with my dark skin and skinny body propelled into a chasm of all things new. I'm supposed to be able to perform slam dunks on a whim, squire women effortlessly while eating a sumo wrestler's portion of food and drink enough beer to get a team of college students drunk. But I wasn't any of that. Lying on a street somewhere in Tokyo, a man in his sixties had basically called me a pussy.

These thoughts were replaced by a cold fear as I stood up. My feet felt heavy, and slight tremors started in my hand when I looked at the office building for my former company only thirty feet away. It stared at me blankly, also invulnerable to invisible forces. I became envious of its inanimate life, its inability to feel pressure or exert any. It would stand there until it was destroyed, saying nothing and feeling nothing, completely fulfilling its exact purpose.

The man handed me a bottle of water and I thanked him, as waves of embarrassment went through my system. What had just happened? Immediately I did a web search for my symptoms on the phone.

Panic Attack

That result came up more than anything else, and I was shocked to see the similarities with what I had felt. I had to do something. The little town I lived in had exposed a strange, raw nerve, but it had grown into something else. Something that simple steps wouldn't be able to fix. Using the same search engine, I typed "psychiatrist" and "Tokyo" and found place of repute based on a simple index of customer satisfaction reviews. My arms were shaking as I walked off the train the next day, still seeing the face of the older man looking at me, the sun slightly hidden behind his towel wrap, creating a tiny halo over his head. The only thing that could calm me down now was a drink. It always took me back into the real world; that hiss of the carbonated beverage as the tab popped open, the cool touch of the can on my lips and the little drops of condensation that wet my palm as I held it. Drinking from the can I was whole, for a minute or two, as things around me felt fragmented.

I tossed the can into the trash and walked into the building. It was two stories high, with a dark brown roof and pastel walls. Inside was cool and dimly lit. Some new age type of music played from an invisible source. A young woman with a pleasant face handed me a pad with some basic information to fill out. Sometime later a woman came by the front desk. She introduced herself as Carmen, and gestured for me to follow her to a room at the end of a hallway to the left of the waiting area.

She was dressed in simple brown shoes, with a long summer skirt that went far below her knees. Her hair, hung loosely just above her shoulders, reflected neither style nor simplicity. We walked into her office, which was equally as plain as her attire, with no decorations on the wall except a faded diploma in a cheap frame. This faced a desk with only a notepad and a pen on its surface. She motioned for me to sit in a chair near the desk. Her eyes were a dark and gentle green.

"I see you said you had a panic attack recently, how are you feeling now?" she asked.

"I'm feeling better," I said, remembering the drink I had downed just minutes before going into the building.

"I see. Well, we do things pretty simply here. I can see on your form that you haven't had any prior attacks. Is there something you feel triggered this?"

"I guess so," I replied.

"Well in this description here you said you fainted, that sounds pretty serious."

"Well, that is true."

Internally, I felt quite comfortable. The chair was soft and relaxing, and the office had no distractions to occupy my mind.

Yet I could feel the slight twinge of bothered energy in my hands, and I was clenching my toes tightly in my socks.

"One second," Carmen said, standing up.

She pulled a small ottoman from behind her desk and placed it in front of me. "You look tense," she said. I raised my legs up, and immediately felt much better. She sat down and gave me a quiet look as the air settled between us like falling snow.

"Most people know the exact reason why they come here, so instead of me asking you a lot of questions and taking things down the wrong street, could you tell me a bit about yourself and what brought you here today?"

Fair enough, I said to myself. Especially since the one hour session would cost me nine thousand yen. I started by telling her about the genesis of my Tokyo trip, retelling in detail my daily routine as a teacher. The people, I told her, were just *so quiet* it was unnerving, and though the kids were cute and loved high-fiving me, I felt like a spectacle more than someone just going through the motions of doing work. I told her about barely speaking to anyone around me, and how I spent most of my time watching the clock.

"Was that stressful for you? Watching the clock count down slowly?" she asked.

I thought about it.

"In a sense, yes. I mean, time moves slowly during the day but when I was at the school it was as if time was even slower for me. A minute was more like five minutes, and the sun felt like it was in the sky much longer than normal."

She nodded as I continued speaking about the subsequent development of chest pains, sleeplessness, and the first signs of what would lead to my anxiety attack. I told her about the doctors I saw, telling a brief joke about the cardiologist that looked like a movie star, and how the symptoms had all hinted at some underlying issue, possibly depression.

"So when they told you that you were probably depressed did you do anything? Exercise, go out on the town chasing girls, anything like that?"

"Well I'm not one to really run around chasing girls like that," I said.

"Why not? Many a Japanese woman has a soft spot for young men who travel to this country."

"True but, I didn't really see myself as this guy that could run around town and do whatever he wants like some of the other teachers."

"The other teachers?"

"Yeah, guys from the states, Canada and Australia. These guys had girls every other week, living like rock stars."

She offered me a bottle of water, which I opened and took a sip of.

"So why couldn't you do what they did?" she asked.

Her expression was flat with a hint of emotion.

"I guess… I'm not like that," I replied, shuffling my toes in my shoes.

"Well, I've only just met you, but I can see that when you refer to yourself, particularly as it refers to social situations, you get tense," she said, pointing forward. I looked at where her hands were pointed and to my surprise I saw my hands clenched into fists in my lap.

Chuckling nervously I said, " You might be right about that."

I opened my clenched hands slowly.

"So tell me more about how you felt back where you used to live. Did you feel powerless in some way? I'm stretching here, but in the way you said you didn't feel like you had the swagger or bravado of those other guys in your town, did you feel some kind of lack, like you were being drained?"

Yes I did, I told her. The analogy I used was being the Lion in a zoo knowing he will never leave it. Whenever I went on the school roof and took a look at the horizon, I knew I would never be out there chasing the gazelles, roaming and roaring at the setting sun. I spoke at length for a while about this view-point, the idea of being trapped. She looked at me quietly as I spoke, and I noticed, did not take any notes.

"I understand how you felt. Your descriptions are very vivid, you sound like a writer," she said. "But tell me, what did you *do* once you figured you were trapped like, 'the Lion' as you say? Why didn't you just leave and go home?"

As she said this, another quiet silence fell between us, so low that I could hear her breathing. I'd never really thought this part though. Whatever work situation I'd found myself in before, I was always determined to do my best, tough it out and see it through.

"I signed a contract with the government," I told her.

"Okay, what does that mean?"

"What do you mean? It's pretty serious. Not only was I accountable to my head teacher, but I was also accountable to the students, the vice principal and the principal. I had to report to my company every day and also send reports to the government. In my training I was told that the entire school year is planned out in advance, and they take things very seriously over here. They even told me I was representing my country and to act badly would reflect badly on where I'm from. I was a *sensei* dammit, and that meant I was some parent-teacher hybrid which meant even more eyes, and more people watching over my damn shoulder each day."

My voice bubbled with indignation, and I took my feet off the ottoman.

"I'm sorry, I didn't mean to go off like that," I said.

Carmen looked at me for a few moments before responding.

"That sounds like a lot of pressure. Representing company, country and so many other things. So you felt you had to rough it, or else face a worst case scenario?"

"It was what I was thinking at the time," I said, glancing at her diploma on the wall.

"So tell me how you felt about messing up," she said.

"I never missed a day of work the entire time I was—"

"Hypothetically I mean. What was a situation that you felt could possibly happen which would negatively reflect on you to the extreme."

It wasn't that clear, I said to her, because during my training, I'd been told all these horror stories of people getting fired for touching students, or a branch of the company losing an entire prefecture's worth of contracts because some teacher rolled into a school staff room drunk from a bender the night before. There were also these nagging tales about promiscuous teachers hitting on the women in the staffroom, causing more issues.

"But let's say you had a breakdown, a panic attack or something like that and had to leave, what would happen?"

I thought about it.

"They would send a replacement teacher to fill in for me," I said.

"And this teacher, would he or she take over your position until your return?" Carmen asked.

"I guess so, I mean, if it *were* to happen," I replied.

"Does that happen? I mean it must happen every now and then," she said, leaning back slightly in her chair.

"Well, if there is an emergency of some sort, possibly."

Carmen took in a breath and took a sip of water from a green plastic bottle that must have been at the foot her chair. She raised her voice slightly. "Let's say it had nothing to do with a psychological situation like yours. So you aren't at school fainting in the staffroom because of a panic attack. You are riding your bike to school and a car hits you. You need to be hospitalized and cannot work. What then?"

Almost proudly, I replied that the company would dispatch a new teacher or work with the school to create a modified curriculum. If my injuries were serious and lasted longer than a month, the company would cover my insurance but pay for me to leave if I needed additional care or time off. Carmen nodded as I said this, her face still calm and devoid of significant emotion.

"So in essence, things would keep going as they always had," she said.

"Well, yes," I replied.

She rubbed a hand across the surface of the desk, as if petting it.

"You know," she said. "Anxiety can be triggered by things we can process and pinpoint easily. A traumatic event for example, like a car accident that gives you an extreme fear of driving, or a dangerous situation like being robbed. These things make logical sense, but more often than not, extreme anxiety like yours, is caused by the constant focus on situations that have never happened, and probably never will happen.

"In a way these types of anxieties have more power, because these fears can haunt you. You might avoid driving in a car, or walk on more brightly lit streets to avoid the wrong kind of people, but you can't leave your own mind alone, nor the thoughts of constant pressure when you feel that you have so many people relying on you. This thought process is what really follows you around, long after you've left work, wherever you are."

I sat there for a few moments, staring at the floor. The clear memory of being anxious during my training was at the forefront of my mind. As other trainees had laughed at the carefree jokes of a particularly humorous trainer, I'd sat there, nervously wondering if I would be the one to make an egregious error, if I'd be the person getting an under the table reprimand from a vice principal, a head English teacher or an angry kid with an axe to grind. As I'd learned how to teach, did workshops and sat through the various sessions on cultural norms I'd never felt fully comfortable, because one day I knew I'd be out there, stripped bare in the eyes of people I'd never met. That logic seemed a bit warped now, because at the school, there wasn't even that much to do and teachers were often so busy they could barely handle their individual workloads. The kids were friendly and welcoming (except the one creep who kept asking me how big my penis was) and none of the female teachers took an obvious sexual liking to me. As I sat there in the little office in Omotesando, I saw myself in the past, alone and stressed, shadowed by Carmen's supposed ghost, watching the clock and doodling on scrap paper. Now here I was in Tokyo, without structure and a plan, far away from the company and all those watchful eyes. Maybe I had made a step forward. I wanted to know what Carmen thought of this, when she smiled and said to me. "That's our time for today."

I thanked her and walked out of the office, saying a quick goodbye to the receptionist who gave me a meek bow after I paid my bill. A few streets away, near the train station, I sat at a café, nibbling on a small bowl of *oyakudon*. The session had been extremely revealing. As I'd left the counseling center, I'd walked with lighter, quicker steps. In some way I felt proud I'd made the decision to leave the toxic environment I'd been in, whether I mentally created it or not. I'd left Carmen's ghost behind and followed the sound of the crow, all the way to Tokyo. Near where I was sitting, a few kids in baggy hip-hop gear practiced dance moves in front of the large window of a store covered with signs that read, "Opening soon!"

My good feeling only lasted until I went back into the train station. I sat in a chair by myself, looking idly at commercials playing on a screen beside the train doors. I'd already spent over one hundred and forty thousand yen from my nest egg, over ten percent of my savings, in just four weeks.

Chapter 10

Another morning greeted me with open eyes. I'd spent most of the night in the entertainment room with the TV and a few cans of beer for company. For the last several hours I'd been watching a marathon of a food program. The host went to different reputable restaurants in Tokyo, constantly exclaiming how good everything was as he ate it. The fellow looked personable, and the extreme close up shots of delicious food made my stomach growl. Dubz was right about the house and its rhythms. In the early hours of the morning, I was free to stroll the through the premises, rarely seeing anyone come or go, most of the time doing this with a beer in my hand, listening to the sound of my sweatpants *swish* throughout the hallways. I eased back onto my pillow. Now, the food show guy was at some waterfront side restaurant. A plate of steaming Octopus parts were brought to his table and placed in front of him. He excitedly chatted about the meal and how it was prepared, then took a bite into a long, slimy tentacle, exclaiming, "Oh my! It's so good!" I heard the door open. Dubz was peering into the room, smiling at me. He was sharply dressed, in a black suit jacket over a dark blue dress shirt, with matching black slacks and black dress shoes.

"The man doesn't sleep I see," Dubz said.

"Sleep is ever elusive, traipsing through the hollows of reality, spinning but never stopping," I said.

"Is that a poem? Sounds good," Dubz asked.

"No I just made it up," I replied.

"Funny guy. I have to go man, gotta make this money! Catch you later."

He left the room, walking in strong strides towards the door. The body language he projected reminded me of the young man I saw near the company office the day before I fainted. There was a sense of purpose in those steps, fearlessness in the way the legs tensed and the shoulders pitched strongly from left to right. That solid arch of the neck and the half smile, half serious face that gave enough emotion to portray the light playfulness that made a life of teaching a little easier. Dubz had it, that resolve to face the world and make it happen, while I sat there drinking beer at seven a.m, lounging on throw pillows. I heard the *ping* of the elevator and saw Mr. Oba walk out. He was wearing dark yellow leather pants and a colourful silk shirt patterned with roses. Following closely behind him, were two tall, handsome young men, both dressed in tight jeans and sharp suit jackets. I didn't hear what they said as they walked quickly past the transparent door of the entertainment room, ignorant of my eyes on them, and went outside.

I'd forgone walking to convenience stores to buy my early morning meals. There was a market a few streets away that Mick told me about, and there I bought vegetables, onions, a few cloves of garlic and cheap ground meat. The streets were relatively quiet today and the sensation of the clear morning with its light cool reminded me of the past as a boy waking up at dawn to go to school, dreading the insufferably hot day ahead. But at that time, around five a.m, when I was wiping the night's crust from my eyes, lumbering slowly to the bathroom, I would always note the feeling of the cold tiles on my feet, and the icy pinch of the morning air on my skin as I came out of the shower. I would always cling to this temporary frigidity, before the sun spread across the land, chasing away the cool fingers of the night before. The mornings still held that for me, that little space between the dark and the light, a median I could cling to, before the light of day shined a spotlight on reality.

The session with the therapist had left me pensive for two days afterward. I'd started making notes in a journal, as Carmen had suggested to me when I was leaving, but it was hard to write. I kept imagining myself in that little toxic world, going stir crazy from thoughts I had personally created. I could see the ghost she had said represented my anxiety, following behind me slowly as I walked to the school. I could see it in the sweaty locker room, drifting closer and closer, as I got more tense. My ghost, my little creation, stifling me without me even being aware of it. I looked so weak in this daydream, so thin and wispy, ready to be blown over by the slightest gust of life's wind.

To combat this weakness, I had to channel the energy of Mick and Dubz in Shibuya. I needed an iota of Zeus' endless confidence. I wanted it all to ooze from me in a dense mist of pheromones. I thought about Yumi. The gulf between us was my invention as well, a perceptual canyon filled with the empty space of intangible ideas.

The girl from Camelot was my first exercise in this new mission of personal change. One thought of her stood out in my memory; the first time she walked past me. I could see the slender curves of her body, and the curly black hair pulled into a tight ponytail. Her neck was visible in this image as well, slim and pale, dotted slightly with freckles. There was no clear memory of her face, but her voice was distinct in my mind; a sharp Canadian accent, and I could also feel her hands on my back as she had hugged me goodbye, the soft hands of a woman. This uncertainty of how she looked gave our second meeting a sense of thrill.

On my way to meet her in Shibuya, I answered my phone on the train when she called me to tell me which exit she'd be coming from. Her voice was cheerful. Seeing her for the second time, she was quite attractive, with dark sensual eyes and slightly pouty lips. There was a strong artistic energy about her, particularly her manner of dress, which favoured black rock band t-shirts and grey thigh hugging jeans. I had invited her to an improvisation show I'd seen advertise on the internet.

The show was hilarious, and as we sat there, laughing at antics of a mixed performance group of Japanese people and foreigners I tried to actively fantasize about her. As she let out another laugh, I could see her naked on her futon in a small apartment somewhere, as we laughed at an esoteric joke, sipping on green tea from small cups. She rested her hands atop mine a few times during the performance as she looked forward, chuckling occasionally. I took in her side profile, liking the round tip of her nose, and her expressive lips. Where would the first kiss be and who would make that step? Should I drop a subtle hint about going back to my place, or would she do the honours? I liked the pleasant mood and the atmosphere, but I felt nervous. Could I even handle a relationship with her, or the requirements of the dinners, bar outings and parties that come with this territory? As the crowd laughed heartily at another comedy routine, I thought about my yellow money pouch in my room, getting lighter by the day.

She stood up to go to the bathroom, and her shirt rose slightly, revealing a thin line of pale skin. This glimpse created the stirrings of an erection in my pants. While she walked away and I admired the taper of her butt through her jeans I envisioned her naked and lying under me, sweat from my body dripping onto her chest.

After the show we chatted near a convenience store that orbited a video arcade. She drank from a large can of Sapporo, which looked enormous in her small hands. She told me she was from Toronto, making sure to emphasize she was *not* from Montreal. We laughed about little things, our Victorian educational systems and her dancing ability. Apparently she was a top-notch freestyle dancer, which was hard for me to believe. We finished out beers and walked with arms locked toward the train station. We had made a bet previously about naming our respective national dishes. I guessed Poutine correctly for Canada and she was stumped by my local delicacy, a common morning meal called Ackee and Salt fish. The bet was a kiss on the cheek, and her lips felt incredibly soft on my cheek. The evening had passed in a calm wave, and as I waved goodbye to her, I wondered if I had done things right. This was because the same night I had met this girl, Dubz met a girl at the same club and took her home. In graphic detail he explained how he ravaged her insatiable demands, having sex with her no less than three times before morning. He also said they had made a video and offered to show it to me, but I said it wasn't necessary. She had taken him to breakfast afterwards he also said, as they laughed and chatted about her questionable fashion choices. Dubz told this story with the passion of a child who has received the ultimate gift for his birthday. It was a regular part of his life, he said. The girl had approached him and said hello, and soon after he suggested they leave and eventually they ended up at the guesthouse.

"When girls come here man, it is just *over*," Dubz had emphasized. "Once they step through those sliding doors, is like they already naked."

I didn't share these sentiments. Though I'd had a similar night or two myself in the past, they had always been predicated on the urgent need to escape my slow life in the small town I lived in. If I came to Tokyo, it was to rage and drink, party and meet people without any real thoughts or considerations. I had always lived in the margins in my normal ways of being, and I couldn't imagine myself telling a girl to come home with me minutes after meeting her. If something did happen with a girl it tended to feel like blind luck, not something done on purpose. But standing there at the west side of Shibuya station where the girl took the train home, I had the feeling I could have made that proposal to this attractive dancer from Toronto, and she would have said yes.

When I reached home, I saw Mick and two of the Italian girls in the entertainment room. He waved at me and I waved back. Down the hall, standing in front of the door to my suite, was Melodie. She was in a pair of black leggings that stopped at her ankles, and a slightly oversized tank top with the image of a man wearing 3D glasses printed on it. She wasn't wearing a brassiere, the impressions of her nipples obvious under the thin cloth of her shirt. She looked at me briefly, any recognition of who I was undetectable in her eyes, then turned around and walked slowly to one of the bathrooms at the end of the hall, her narrow waist barely moving with each step she took. I went into the room and lay on the bed and started reading an old novel.

Hungry a few hours later, I went to cook some food. I packed a few of my vegetables and some of the ground meat into a small silver bucket that served as my food transport device from my room to the kitchen. Spreading the vegetables out on the large counter in the kitchen, I started chopping onions and preparing the stove. The kitchen had everything a person could need, with multiple rice cookers to the left of the stove, and a wide assortment of pots and pans underneath the cupboard. There was also a shelf filled with large black plates, and drawers with the usual tools of the culinary trade: spatulas, sieves, shredders and strainers. I dropped a few onions and okra into the pan and let it simmer. I heard voices and the bustle of people coming into the lobby. I didn't look up to see who it was. As the smell of the frying vegetables filled the air, I stared at the vegetables, watching them shake with heat.

Whoever had come into the house was very loud, despite the fact that it was almost one in the morning. I made out the excited voice of Hans, chatting broken English and German in rapid bursts. A voice responded in German, a girl's voice, and then I heard the group laugh. The voices stopped, and I heard the shuffle of feet move away from the kitchen signaling a move into the entertainment room. I opened the bag of ground meat and poured it in with the onions and the okra. I sprinkled black pepper on the quickly browning meat and looked into my silver bucket. My last and most important ingredient, a bottle of soy sauce, was missing. I exited the kitchen and almost walked into a girl right by the door. From where she was standing, she must have been watching me cook. She was tall, almost my height, with an athletic physical build. Her face was sharp and angular in that eastern European way, but not harshly so. She had short, jet black hair styled with intermittent streaks of blonde and purple. I could see the rise of her generous chest from her form fitting black shirt, which she wore with black jeans tucked into pair of small boots. She extended a long arm.

"Hey, I'm Steffi!" she said with a smile.

We spoke for a few minutes. Her voice and her face indicated that she's was little drunk—but the way she waited for me to reply, standing there with a constant smile and somewhat fidgety energy, telegraphed significant interest. I shook her hand and excused myself to run and get the soy sauce from my room. Back in the kitchen, she was sitting on the counter, lifting her legs up and down in brief kicks. As I poured oily, black drops of the sauce into the pan, I saw her move a rogue bang of hair from in front of her eyes, blue eyes, grinning still.

"That smells good," she said.

I smiled in agreement.

"Can I have some?" she asked.

"Sorry, I think I only made enough for myself," I replied.

"Well then fuck you," she said.

"If I'm 'fuck you' then your name is 'fuck off'. So you are FO and I'm FY okay?" I said. Watching the improv show earlier had taught me a few tricks.

She chuckled and hopped off the counter, mentioned something about the entertainment room and left the kitchen.

The food was ready, and I tossed it all into a large bowl, grabbed a fork and headed to the entertainment room. I took a seat on one of the couches near the rear of the room. In there with me was Hans, one of his friends from our Camelot night and several new faces. Steffi was the only girl in the group, sitting a few feet in front of me. She turned around several times, fully engaging me in conversation.

"My hands are big!" she exclaimed. "Guys hate it because my hands make their dick look small."

I laughed at this revelation. She then went on to explain why she didn't like Japanese men.

"They all act like twelve year old children, and their junk is too small. I like a big strong guy, it is just how I am," she said.

This was how the conversation went for some time after I'd finished my meal and the bowl sat empty at the foot of my chair; a raw mixture of harsh sexual jokes and statements filled with curse words. With each bizarre comment or statement, I felt my sense of intrigue about her increase. I took a better look at her face and features, the ample bosom, her tanned arms and her eyes.

The guys beside us were talking amongst themselves, but occasionally paused to watch our exchange. I could see one of them gesturing and smiling at us, possibly wondering why she was speaking to me for so long after just meeting me. Should someone have asked me that question, I would be unable to answer. I told her I was going to get a drink at the convenience store up the road and she excitedly hopped up, saying she'd follow me there. As she stood up, she knocked over two beer cans beside her. As the suds starting spreading across the light carpeting near the TV, I went to the kitchen, and grabbed a cleaning rag. Hans came with me as well, looking slightly concerned. We went back to the room and she grabbed the rag from me and started scrubbing the floor intensely.

I was in a stooped position beside her as she worked, and I could smell something sweet on her skin. The spill was now cleaned, and I took the rag from her and walked to the kitchen. She followed me there.

"I wanted to make out with you on the carpet," she said.

I smiled at her. "Really? Why?"

"I think it was the perfect moment. We were on our knees so close I thought it would be nice to make out."

I smirked at this statement, and she walked away, telling everyone in the entertainment room loudly what she had just told me. I played along, not taking it seriously. Historically, there had been little value for me in a drunk woman's advances. Sometimes alcohol-fueled directness can be fun and even flattering, but I knew the next day, when Steffi woke up, she probably wouldn't remember who I was. I'd be a dark blur in a night of blurs. I put the rag under the sink. Steffi was sitting where I had been sitting previously. I sat beside her.

"So you like me?" I asked.

"Of course. You are good looking and you have a beautiful body. I haven't seen your cock yet, so I cannot be sure if I *really* like you, but yeah."

I laughed loudly. There might have been a touch of possible truth in what she was saying, but who knows.

"I'll be more inclined to believe you when I meet you again and you are sober," I said to her.

"I'm going to a bar tomorrow night. They serve fifty yen beers there. You should come," she said, leaning on me slightly.

For the next hour, she peppered me with questions and our dialogue integrated us with the larger group, who were now watching music videos on the TV. When she went outside to have a cigarette, I caught Hans looking at me, with a huge smile on his face. I could smell the beer on him from where I was sitting.

"You are a monster," he said.

I smiled as he said this. Mick came into the room in sweats and a black t-shirt and flopped on some of the throw pillows near the TV.

"Best thing after a run is a drink. Can I have this beer?" he said to Hans, pointing at an unopened can in a box of Asahi.

"Of course," Hans replied.

Steffi soon walked back into the room, all attitude. She immediately picked a fight with Mick over his throw pillow. Initially, Mick refused to give her the pillow unless she told him what her opinion of him was.

"I want the pillow, not to give you some fucking opinion of yourself," she said.

"You'll get the pillow once you tell me," Mick said, his eyes gleaming with the same energy I'd seen on that night we went to Shibuya.

"Honestly, when I walked in here I thought you looked like a friendly gay guy, so I thought you'd give me the pillow without any problem."

The room erupted into laughter, including Mick, who smiled and shrugged his shoulders as he gave her the pillow.

"Fuck you," Steffi said. "I've got my own now."

She was holding a beer in her hand. No one decided to remind her that the entire conversation had started on the topic of a throw pillow. More time passed, and the crowd left, leaving her alone in the room, passed out on the floor. Sometime later I tried to wake her up, to give her a blanket, but she was dead to the world. Sprawled out on the floor with one leg hidden under two throw pillows, she still managed to look peaceful. I took a walk up to the convenience store, bought a beer and went back to the house. When I went to my room, sleep came for me quickly. I woke up at five, and stepped outside to see if Steffi was still sleeping in the TV room, but she was gone.

Chapter 11

Naturally, the next day, she had little to no memory of me. I showed up to the *Izakaya* fifty yen drink up she had invited me to. Steffi and a group of students including Hans were all sitting around an extremely long table. When I said hello, she gave me a sober smile and a lingering stare. Nothing registered in those blue eyes of hers. More than a bit annoyed with myself, I soon left the restaurant, going to a video arcade in Shibuya where I played Street Fighter until my fingers hurt and beside my foot were five empty cans of Chu-Hi. I had canceled a potential outing with the artsy girl from Camelot to go to the restaurant to meet her.

Sometime later after I'd reached home, I'd started cooking. I stood there in the kitchen waiting for the food to cook, glancing at the occasional tenant coming into the house. Hans walked into the kitchen, his face a little red but without the leery smile that indicated he was extremely drunk.

"Hey man, what time did you leave the party? Steffi asked for you and we couldn't find you," he said.

"Oh?"

"Yes, she was telling me that you were not… ah, were not such a good guy for running away from her. I told her that you are a cool guy, and then she asked more about last night. I know that you guys were talking in the kitchen, and when I mentioned that, I think she remembered who you were."

"She must have been drunker than I thought," I said.

"We were all so wasted man. Anyway, she told me to tell you that you should text her."

I tried to imagine this scenario as Hans said it, seeing Steffi gently ask him to relay a message to me. I didn't think this was possible; I'm sure whatever version of this message he was giving me was heavily censored. I pulled out my phone and sent Steffi a text message. In seconds, I received a response.

Hello there, little pussy!

The following night, we met at the train station closest to the Greenleaf house. As I walked over to her, she poked a rod-like finger into my chest. "I was about to leave you. You are late!" she said. I laughed and then looked at her. In a hoody, jeans and funky multicolored sneakers, she looked nice.

"Coffee?" I said.

"No, we don't need coffee. After today, I think I need a drink. Shinjuku?" she asked.

Sure, I said. As we walked down the stairs, I made fun of her outfit. "You look like a sexy Unabomber with that hoody on." She laughed and pulled the hood off, the bright fluorescent lights in the station sending streaks of white across her black hair.

"I had a bad day today," she said once we were on the train.

She told me about the project she was working on, and how she was on a deadline to summarize ten pages of data, but she had only read two pages so far. She was here doing some kind of pre-architectural internship, that, like Hans' language school didn't seem to take up much of her time during the day. Her face looked more serious as she spoke, talking about her interest in Japanese architecture, and how things like the Mori building were projects she aspired to work on.

"Do you put a lot of pressure on yourself?" I asked her.

She shook her head saying no.

We were in a sharp contrast to the people on the train on that time of the day. There were mostly men on board, standing quietly in a range of dark suits, with almost every man's eyes fixed directly on their cell phones. They fit perfectly, as much a part of the train as the bolts that held the standing rails upright. In there in the middle of it all were Steffi and I, chatting and laughing. Our conversation was a consistent cycle of her making whatever I said seem silly, laughing at me, throwing a subtle insult, asking a question of genuine interest, and then doing it all over again. The mind buzzing under that head of stylish black hair was sprinting at full gallop, leaving everything behind in the past tense.

"I think I felt bad the other night for not remembering who you are," she said with a smirk.

"Oh, so this is just a courtesy meeting?" I asked.

"I think so, yes. Remember I haven't seen your cock yet, I don't know if I really like you," she said flatly.

A whooping laugh escaped my mouth, startling a man beside me. The train was slowing down now, coasting into Shinjuku station. We had no real destination. I didn't go to Shinjuku very often, but Steffi was a veteran.

"Let's just find an exit," she said.

We headed out into the night, seeing that cool Shinjuku cityscape of lights and dark alleys. We walked towards Golden Gai, a little road with tons of tiny bars with high table sitting fees and overpriced drinks. This area felt like the darker, dirtier Tokyo people read about; the small streets with black asphalt illuminated by the dull glow of the signs for each establishment, the super contiguous fixture of cool shops that could only hold about ten patrons at a time, and the scattered array of hanging lamps that cast blood-red light on the blood-red faces of men walking under them. In one of these alleys, we saw two men walking nearby, both foreigners obviously looking for something. They were tall, broad-chested men dressed in plain Dockers and short-sleeved shirts who looked to be in their late forties. One walked up to us.

"English right? Good," he said.

"Yes I speak English," Steffi replied.

"Do y'know where any gay bars are?" he asked.

Steffi, obviously knowing these sorts of things, directed the men to an address on Shinjuku Ni-chome, a few streets away.

"I hope I told them the right place!" she said with a giggle.

We walked in a circle around the same street three times. She initially suggested going to Albatross, a bar she knew. I said it was fine, but as we walked past the same establishments she kept suggesting other places. Each place she recommended was fine with me, but not for her. This went on for twenty minutes, a bizarre ritual that left me sighing as we prepared to circle the street for the fourth time. Finally, she chose a place.

It was a tiny bar with an interior of red velvet. The bartender was a young man with a friendly face. He gave us both a confident, knowing smile that immediately stripped us of all identity. Within that smile, we were anyone on a given night that happened to come into this bar, faceless mannequins with holes in our faces for liquor and outstretched hands waving money. We ordered a few drinks and I balked slightly at the eight hundred yen price tag for my short glass of Bacardi and coke. I felt more chatty than usual, and explained to her the depth of the movie, *The Lion King*.

"It always shocks me how people don't get how deep Lion King really was," I said.

Steffi nodded and took a deep gulp of her drink and waved to the bartender to bring us two more. Swallowing the last of my drink, I continued. "I mean, it tackles all the major issues about life in a way a kid can easily understand. You have the death of the father, which was just *major*. I still get chills seeing Mufasa fall off that rock face."

"I cried during that scene," she said.

"Exactly! But before that, we get that excellent summary of their concept of eternity when he tells Simba that should he die, he'll be in the stars watching him and guiding him."

"But he didn't say he was going to die," Steffi noted in a firm tone.

"I know, I know, but that is why Mufasa's death was even more powerful. Because now, his son was prepared to deal with it mentally. I mean, it's crazy, the film is filled with betrayal and talks about love, teaches you about the value of family and also having real friends watch your back."

I'd never spoken this passionately about any movie and I eyed my drink carefully. The bartender came back over with the two new drinks. I took out some money, but Steffi stopped me.

"I got it," Steffi said with a smile.

In that smile, I saw the first sign of calm in the maelstrom of her mind. Her eyes didn't look significantly probing, and there was no insult waiting for me in the rafters. As we wet our throats, she told me about her love for horror movies, and how she cried watching *Dracula* as a child. We left the bar soon afterward.

"I normally bomb the Family Mart for drinks before I head anywhere," I said to her. Back on the Golden Gai, I spotted the familiar green and white colours of the establishment in the distance. As we walked towards it, I thought about a moment earlier in the evening, when I had touched her on her shoulder while we were speaking at Shinjuku station. She had literally jumped back.

"I don't like touching," she had said. "I'm not a touchy feely person."

At the time, I had ignored the statement, assuming it was one of her combative quirks. But at the bar we just went to, when we were having our first drinks, I touched her knee, and she had jerked it away. Her discomfort with being touched wasn't something I wanted to make an issue of, and I told her I wouldn't touch her again for the remainder of the night. There was a visible shift in her face as I said this, particularly in her eyebrows, which frowned slightly. After that, she became more relaxed.

After popping into Family Mart and grabbing two fresh beers, we stood outside a love hotel, people watching.

"Salary man," I said, pointing to a man in a black suit with a neat haircut walking with a suitcase.

"Drug dealer," Steffi said, gesturing with her nose at a young man with baggy pants and an oversized shirt walking past the love hotel.

"Why do you say that?" I asked.

"Obviously he is hiding drugs in those pants," she replied. After pointing out a supposed drag queen, karaoke king and a pervert, we left that spot and roamed up an adjacent street.

"I love these guys!" Steffi said, pointing at a large billboard of young men with extravagant hairstyles. The men in the image all had a very similar look; slim handsome faces with small lips, their hair dyed in various shades of brown set into gangly spikes or long, elaborate curls.

"Are they in a band or something?"

"No they are hostess boys," Steffi replied.

That information was genuinely interesting to me. Life lived as a pretty man, spending your nights entertaining women with loads of disposable income in a dark, quiet bar. Steffi explained to me again her disdain for Japanese guys, launching into a story about the first Japanese guy she slept with.

"It wasn't so bad, but he was so feminine," she said.

I listened to the story, but didn't really hear all the details. An usually strong buzz was hitting me. Her mouth was moving, and I saw her gesturing and laughing, but the words weren't clear. A light drizzle began and we ran back to the Family Mart and bought a cheap umbrella. After the rain stopped we snapped pictures on our phones with a few of the hostess boys, one of whom said he was a part-time baseball player. Twice Steffi ran behind an old car in an abandoned parking lot to take a piss on the street. I laughed a lot with her that evening. The street was ours, and it could be ours forever as long as we had alcohol and time.

As we kept drinking I found it harder to keep up with her unceasing barrage of insults and emotional pushes and pulls. She would say I'm attractive and then immediately afterwards say something rude, usually with a dirty word involved. The initial hilarity of her brusque style of interaction chewed slowly into the good feeling of the moment. The street wasn't ours anymore, and our forever was washing away in a bucket of cocks and pussies. I believe she noticed I wasn't paying her words much attention. She stopped speaking, pulled me towards her aggressively and shoved her tongue into my mouth. The kiss was long and wet.

"Do you want to come to Shimokitazawa?" she said.

That's where she lived.

"What time is it?" I asked.

She checked her phone and told me it was a few minutes past eleven. I nodded and we walked back to the station, my arm around her shoulders. After coming off the train at her stop and leaving the station, I spent a minute with a young Japanese guy on the street who was playing guitar. I'd fiddled with the instrument in the past, and I tried to play, but my head wasn't clear and I clumsily plunked the strings before handing it back to him. Steffi walked *very* fast up the road, and I had trouble keeping up with her. I stopped at a 7-11 and bought a bottle of water to curb my impending nausea, a bottle that Steffi drank on the way to her place. She lived in a house off the main street with a small front yard. In the kitchen, she made a small sandwich for me.

"No thanks," I said.

The world around me was a constant wobble, and if I sat down her kitchen became a visual merry-go-round. I followed her up a short flight of stairs. In front of a large brown door she turned to me and said, "If you think you were going to have sex with me, forget about it. The Red Army is visiting."

"I didn't say anything about sex, I need a place to—wait, what's the Red Army?"

"You know, the *Red Army* is in town."

Oh, I thought, her period.

We went into her room, which was spacious with only a futon on the ground, a threadbare closet and high ceilings. She took off her pants, revealing an extremely toned pair of thighs and a tight rear end.

"Take off your pants," she commanded, resting a hand on the band of her black panties.

"Not yet," I replied, standing by the door. In my vision, I saw two Steffies looking at me.

"Go out on the balcony if you feel sick. If you puke in my room, I will fucking kill you," she said with a smile.

"I won't puke here. Man, I think the guy at that bar in Shinjuku gave me some strange drink," I said.

She laughed with no pity. "Whatever you say, pussy."

She slipped on a pair of colourful boxers and lay down onto the futon. I decided to go outside. She giggled as I stepped over the bed and outside to the balcony. From her window, the streets were dark and quiet. I took several deep breaths in an attempt to collect myself, but nothing changed. The few streetlights that I could see were in blurry doubles. A small red chair was on the balcony, and I sat there for a few seconds, until everything around me started spinning again. *Dammit*, I thought. Steffi was lying stomach down on the bed, her bronzed skin and perfect butt teasing me with promise.

"Cuddle with me," she said without turning around.

I didn't respond, because I was heading out the door and down the stairs. My mind raged. *Fuck beers, Fuck Sake, Fuck Vodka!* In the bathroom downstairs, I leaned over the toilet and heaved, but only a trickle of bile came up. Like the kitchen, the bathroom was also a merry-go-round, this one set on the maximum speed. I pushed two fingers in my mouth, activating my gag reflex. Now, a clear stream of liquid blasted from my stomach up through my throat and into the bowl. I did this three times, and immediately my head felt clearer. Luckily, I hadn't made a mess, and the entire process took about two minutes. After flushing the toilet, I wiped the seat clean and washed my mouth. I went back upstairs, to the complete darkness of Steffi's room. I took off my clothes quickly and fell heavily on the futon beside her, immediately passing out.

The next morning, I woke up very alert and refreshed at about six a.m. For a second I didn't know where I was, until I turned to see Steffi smiling at me. The morning light bounced off her bronze skin, revealing the tiny hairs on her forearm. She teased me about being drunk in a warm, heavy breath. She stood up and walked to the balcony door and began smoking a cigarette. When she lay back down, I gave her a foot massage and told her a funny story, playing with her toes and making them argue with each other. She smiled throughout this monologue of mine, as I occasionally looked up from my puppet show, through the mounds that were her breasts and into her eyes. Then, I felt tired again, and held her beside me, feeling her hands slip around my back. Before I blacked out again, I saw her eyes with that serious look. The look she gave me when she didn't want me to touch her knee. This image stayed in my mind for a few seconds, before I fell into the darkness of sleep again.

I woke up to see her standing by the door. She wore a dark yellow skirt that stopped below her knees, and long brown boots. Her purse was large and blue, dotted with rhinestones and stickers. Hung over her shoulder was a thin black sweater.

"Come I have to go to class. Get up sleepy boy," she said, slipping on a pair of giant dark glasses.

I groggily put on my pants and shirt, and headed out with her.

"I can't believe I made you a sandwich and you didn't eat it! I cannot see you again!"

This was the theme of our walk to the train station, her constant declaration that she wouldn't see me again. She spoke in her normal voice, but there was a strange insistence underlying the energy she put into her words. I walked beside her quietly, still feeling quite tired. Steffi was walking at her breakneck pace again, and I barely kept up. On the train back to Shinjuku, I remained quiet. Steffi's naturally high, almost manic energy was very real. I initially thought it was some kind of screening mask to drown out people she didn't like, but I could tell it was the result of a natural adventurousness. Also, I saw that her way of expressing that she liked me was by a series of verbal disqualifications, which differed greatly from her actions. Then, I noticed that when I retreated mentally because I was tiring of her way of showing affection, her face would reflect a very different mental dialogue. In her eyes I could see she was trying to figure out how to keep things right, and if she had pushed too far with her sarcasm.

Every now and then she'd ask me a question, to which I gave a simple and standard answer. She looked down at her feet a few times, unsmiling. When our train stopped we exited at the same terminal. She gave me a kiss on the cheek and turned quickly away. I turned back around to say something to her, but she was already several feet away, walking rapidly towards a set of steps that led to another train line.

Then, I understood. Regardless of her attitude, sarcasm and jokes, some part of her had wanted the night to go well. I thought about what to say to her in a text message, particularly after the embarrassment of getting so drunk on our first outing together. When I reached home, she had already sent me a message. A little text, telling me she had a great time with me. My somber morning mood must have bothered her, and from the sea of profanity laced conversations and endless drinks Steffi seemed to be used to, the calmer girl inside her had risen to the surface briefly, and looked directly into my eyes.

Chapter 12

It's midday and I was in the Mori building, having lunch with Zeus. We were in an upscale café, filled with a mix of patrons. I peered over the menu, which had an assortment of tasty meals, but none cheaper than fifteen hundred yen per plate. Zeus ordered quickly, and noticing my constant gaze at the menu, tapped me on the shoulder.

"Don't worry man, I got this," he said. "You gave me a good reason to get out of that mad office."

I ordered a chicken pasta salad. As usual, he was well dressed, sitting in a black suit that rippled with color with each shift of his broad shoulders. He removed his jacket and slung it around the back of his chair.

"The material on this suit is called Bird Eye," Zeus said. "They actually weave two slightly different colours of fabric together. Here, take a look."

I held the jacket, which felt cool and soft in my hand. Up close, the cloth had an intricate interwoven pattern filled with little dots of a slightly lighter colour.

"The dots are the eyes. From afar your suit looks solid, but after people start walking closer the colour begins changing," Zeus said with a big smile.

"You are pretty serious about your suits," I said.

"Not really. I do have a tailor, but if I'm feeling lazy I just go to Zara, or the Armani store. But I was watching *Mission Impossible 4* the other day and saw Tom Cruise in this badass blue suit."

"Yes, I remember that," I said.

"After I saw the suit in that movie, I had to get that shit!" Zeus said with a laugh.

I handed him the jacket and soon afterward the waiter came with our food. It was delicious, and I made a mental note to come here again. We chatted about light things, such as a recent rugby game at the Tokyo stadium and Zeus' upcoming trip for a week to Korea. I gave him the rundown on the Greenleaf house, telling him about the tenants, the layout and my creepy dream about Mr. Oba. Zeus laughed heartily, his voice booming throughout the restaurant.

"Price okay?" he asked me.

I chuckled and continued, telling him about the assortment of people in the house. Explaining some of the hesitance I was feeling generally, I mentioned the girl from Camelot and my encounter with Steffi. At the mention of these women's names, Zeus' face became more serious.

"It takes everyone a little while to settle down mentally here," he said. "I had to work like a dog for about two years before I started looking at things a little differently. But this girl you mentioned, Steffi, have you slept with her yet?"

"No," I replied.

"You should," Zeus said.

He eased back into his chair, fanning out his shoulders.

"Remember when I told you the first day you came here that Tokyo would be good for you, because a city like this favours certain kinds of risk. Risk in business, risk in choices and this leads to a strengthening of character. With women, I don't want to calculate anything or think about where I'm going with her. In my life, I know where I am and what I am doing. If a girl is interested in me, she needs to reflect that. It doesn't have to be immediate, but usually I draw them into what me and some of my boys call the 'Event Horizon' and that is enough."

"The Event Horizon?"

"Yes," Zeus said with a sly smile. "In physics, the event horizon is the outermost part of a black hole from which nothing can escape. Before even perceiving it, you are in it. It is the *de facto* point of no return. Basically we are dealing with your personal gravity well. Women decide long before you sleep with them that they want you, but some guys, very specific guys, have enough gravity to always ensure this. Develop enough gravity with women, draw them into your little void, and you won't be worried about whether she likes your skinny jeans or your Thursday underwear. You'll be free to focus on bigger and better things, and if she tags along for the ride, so be it. Oh, this place has great garlic bread by the way."

He waved to the waiter. "A few pieces of garlic bread please."

The waiter arrived a minute later with a large plate with ten small slices of bread next to a tray of butter. Zeus took a hefty bite into one.

"You have to ask yourself," he said between munches. "Are you here just to chase tail, or are you here to survive? The prevailing thought in any decision must be the most important. This is how you stay grounded and don't get lost in the chaos."

I'd never heard him speak like this. But looking on him, happily eating his garlic bread, nothing suggested this was out of the ordinary for him. Since I'd made the move to come to Tokyo with nothing but my savings, it is possible that he saw me as a warrior like him as we stood together in loin cloths, tossing spears around Tokyo.

"Survival is the most important thing," I said, thinking about my panic attack.

"In this quest," he said, taking another piece of bread and dipping it into the tray of butter. "We are basically alone dude. It's just us, and our ideas and then there is reality. In this reality, there are people and their dreams and desires. But it is *our* dream, *our* desire that is the most important, because hey, it's my life. So maybe one day I'll relax and get some little cottage in Hakone, or go back home and spend a few years popping out kids and relaxing, but that isn't why I'm here, and I think, it isn't why you are here either."

We sat silently for a while after this, eating the rest of the garlic bread. Zeus was quite a few levels above me in terms of this thinking process, I noted. I'd never thought much about life in its entirety, just getting a job, having a few drinks when I was stressed and occasionally trying to find a girl. Here he was talking about society, people and purpose, all things that shadowed the *intent* that seemed be following me around Tokyo.

"Either way man, don't sweat it, just have fun, and you'll figure it out," he said.

He stood up and slipped on his jacket.

"We'll meet up soon yeah? Time to get back to the grind," Zeus said.

"Definitely, and thanks for lunch," I said.

He nodded and walked outside into the hallway, turning left and out of sight. I left soon afterwards, walking around Roppongi in no particular direction. I walked for quite some time, following the different roads, walking under huge underpasses, and over pedestrian walkways. Zeus' speech made a modicum of sense to me. A person needs to establish their own identity separate and apart from just the pursuit of identity. The gravity well business made some sort of sense; Mick and Dubz had some version of that.

The roads had taken me up to Yoyogi, and I circled the park, ending up at the Meiji shrine. The sudden appearance of dense foliage in the concrete landscape of Tokyo drew me back to Shizuoka, as I was driving with Yumi to an event. The breeze had blown through the window onto my face, heavy with the smell of the nearby sea. Rock music had been playing on the radio, and Yumi had been singing along, her hair flapping in her face. We were heading to a barbeque at a public site near the sea, close to a pier that went out into the watery depths for thirty feet. It was a gathering of interesting people, and I ate until I was full. After the sun had set, I took a walk to the pier, to see Yumi there. She was sitting in the darkness, her long hair like a veil. Her shoes were off and the floral patterns on her dress became spider webs in the dark. Some distance away, a father and son were fishing together. They both walked along the shoreline with flashlights hung on string around their necks, casting jerky, oscillating beams with each step they took.

I had walked over and sat beside Yumi, looking out into the blackness that was the sea. That was the day she told me about giving up on her dreams to play piano, and studying psychology. Something about the pressure of being perfect had affected her, she said. Though she had ideas for music, and liked music, there was a point in time when the desire left her in a huff, and she could no longer sit for hours at a time in front of the piano. She spoke about taking meditation classes to try and settle her mind, to see if the cause of her disinterest was due to a lack of focus, but it didn't help. As she searched more and more for this core reason, it was then she became interested in psychology and the nature of thought itself. This was long after she had finished school, and had been working a simple job. As I sat there, listening to her explain the slow dissolution of her dreams through simple situations, I was tempted to believe we could be more than friends. But I was still in between that barrier of time and culture, afraid to touch the soft hands resting on the pier only inches from mine.

We sat there until it was so dark that only the lights of some distant vending machines were able to guide us back to the car. When we were walking back, she tripped on a stone in the dark, falling forward. She instinctively grabbed my arm and I held her, feeling her body close to me for the first time. Laughing at herself and straightening up, she thanked me for preventing her from being truly embarrassed. In my mind, I kept that feeling of her touch; the unresisting softness of her flesh on my fingers, and the taut smoothness of her hips that I felt upon catching her. Her hair had brushed my arm, and I could feel the strength in her legs as she tensed to straighten up.

My mind returned to the present moment as I walked through the Meiji shrine. Back then Yumi had almost fallen in the dark, face first into the black of night. It was good that I was there at that time. She had sat there thinking about her dreams in the dark, and here I was thinking about my future in the light. A large stone stood in my path and I kicked it. It was all extremely quiet. In front and behind me I could see no one. I was far from any seaside piers that could give me any insights into my inner realities. I looked up at the tops of the giant trees around me and imagined the crow. With its clear all-seeing eye, it was the only thing watching me as I walked, but I know it would never catch me if I fell.

Chapter 13

Talent, Carmen told me, is not necessarily a guide to a person's path. Not everyone has something specific they can use to make a lot of what they want from life happen. But, talents can be honed and shaped in ways that allow for different strategies in the approach to enjoying and evaluating one's life. I listened to her as she said this during our second session, as I sipped on the usual complimentary bottle of water she had given to me.

"The last time we had spoken, remember I asked you about what did you do when you realized you were unhappy. You told me that you had to stick it out, to honour your government contract, and so on."

I nodded in agreement.

"After you left, I thought for a while about what you said. Tell me, what do you do recreationally?"

I thought about this for a moment. "Nothing really."

"How do you relieve stress? Do you exercise, party, or drink?"

"I guess just drink mostly."

She rubbed the desk while looking at me.

"So you know that with people that have anxiety in the manner you do, many doctors often recommend moderate exercise as a way to deal with stress."

"So I've heard," I replied. "But I haven't been doing any heavy exercise since I've been here."

Carmen told me about a research study done on relatively happy people. In this study she said, the people who claimed to be the happiest, generally tended to do more things than the average person. They were interested in multiple activities that engaged their minds in a different way. People who said they were not as happy, tended to do far less things, usually nothing more than work, returning home or watching the television.

"We know that thinking about things can have a physical effect on the body. In the same way you feel pleasure you can create pain and tension. But say you were doing just a handful of things to ease some of that pressure, how do you think that would help you?"

I responded by saying that it would most likely distract you from what is eating you on the inside.

"Do you see yourself in five years doing the same things you are doing now?" she asked.

"No, definitely not," I replied.

"Then I would say at the very least, look at the advantages around you instead of the limitations. Tokyo is a big city, with lots to do. Why not live in it, instead of living in your head?"

Living in your head.

The words made me pause for quite some time.

"Are you all right?" Carmen asked me.

"Living in your head," I began. "Were the last words my grandfather said to me."

He picked me up often from school in his old Honda Civic I told Carmen, and he'd drive me back home, usually stopping to get me a snack of some kind from a wholesale shop near my house. There was nothing unusual about the routine. I mean, I was a child and there isn't much a child worries about. But I do remember being a little different. I was a quiet kid, constantly thinking about things around me, life and people. Sometimes I'd get into the car and not want to say anything, and my grandfather would pat me on the shoulder and say what he always said: stop living in your head. He said that to me one evening when I was in a somber mood, as he drove near the wholesale store to get me something to cheer me up. We never made it there, because a truck trying to avoid a pothole drove into our lane and smashed into the car, killing him instantly. I hit my head on the side of the door, which knocked me unconscious.

"That must have been terrible," Carmen said.

"I guess. It was a long time ago."

If anything, I said to her, it made me get more into my head. The subsequent funeral and the wailing of family as I had stood there, unable to process it all, sinking deeper into myself.

"So you didn't cry or anything?"

"No. I've thought about this and I think at the time I was very curious about life. I was trying to make sense of the world, and his death fractured that thought process. After that life just felt dangerous and uncertain and wasn't anything I could easily figure out."

"Often people blame themselves for circumstances outside of their control. Did you blame yourself for his death?"

"In a logical way. If I wasn't in a bad mood, then he probably wouldn't have been driving to the shop to get me something, but at the end of it all, who knows."

"You've made this step towards change," Carmen said. "Perhaps you should do something with it. From what you've told me today I can see you have a strong ability to keep pressure in, but your anxieties might hint at that wall starting to crack. It might be time to go out there and switch things up."

That statement more than anything, was what stuck with me long after I'd left our session. After six weeks in Tokyo I'd spent most of my time in dark bars, or at the house, lounging in the entertainment room, shuffling about during the early morning because I couldn't sleep. I'd sent a few messages to the girl I'd met at Camelot, but I hadn't received any timely responses. My window with her was closed, as I was already out of her sight on that rapidly moving social conveyer belt of the city.

Steffi wanted to see me at some party tonight in Roppongi at a spot I'd never been to called The New Lex. We met by the Friday's restaurant and walked to a 7-11 across the road to snag some early drinks.

"This is a good strategy," she said to me with a smile, pointing to her long can of Asahi.

The party at the club was some all you can drink in three hours event, which would prove interesting to observe, knowing how expensive drinks were here. We moved away from the convenience store and sat on a stoop near a public bathroom in Roppongi.

"Oh my god that girl is sooo skinny!" she said.

The woman she was referring to was a wispy, unnaturally thin Japanese woman wearing a long, dark brown dress some feet away from us. Her bones were visible through the cloth; she was a walking epitome of malnutrition. She walked away, disappearing around a corner as Steffi gawked at a man with broad shoulders wearing a spaghetti strap dress stroll by. While she chatted about him I looked at her profile, remembering the sunlight only a few days ago that fell on her arms, arms that had hugged me while I slept. The armour she wore had been dented that evening, but whatever connection I made had lost much of its strength. Upon meeting tonight, she refused a hug and made sure to call me a "pussy" as least twice before complimenting me on my shoes. Slightly annoyed, I'd felt less of a desire to follow her to the party. I knew it was all you could drink for three thousand yen, but I could easily get drunk on less than a thousand. The only thing that had brought me out tonight was a hint of that initial intrigue I'd had about Steffi when she first strolled into the house in a stream of curse words and sexual innuendo.

"I'm not sure if I want to go," I told her.

"Come with me, I guarantee you will enjoy yourself," Steffi said, pinching me on my arm.

"I get the distinct feeling you just want me to come to entertain you," I replied.

"Of course, why do you think I invited you out tonight?" she said with a laugh.

I wasn't sure what to believe, but didn't care that much. I'd already left the house and it was after eleven o' clock, and trains would stop running soon. We walked down the street and took a left near the top of the trip. I could see a large number of people waiting in line, lots of attractive girls and dressed up nightlife city boys. Entering the club I saw a photo gallery of the glitzy patronage that thought it good to bless Tokyo with their presence. From the Backstreet Boys to Paris Hilton, Ben Affleck and Chad Kroeger, it looked like *everybody* had been to the New Lex. Now I was one of those people. Well, sort of.

The V.IP area looked a bit shoddy, and on top of the crowded bar space, there was a non-existent men's bathroom. My mind was echoing complaints that no doubt many a person were at this point in time. Whatever the cool factor was, it wasn't immediately apparent to me. Steffi however, was in her element; a mermaid effortlessly balancing on a wave in the middle of a maelstrom. Between doing shots and running in and out of the V.I.P area, there wasn't a person she didn't laugh with, slap on the shoulder, or give the sexy eye. A bunch of people from her school program were there, as were Hans and his usual friends. But this number paled in comparison to the mish mash of steely-eyed Russian hostesses, heavily mani-cured and face-painted Roppongi regulars; young men who ran the gamut of stylish and tacky, and a few *Gyaru* with their brown hair and fake eyelashes. There were some banker types, dressed in expensive sweaters and suit jackets, then people who seemed a little out of place, standing uncomfortably with their drinks held to their chest, smiling at no one.

The bar situation wasn't very fluid, and I had to muscle be-tween a few sour-faced Americans blocking the bar who kept saying "Easy bro," each time I reached between their group to ask the bartender for a drink. The music was good and throughout the crowd I could see the smiling faces of a few folks preparing to seal the deal. Standing quietly near a column, I was reminded of the John Donne quote, "No Man is an island", but there I was, with people as sand, and the club as the lone tree, offering shade. While I sipped on a Gin and Tonic, I noticed a flurry of movement at the door, and many people left the bar to go and see what was happening. I took advantage of this lull, and the bartender happily gave me sev-eral shots. One of the Americans at the bar tapped me on the shoulder.

"I know who's here," he said. "I fucking hate his movies."

Mildly interested, I looked at the door, where the already plentiful club congregation had swelled into a pit of meshed bodies. The lights of cell phone cameras flashed for some time, then the crowd split open, and several tall, well-built men ush-ered someone into the V.I.P. From where I was standing, I didn't see more than someone of average height, with black hair, in a white shirt and brown leather pants, his face partially hidden by a pair of large glasses. After the crowd split up from their paparazzi revelry, I ordered another drink. The bartender made good mixes, and I raised my glass in salute to him. Many of the girls in the club were now shadowing the V.I.P section, making it even harder to see which celebrity was inside. But based on the energy of the establishment, most of the crowd didn't seem to know there was a celeb there, or didn't care. I saw Steffi about ten feet from where I was, being held at the waist by a tall guy. She was looking up at him, deeply into his eyes, while his lips moved and she smirked and grinned. They stood like this for a while, not dancing, only talking. Then, the tall young man leaned downwards, and whispered something into her ear. Steffi's body language immediately changed, and I could see her hands drift to the small of his back, then up under his armpits and over his neck. She kissed him passionately, and they leaned heavily on the wall, all tongue and strobe lights. They broke the kiss and he took her by the hand and started walking towards the exit. I saw her glance left and right, as if she'd lost something. Then, her eyes caught mine staring at her, and she paused. She was smiling broadly with her face still red and flushed from the drinking and kissing. The smile wavered in its intensity, and I saw the look in her eyes change. Someone passed in front of me, and then she and the tall young man were gone.

I felt a warm anger fill me, but I stood at the column, drinking the last of my well-manicured cocktail. I stayed there until drinks were pay per drink again, then I walked outside. Lining the entrance of the club, were dozens of people wading through a creek of inebriety. One of the cute *Gyaru* I had seen earlier was face down on the pavement, her friends struggling to sit upright on the sidewalk. They dropped their phones constantly, and refused the assistance of a young man (who I realized was one of the Americans at the bar) trying to hand her a bottle of water. A few young men, handsome and shining with the cool gloss of youth, sat chatting to girls on a railing parallel to the club's entrance. It was a menagerie of quick pickups and happy endings. The girls, whether they were foreign or Japanese, seemed reasonably enamored by whomever they were talking to, or were feigning interest to get laid. I looked at this social spectacle before turning around, and walked up the road. Not bothering to wait for the train, I made the lengthy trod back to the Guesthouse.

A trenchant worthlessness was all I felt as I walked with nothing but the night as my company. Why hadn't I reached out once to touch her as she did her social rounds? I processed how I had felt in the club, noting how cemented I was to my location. To me, I didn't possess that slick hipness, or the testosterone fueled sense of obligation that I felt from the other men around me. There was no difference between me and the awkward men I'd seen scattered about, as they smiled and nodded at no one, trying too hard to act as if they belonged. Mice in the wild get caught by snakes that hold their gaze, so paralyzed by the idea of capture they cannot move. Fear is paralytic and hypnotic, I reasoned, walking past a group of workmen repaving a section of the road. The men worked with energetic purpose and strong body language; completely focused. I looked at them for a minute before walking away. Undeserving, was the word, I said. That was the best way to describe being in the margins or whatever I liked to call it. There was nothing pushing me to expand and grow past where I was emotionally. This hesitance, like my anxiety, was linked to roots so deep I had no idea if I could remove them. I sighed.

Twenty minutes had passed and I was nowhere near Yotsuya. I regretted my rash decision to walk home, but I was already in limbo. My anger eventually gave way to the demands of the long walk on my body, and it was replaced by a pounding sadness. Moments and connections were merely brief sparks in Tokyo's lightning storm, where everything was for sale and everyone was replaceable.

When I finally neared the house, my mind welcomed the quiet Yotsuya cobblestone back streets. I went inside in the lobby and heard laughing to my right. The entertainment room was alive with activity. In there I saw Dubz and Mick with two girls and the remains of several beers and snacks.

"Hey what's going on my man!" Mick said in an eager voice.

"Nothing much, just came in, is all," I replied.

I have a story to tell you later boss, how these girls are and what happened tonight! Dubz said to me in rapid patois.

"What did you say to him?" asked one of the girls. She had a plain face, but an extremely curvy body.

"I told him you were beautiful," Dubz replied.

"Liar!" she said with a laugh, slapping him on the shoulder.

"Damn right!" Mick replied.

The other girl, who was slim with a cute face, laughed loudly in a slight squeak. I left the group and went to my room, hearing the echo of laughter from the group outside seep slightly through the walls, sounding like a TV with the volume turned down very low.

Chapter 14

In the kitchen, a pot of tea was boiling in front of me. It was about five a.m and as usual for me, sleep was elusive. I'd bought the tea at the market down the road the day before, along with a small bottle of honey. I stood in sweatpants and a baggy t-shirt by the kitchen counter. After the tea finished boiling, I poured it inside a large pink cup with a smiley face on it, and walked into the entertainment room. A few remnants of the previous evening were there, a cigarette stub barely visible under a pillow, a beer can or two and a crumpled snack bag.

I walked outside with the cup of tea in my hand, looking upwards at the deep dark of the morning sky. It was chilly, and goose bumps rose on my arms as I walked through the large gate leading off the property. The familiarity of this activity rang lightly in my mind, like a bell far away. Some of the buildings around me had a similar tone and layout as the ones in my previous neighbourhood. Here, walking along in the morning, I did not feel as if I was in a city of thirty-six million people. I was just one man with a cup of tea, who could walk for miles without seeing anything of significance. I passed by some older buildings and a few small but stylish houses. Parked in many of these driveways were expensive European cars. I passed through a small alleyway that went down a steep hill. I stopped there, looking at the quiet sprawl of Yotsuya in that webbed lens of electric poles, wires and television antennas. The tea was finished now, and I made the slow walk back to the house, and went inside to put another pot on the stove.

I took a walk down to the lower level with the basement apartments. I passed by a few suite doors, and stepped into the laundry room. It was very large, with seven washing machines and two dryers. The floor was a dark spotted tile. Someone had put a chair in there, a small green chair that looked out of place in the sea of blinding white machines. I left the room and went back upstairs, and made myself another cup of tea. I sat in the entertainment room and closed my eyes, as the minutes turned into hours and the light of the sun began to brighten the lobby.

A voice called to me, and I saw Dubz, dressed for work, smiling broadly. He started telling me about the girls from the night before, but I didn't really listen, just nodding along as he laughed and mentioned how they met and some trick that Mick pulled off to get them back at the house. I don't even remember when he left, and I sighed as I saw the bright morning sun, filled with purpose, reflecting my lack of it. At the convenience store at the top of the road, I bought a chicken bento and several Chu-His. I walked back to my room, leaving the bento on my little sink and drank the Chu-His, one after the other, quickly.

My eyes got heavy, and I drifted into a light sleep, the can still in my hand, while I sat on the floor. The guesthouse rippled and the walls tore away. I was flying at high speed through a bright white sky, and then I felt my feet hit solid ground. I was in a field on a dark Caribbean evening with a cricket bat in my hands, waiting. A ball was thrown at me and I tensed my thighs, waiting for its impact. I hit the ball with a *crack,* and set off running to the next wicket. I had no fellow batsman on the pitch with me, and as I quickly reached the second wicket, I saw my grandfather doing a light jog towards me.

"Come sir, you can't beat me," he said.

I smiled as I looked at him, feeling a sense of familiarity remembering a gift he had given me as a child. It was a small wooden chair, perfect for the size of my body at that time. It had accompanied me on several missions in the backyard, served as a buttress for my feet as I scrawled drawings on paper inside my room, or watched cartoons on TV. The chair had been a fixture in my life until I broke two of the legs with my weight some years later.

I'm back at the wicket now, and my Grandfather pointed to men around the field, who had appeared in swirls of mist. The hand signals he gave them were motioning them to come closer. I knew this meant he was going to do a fast pitch with some bounce. He reared up, running at full speed towards me and hurled the ball. I took a defensive stance and pushed the bat forward, hearing the ball hit the wood hard. It popped up into the air, and one of the faceless men caught it, and they all cheered. My Grandmother was nearby. I did not see her, but I could sense her. I saw the smiles; I heard the laughs and little giggles from my then-tiny body being tickled by her large, dark hands. My grandfather walked towards me, saying something but I couldn't hear the words over the shouting voices of the men around us. He threw the ball to me, smiling as he did this, and then the field disappeared and I reappeared inside my grandparent's house. It was dark, but I felt comfortable. They were sitting in the shadows near me, with only their hands visible, resting on their knees from an overhead spotlight. The shadowy outlines of my grandparents watched me quietly, and I felt a growing sense of discomfort. I looked at their silhouettes, but could not see their faces.

"This moment isn't forever," came the voice of my grandmother.

I was startled, because her voice didn't come from the direction of where she was sitting, but everywhere, loud and omnipresent.

"What do you mean?" I asked, looking at their hands, still rigidly unmoving.

"This moment isn't forever," came the voice of my grandfather.

Then the chair I was sitting in began to sink into the ground, and I reached up at nothing, feeling my legs stuck as I fell into the house itself, looking up at the ceiling, which was actually a sky without stars, until everything became black.

I woke up soon afterward in the quietness of my room. Shutting my eyes again, I lay down on the bed, attempting to sleep and dream again. I wanted to hold on to that sensation of my grandparents, but it didn't work. I was here, in the guesthouse, back in the real world, away from both of them.

Getting up off the bed, I ate the Bento meal, while drinking a half can of lukewarm beer. I went outside and into the lobby, to see Briggs standing in a full yellow jumpsuit, with a pair of large dark glasses pulled up and over his hair. The outfit wasn't exactly skintight, but it fit the contours of his body well. He smiled as he saw me.

"Hey man, great day isn't it?" he asked.

Bright light streamed into the lobby, and my mind created the image of a clear blue sky outside. I nodded in agreement, and asked him about his outfit.

"I'm doing a little publicity stunt for my series. If you aren't doing anything you should tag along, it always helps to have someone there when I'm making videos. Are you good with a camera?"

"I actually have a camera, but I haven't used it in a while," I replied.

"That's no problem, bring it along and we'll have a good time," he said.

Briggs warm energy was a welcome escape from the somber mood of the house, and I decided to follow him. I went back to my room and reached into one of the suitcases I'd barely touched upon coming to Tokyo. Under some clothing and books I'd probably never read, was my camera, which I had purchased after a few months in Japan. It was an impulse buy, something I thought I'd need to capture everything around me, but I had barely taken ten photos before I lost interest, putting it in its box and leaving it in my suitcase. Holding it in my hand, I could smell its newness and remembered the one thing I'd always like about it was its weight. I changed into a normal set of clothes and walked outside with Briggs.

We walked to the station, and I noticed all the eyes on Briggs. Several people, including a set of giggling teenage girls, whipped out their phones to take pictures of him as he passed. More than once, he strolled over to these persons, saying a very polite hello and asking if they wanted to take pictures with him. They mostly said yes, and at this point, I would take one of the girl's phones, and snap a picture of him with them. Each time, he made a bizarre pose. He would crouch like a sumo wrestler, or open his mouth so wide his face turned into a gaping hole surrounded by wrinkles. This exaggerated behaviour caused the folks Briggs was taking these pictures with to giggle. Afterwards, he gave everyone a business card from a yellow pouch around his waist, bowed and kept walking. As we boarded the train to head to Ginza, where he'd be shooting the episode today, a girl walked over.

"Tokyo Rover?" she asked.

"That's me," Briggs replied with his gentle smile.

The young woman was Japanese but had grown up in London and was a big fan of his web series. She also took a picture with him, walking quickly back to her friend to show her the image.

"When I came to Japan I was nobody," Briggs said. "Like most people I was just wearing the suit and tie, doing the rounds of teaching English, but I didn't like it so much."

"I think I'm in that position now," I said to him.

"Well, everything is about a choice in my opinion. I mean, here I am in a yellow jumpsuit on a train filled with people! But I learned pretty quickly that here, you can do this sort of thing without much hassle, and now I'm pretty comfortable doing it."

"Why the jumpsuit?"

He made a comical face that resembled a stern old man and pointed a finger at me.

"I guess you didn't watch any of my videos," he said in a slightly modified voice.

"No, sorry, I haven't had the time," I responded.

His face changed back to normal.

"No problem my friend. I started this web series as a way to just break the monotony of my day. Y'know, you wake up, put on the suit, you go to teach all these loud yammering kids and you are basically just a clown for hire.

"So I said, why not clown around and feel good about it? So I was watching *Kill Bill* and I saw that suit Uma Thurman was wearing, then I remembered that it was based on the classic Bruce Lee costume from *The Game Of Death*. So I know I'm not ripped or anything, but I thought I'd wear my costume and just go around town doing crazy things and getting it on camera."

The train slowed, and as a stream of new people entered, we moved to a pair of open seats.

"Why Tokyo Roving?"

"Well you know how they used to call people roving reporters? I took it from that. I'm not a reporter by any means, but I was roving around town, so the name just made sense. More than anything though, what started to change for me, was just how I felt. I loved the way people responded to me, even if they were making fun of me. It was better than some kid throwing snotty paper balls at me from the back of a classroom. So I made some videos and one or two really took off. I made this one called the Shinjuku Shutdown—"

"I saw that one," I interjected.

"Awesome! So in that video, me and a guy wear matching jumpsuits and we go to Shinjuku and just hit on girls and act silly. I was pretty scared when I did it, but I said what the hell man, I'm in Tokyo. So we went to some bars, hung around the station and even got into a club dressed the way we were."

His voice was easy and light, even though he gestured frantically as he spoke. There was a brightness in his eyes as he continued the story. A similar brightness that I'd seen with Dubz, Mick and Zeus.

"But those early videos were terrible," Briggs said. "I was shooting on a camera phone that didn't have the best resolution. The stuff was a bit jerky, and some shots were very dark. Now, I try and do things a little better based on what I've learned, but what was cool was that even though the videos (to me) were bad, they still got loads of views on YouTube."

We stood up from our seats as we exited the station that took us into Ginza. Again, some people smiled as he walked past, took pictures of him, or took pictures with him. I'd already snapped over a dozen of him in these poses with these random people. He also asked me to take pictures of him humping a post, high fiving a policeman and asking a girl to pretend she was choking him. I was surprised this happened so quickly. From his little yellow pouch, he pulled out a small camcorder.

"So we got some cool stuff yeah? That's just material I drop on the blog on my web page. So what I do now is just talk a bit to the camera and swap the *eigo* and the Japanese to make sure I keep my audience together and then, I rove."

He showed me how to hold the camera and keep it in frame as he spoke. A few times, he told me to shoot him while he was walking, talking about the environment. He effortlessly switched from English to Japanese as we met several new people, whom he interviewed about things like their clothing and favourite music. I couldn't help laughing when he chatted to a slightly older woman with a heavy voice, who pestered Briggs about his favourite sexual position.

"Can you believe that *oba-chan* is still so frisky? I love this stuff!" Briggs shouted.

After we finished filming, we went into a small bar near the station, where we ordered some noodles and beers. This was the first time I saw Briggs be completely silent, as he held his camera, looking through the footage I'd shot. I sipped quietly on my beer, wondering if the happy-go-lucky side of him would morph into a diva screaming at me about how badly I shot the footage.

"This is pretty good man," Briggs said. "Usually people I walk with shake the camera all over the place, and I need to spend a lot of time when I'm editing adjusting for that. But you captured it well. You ever done videography?"

"No," I replied.

"Maybe you should think about it, lots of need for guys like you here."

We ate our meal quietly for a while, and then Briggs explained his dream to me.

"I want this to be a real show, with a real team and so on. I just need to keep focused, and see if I can get my skills to where I want them to be."

He told me about his website and the user counts he'd gauge each day. He talked about things I didn't really know like Search Engine Optimization and ad placement. There was information he gave on affiliate programs, formatting data, Klout scores, social media presence and targeted marketing. When he finished speaking, my head throbbed.

"Hey man, sorry if I went off on a tangent there," he said. "But living in that house, there are all these types that come and go. You get a vibe from some people, and other's you don't. There is a drifter kind of vibe about you. I've seen you around the house all quiet like, and every now and then I catch you walking around the neighbourhood. You are our Yotsuya *Ronin*, the wandering Jamaican samurai haha!"

I was surprised to hear this, and then I felt silly. Whatever reasons I'd given myself for completely believing I was just a fly on the wall was slowly becoming an illogical perspective. Especially as I was sitting in a café with a man dressed in a yellow jumpsuit, telling me about personal marketing strategies. The crow was nearby, and I could almost hear it laughing.

We went back to the house. Briggs thanked me profusely for helping him out with his episode, of which he'd be sure to credit me in when he put it online. I smiled as I watched him go down the stairs, shouting a hearty hello to someone I couldn't see. With a slightly renewed energy, I went into the kitchen and began cooking, remembering my slothful crawl to the convenience store earlier in the day. As the okra sizzled and the ground meat simmered, I felt my phone vibrate in my pocket. It was a message from Yumi; she was coming to Tokyo tomorrow.

Chapter 15

Yumi was coming to see some friends that lived in Saitaima, in a suburb just outside the city. On the phone, she explained they were having some kind of meet up and a barbeque, and that I was invited if I'd like to come. I agreed to go, and soon I was on the train headed to Hatogaya, to meet up with her.

As I exited the station I immediately saw her waving at me. She was standing beside a white corolla with a tall, grizzly young man smoking a cigarette. I walked over quickly, giving her a light hug before shaking the hand of the young man, who gave me a sly smile.

"Tatsuya is my name," he said.

"Yes, this is one of my friends who I told you about," Yumi added. "He moved to Tokyo a few years ago, so it has been a while since we've seen each other."

The drive to their house was a revelation. The low rolling hills in the distance and the sea of green rice fields between the roadways felt exactly like Shizuoka. I felt very calm taking in the scenery. Yumi told me that she and Tatsuya had gone to the same high school, and had been neighbours. Soon after leaving high school, he moved to Tokyo.

"I'm a country boy, but I'm not a country boy," Tatsuya said with a laugh.

Tatsuya lived with his girlfriend in a small house near an elementary school. As we walked in and removed our shoes by the door, I smelled chicken and beef. Several people were inside, mostly people from the area. Tatsuya's girlfriend, a slim, round-faced girl named Erika was the resident DJ. She moved constantly from a laptop atop a small desk in the living room to the kitchen. A random selection of YouTube music videos was the background music for the gathering. As their faces slowly became red from drinking and everyone sat in little groups on the floor, I went into the past. I had always been in these situations with Yumi, sitting with friendly people, watching the evening turn to night with a drink in my hand, my stomach full of food. I chatted with a few people, some of who made noises of surprise when I told them I lived in Yotsuya.

"You are rich," one girl in a straw hat said.

"No, no, I live in a guesthouse, I'm just lucky," I said.

After a little while, I went outside with Yumi and we sat on a pair of chairs facing a hammock on the porch. After nearly two months of seeing buildings everywhere I turned, the clear evening horizon was refreshing.

"So how is it going? Are you still feeling ill?" Yumi asked, looking at me.

I decided not to tell her about the panic attack I'd had a few weeks before. What I did tell her was about some of the people I'd met at the house, and the recent outing I'd had with Briggs.

"That sounds exciting, maybe he is right," Yumi said.

"Right about what?"

"Well, you said your friend, Mr. Briggs, is doing what he is doing to escape some aspect of his life. Maybe he is right in doing that. Probably that's why you left Shizuoka, to find your own project."

There was some truth to what she was saying, but I couldn't see myself walking around the house in a yellow jumpsuit, much less through the heavily packed streets of Tokyo. We kept talking, and her pointed questions about my life reminded me of our last meeting, when she hummed along with the Tina Turner song and didn't look at me for a while before we shared a kiss.

"I've missed your company," I said.

Yumi smiled, and patted me on the forearm.

"Me too! It was so strange when you left Shizuoka, but I thought if you made that choice, then it was what you wanted to do."

"I guess so," I replied, sipping more of my beer.

My head was clear this evening. Though the folks around me were drinking heavily, I'd only had two beers. Around Yumi, I didn't feel the need to escape in the comfortably fuzzy blanket of heavy drinking. I liked the sharp contours of relative sobriety; feeling the cool wood of the chair against my thighs and the slight chill of the night.

"I think I might try some new things," I said to her. "Since coming here I've met so many people doing different kinds of stuff. Tokyo is different."

"Yes, it is," Yumi said.

This statement from her felt a bit enigmatic, but I figured not to ask her what she meant. I couldn't be the only person who had come to Tokyo to rage and let loose. She touched my forearm again and looked into my eyes. I could see the spark that I'd seen the day I left, that dance of fire swirling in her eyes.

"Are you busy tomorrow? I'd like to have lunch with you, in Tokyo," she said.

"I'd love that."

"Good, I'm happy," Yumi said, nodding.

"Would you like another beer?" she asked.

"Yes thanks," I replied.

I sat there for a little while longer, and went back inside. The partygoers were now dancing to some hip-hop music. The girl with the straw hat I'd spoken to earlier, was in the center, doing a set of jerky moves while pumping her fist into the air. Her face was astonishingly red but she still maintained a genuine smile. The group forced me into the middle. Smiling, I did a slow fist pump, as they followed my lead, eventually laughing. Yumi gave me my beer and rested her hand on my shoulder.

"You can dance?" she asked.

"Sometimes," I replied.

This is how the night ended, with the echoes of everyone's voices in the air, YouTube videos playing on the screen of a non-descript laptop, and Yumi's face, smiling at me through the spaces of different conversations. Back at the train station, I said goodbye to Tastuya and Yumi, who nodded at me after saying, "Tomorrow." The ride back to Tokyo was uneventful, and by the time I reached home, I went into my room, and fell fast asleep.

We met at a restaurant somewhere in Akasaka. Yumi told me about a restaurant there that had a good curry meal had always wanted to try. As we ate, I commented on her shorter hairstyle, and she laughed saying she wanted to look younger. She said she liked my shirt, which I'd incidentally bought in Tokyo on one of my previous trips. The food was good, and with our stomachs filled, we left the restaurant and stepped outside.

"I have a hotel room nearby," she said to me. "I have something to give you."

"Okay," I replied.

We went to her hotel, a giant high rise with no less than thirty-five floors. We walked in and she told the doorman her name. Upstairs, on the twentieth floor, I was surprised. The room was nice, with a king-sized bed, a bathroom filled with black marble and a TV that rivaled the one in the entertainment room back at the guesthouse.

"I'll be right back," Yumi said, going to the bathroom.

I sat on the bed and turned on the television. *The Matrix* was playing , and I chuckled at Morpheus' comically deep voice in the Japanese dub. The bed felt nice, and I eased back, feeling the comforter hug my arms and neck. I heard water running in the bathroom and went to the window of the hotel. From this view, the licorice stick train lines, intermittently sprinkled sluices and the delicate swirl of the highway system between the mostly grey buildings could be called majestic.

I turned to see Yumi, completely naked, standing by the bathroom door. She gestured for me to come. She had adequate breasts that complimented her narrow waist and long attractive legs. I walked into the bathroom with her, feeling the heat of water vapour from the tub gently settle onto my exposed skin. She stepped towards me, and I held her waist. We kissed, long and sweet.

"Let's take a bath," she said.

I said nothing as I slowly removed my clothes. The entire time, Yumi kept watching me.

"You are making me nervous," I said with a laugh.

"Why? I'd always wondered how you looked naked," she said.

"Really?"

"Yes," Yumi said.

Her eyes took in everything several times, settling on my erect penis more than once. She walked over and squeezed it softly.

"I don't think you are that nervous," she said.

I couldn't help but grin as we went into the bath. It was larger that I'd imagined when I first saw it. We both fit in it comfortably. I kissed her again, splashing water about, my hands slowly going up her thigh under the water. She held my hand firmly and broke the kiss. She took a sponge from behind her and dapped some shower gel on it, motioning for me to turn around. I did so, and she washed me slowly and delicately. Her hands moved in an easy, hypnotic rhythm, and I could feel my knotted muscles relaxing with each sweep of her hands across my back. She rubbed my stomach with her other hand as she washed it, kissing my back with slow, strong kisses. Then, I washed her as well, feeling the delicacy of her wet hair when I ran the sponge on her neck, across the narrow spread of her shoulders, up the tight skin of her back and under the softness of her breasts. I wanted my hands to explore her forever, feeling the water guide my hands noiselessly across her body. I dropped the sponge into the water, kissing her neck and moving my hands between her thighs. She let out a gasp as I found her vagina, slowly moving my fingers around. Soon, she held my hand again with the same firmness and stood up in the water, her supple behind glistening in front of me. I stood up and she handed me a towel. We dried off, and she took another look at my pulsing erection.

"Definitely not nervous," she said smiling.

She took my hand and led me into the room. We stood by the bed, and she told me to close my eyes. I felt her kiss my lips, then my nipples, the skin below my ribs, and then my member. She licked it slightly, and I gasped, the world dark and bright at the same time. She took it into her warm mouth, sucking and slurping as if there was no tomorrow. Gone was the quiet veil, gone was the gulf. The room echoed with the smacking of her lips as she did the motions, moving her head faster and faster. My entire body was stone, frozen and powerless in her grasp as her lips traveled up and down. I exploded in a shockwave, which made Yumi hum with pleasure as she swallowed it all, continuously sucking long after there was nothing else to give.

I was still solidly erect, and Yumi gave the tip of my penis a brief kiss. She lay me back on the bed and immediately mounted me, the sensation of her vagina warm and moist.

With her long legs straddling mine, she grabbed me close, kissing my nipples and gyrating her hips. Her eyes were closed and I saw her grit her teeth, her thighs shaking. Her nails dug into my ribs as she came, her body shuddering so hard I thought she was having a seizure. She flailed her neck and arched her back tightly, as the ripples of her orgasm went through her body into mine. Then she started grinding again, whispering something I couldn't understand properly into my ear, her breath soft. The imagery of it all was intoxicating. The large white sheets billowing around us, the midday light shining in, illuminating her skin, and hair. The clean and sharp edges of the furniture, the only witnesses to our passion. Our bodies collided more and more, my heart racing with each touch of her skin, the taste of her lips, and the occasional look she would give me of complete surrender. The second orgasm for me was more explosive than the first. Like Yumi, I shook incredibly, holding her tightly as her breasts pressed onto my chest, with the thin slick of our sweat clinging us together. The wave barely settled before I felt her touch me again, and my body immediately responded. There was no time, there was just us, and the bed was the world, our bodies everything that mattered. I was awake in a new way, my eyes open to a reality of pleasure I'd never imagined before. This went on for some time, until we were both spent, and my penis ached from use.

We drank water from the mini bar in our room, and silently watched a Harrison Ford movie on the television. She rubbed her toes against mine and occasionally stroked my pubic hair, and gently rubbed my balls. The hours passed, and soon, we both fell asleep.

In the morning, I awoke still naked to see Yumi fully dressed, standing near the bed.

"I'm leaving to go back to Shizuoka now," she said.

"Wait, but why?" I asked.

"I came here to give you something, a gift. Now that I did that, I need to leave."

"Can't you stay a little longer?" I said, feeling a tense disappointment.

She walked over and eased me down with her hands. They felt warm and soft against my chest. She kissed my neck, my chest and my stomach. She slowly licked my balls and then took me in her mouth. I gasped as I became hard, her tongue like soft foam. This time she wasn't frantic with her motions, but slow and deliberating. Everything around me melted away, with nothing left but Yumi's lips. She rubbed my thighs with alternating hands while she sucked it slowly, pushing me closer and closer. Then I came, and she didn't move, continuously rotating her tongue as I shook in spasms. She remained there for a while, savouring and sucking. She pulled my penis out of her mouth and kissed it, then kissed my thighs.

"I wanted to taste you one more time, so I can carry that with me," she said. "I don't know if I am ready to leave my life in Shizuoka, because everything I know is there, but a part of me has always wanted you, to see you and feel you, taste you and touch you the way I have today. When we spent time together last year, I could see that you had some sadness within you, but I didn't know what it was until you left for Tokyo. I know you are trying to make a path for yourself, and find something on your journey. This was my attempt to give you something beautiful on that path, a memory to hold on to as you move forward."

I tried to speak, but she raised a hand to stop me.

"I could love you, very easily, but I know it is not the time."

She came over to me again, leaning in on the bed and lay on top of me. Her dress was thin, and I could feel her body through the fabric. We stayed like this for a few minutes. She raised her head up, and looked me in the eyes. The expression she had was extremely calm, but the fire I'd seen in them before radiated with a different intensity. Her pupils had gained a new luminosity. She kissed me softly on the cheek and stood up, picked up her bag and went out the door.

Chapter 16

The image of Yumi's body burned in my mind long after the bed got cold, long after I'd returned back to my room and couldn't sleep. Two days passed, then three, each time with me in the morning walking further from the house, deeper into the bowels of Yotsuya and the surrounding area. I found myself in libraries and bookstores, museums and streets with ancient buildings on the verge of collapse. Often I looked in the small mirror on the wall in my room at my eyes. The same fire from Yumi's danced in them, swirling around with a hidden purpose.

There was something between us, definitely. The way my body reacted to hers at the slightest touch, and the overwhelming calm that coasted over my body as I had lain beside her watching TV. But I couldn't leave Tokyo. It wasn't that easy, and she was right. She had given me something, a blazing inferno of impetus.

What Carmen said about time was right. What's the point in living if you don't have anything to show for your time here? In the house, that much was clear. These individuals were *living,* even if some were just partying and chasing women. Hans was doing language school and gaining a future skill while raging through seedy bars and clubs. Mick had his collection of running ribbons and a few trophies from events to acknowledge his passion for the craft. Dubz had told me more than once he greatly enjoyed teaching children. Then there was Briggs, with his explosive determination to be more, his videos and semi-celebrity, upbeat energy and focus. I could track his progress and development, from his early low-quality videos, his face tinted with a hint more trepidation, the bravado less outrageous. His evolution was there for everyone to see.

All I had were a growing collection of beer cans in my room, and the empty shells of a dozen bento boxes. If I left Tokyo tomorrow, grabbing my suitcases and leaving the GreenLeaf house forever, there would be no indication I was ever there, except some hidden copy of my identification that only Mr. Oba would have access to. The streets that welcomed me each morning, the convenience stores that I'd spent so much time in, they'd all be left without impression. I'd go away, fading into the sky like a bird in the distance.

I sat on my bed as I thought about this, my body still tense with energy. I reached into my blue suitcase, and pulled out my camera. Because of its lack of use, each time I opened the case I bought for it and the accompanying lenses, I would get the strong smell of new electronics. What I liked the most about it was the camera strap I had purchased, which was red, green and gold. I casually snapped a few photos of my room, fiddling with the settings on the camera, reminding myself of technical matters like aperture, F-stops, and shutter speeds. The camera made a very nice *click* each time I shot a picture. This camera had lain in my bag for the better part of a year, hidden in the world of my confusion, cloaked in as much fear as I'd been. Holding it there in my small room, I felt as if I was with Briggs again, and that anything could happen in the moment. The clicks of the camera would document the things around me, even if I didn't stay here much longer, I needed something to show for it. The looming emptiness of the house now made me feel equally empty.

It was harder to stay inside, lying in the entertainment room with a drink in my hand. I needed to be out there, doing something.

Now as I went out, I always had my camera with me. After a sleepless night, when I walked around the surrounding area, I would take pictures. I'd try to capture the sleepy atmosphere of the early morning contrasted with the dark edges of the city's skyline. I'd follow a man in a suit for a block or two, documenting his steps until he reached a train station. I'd catch young girls in tiny miniskirts spending time with much older men in the evening. Train stations became a delight for this activity; the various kinds of emotion on people's faces a treasure trove. Most people looked forward blankly, but every tenth person had a smile, or an obvious nervous energy. Some people wore bizarre outfits and some fit the casual profile very well. I snapped away, loving the *click click click* of the shutter. In days I easily shot thousands of pictures of people, food, buildings and street art. This photography had taken me one step outside my usual margins and now labeled me as an active participant in the daily minutiae. I was still in my area, on the periphery of things and people, but now where I was had a voice. I'd come home and look through my photos for the day, analyzing the mood and tone of each of them. Some images would give me an immediate thrill, such as the frozen look of surprise in a man's face when he realized I was taking a photo of him, or seeing funny things after the fact, like an older woman wearing a shirt emblazoned with gold letters that read "Fuck Is Good For Release".

Being with Yumi had given me a taste of need. Often, I saw her sitting in the bath in front of me, the slick of the water pasting hair to her face, her eyes gazing at me with that delicate blend of calm and raging desire. For so long, I'd been walking alone, and for a moment, she let me know that someone could hold my hand.

There was no way I could move to Shizuoka. Someday perhaps, but I was invested in Tokyo. If I moved now, it would finish the rest of my savings. Thoughts of her still gave me erections, and after a day of taking photos I'd sometimes find myself with my eyes closed and my hands in my pants, thinking about her lips and her soft body. Then I'd go outside into the lobby and see someone in the kitchen or the entertainment room. I'd talk to Dubz and laugh harder with him about his anecdotes about girls and teaching English. I asked Mick about a running schedule that I could try, to which he enthusiastically responded with an hour's lecture on the art of preparing for running. Some of the women I'd seen around the house, that I'd looked at shyly as they had passed by me before, looked different now. Many of them smiled at me as they went about their day to day, and now I tried smiling back. The energy I had within me was shifting into a new state, and for the first time in my life, I knew I would have to step outside the margins if I was to make significant change for myself. There was no more time to keep the empty bag of despondency and faded resolutions that I'd walked with for so long.

A day after I'd approached Mick about the running schedule, he handed me a sheet of paper filled with information about gauging my heart rate, how to do proper stretches and various distance programs, from short runs to long runs.

"I'll do a quick run with you today if you want," Mick said.

"That would be good," I replied.

I had an old pair of sneakers and some dusty running shorts that I wore with an old t-shirt. Mick came out of his suite in his more advanced gear. He wore slick running tights under a pair of dark shorts, and a quick dry shirt.

"We'll go from here to say... Yoyogi. You seem like a pretty fit guy and the route shouldn't be more than two miles. We can stop anytime you like," Mick said.

His voice had gained a quiet, authoritative tone, dense with focus.

"Okay," I said.

I did the stretches he taught me, and took in several deep breaths as we ran in place for two minutes. It felt strange, doing this on the expensive carpet of the lobby, as our footfalls echoed down the hallway. He motioned to the door, and we ran through the gate, hitting the streets and running up the road. A few paces ahead of me, I could see Mick had excellent form, lifting his legs in long even strides, keeping a constant rhythm. I took the easier route, using my arms and legs minimally while trying to keep up. As the first dots of perspiration appeared on my forehead, I felt a surge of energy throughout my body. The blood rushing around my arms and legs felt good. We didn't speak much as we ran. Mick had ear buds on, while I entertained myself with the sights and sounds around me. This was another quieting sensation; running past the streams of people on their respective daily commutes with Mick, flying by like wraiths in the afternoon.

By the time we reached Yoyogi, I was spent. My heart thundered in my chest, and I fought to keep my breath.

"Not bad," Mick said, looking at his watch. "We did okay time."

Not up to asking what 'okay time' was, I walked over to a vending machine, and got a bottle of water. We were at the southeast side of the park, by the Harajuku gate. I hadn't been in Harajuku since I'd moved to Tokyo, and Mick pointed to a few girls dressed like porcelain dolls walking with parasols. We walked through the Harajuku gate, through the colourful main street and then down to Omotesando.

"I bought my wallet there," Mick said, pointing at the Louis Vuitton store.

"How much did that set you back?" I asked.

"Not that much, about seventy thousand yen," he replied.

"That's one month's rent for me," I said with a laugh.

"The ladies love it," Mick remarked.

I looked at the stores, loud and brazen with their excess of wealth. Burberry, Gucci, Louis Vuitton, Chanel and the rest of them. The buildings were perfect representations of the elite's playthings; an obese display of gaudy storefront installations. These were stores with doormen and private shopping rooms. I'd seen hip young men around town with their long Louis Vuitton wallets, but I didn't know they were so expensive. A month of my existence here was an easy, one-time purchase for Mick.

"Hey, I think that guy knows you," Mick said, pointing across the road.

A short man standing beside a tall garbage bin was waving at us.

"Do you know that guy?" Mick asked.

I squinted my eyes and took a better look at him. The man was dressed sharply in a casual sort of way, in a thin summer sweater and designer jeans. Nervously looking across the road, he ran over to where we were.

"Do you remember me? I am Tako, from F-Bar," he said.

The memory came in a flash. My first night in Tokyo, when I'd walked into the lounge and he'd been wearing a lime green suit.

"Yes, how are you?"

"I'm good, I'm good," he replied, dabbing his forehead with a silk handkerchief. "Hello, I am Tako," he said to Mick, shaking his hand.

Tako looked Mick and I up and down. "I can see that you were running, definitely good for the body."

He said this in a very formulaic manner, making it sound neither positive nor negative.

"I don't want to disturb you for very long, but I wanted to ask you if you were modeling for any agencies here."

"Me? No," I said.

"I run a men's agency here and I think you would be a good fit with us, do you mind coming by and taking some head shots this week? There are many things happening around town in the near future."

He handed me his card and gave a polite bow before walking back across the street. His full name was Tako Suou and the name of his agency was the TS Men's Agency.

"Not a very original name," Mick said, looking at the card. "But the office is in Gaienmae, so they must be doing well."

"Gaienmae?"

"Ah, I forgot you don't know Tokyo that well. It's between Omotesando, where we are, and another wealthy district, Aoyama-itchome."

Mick patted me strongly on the shoulder.

"Looks like you are going to be famous!" he said.

I laughed nervously, fingering the edge of the card with my hand. I placed it carefully into my wallet.

"Okay man, let's head back to the house," Mick said, doing a few light stretches.

As we ran back to the house by a different route, I thought about Tako's card shuffling around in my pocket, and it's potential. There seemed to be so many things happening here, especially in the pulsing undercurrent of the city. A life below the life I could see, buttressing the millions of dreams its inhabitants had.

Chapter 17

Going to Tako's office in Gaienmae, I felt cool. It was the middle of the day, and I wore one of my best dress shirts, the jacket Zeus had given me, my favourite skinny jeans and a pair of black Kenneth Coles I always kept in my emergency suitcase. The office was close to the train station, on the second floor of a swanky building. Inside was enough room to accommodate a small lobby with chairs, two offices, a bathroom and a storage room. On the wall, were pictures of attractive men and women in a variety of ethnicities. A stylized version of the agency's name was on a banner above the pictures. When I walked inside, a tall woman dressed in black with red dyed hair said hello.

"I'm Ayuna Moriako," she said in a cheerful voice. "Mr. Suou was right, you are very handsome."

I blushed inwardly, not sure what to say. From the office closest to a set of windows facing the street, Tako came out. Today he was dressed in burgundy chinos, with dark brown boots and a long-sleeved white shirt.

"I hope you are well today," he said with a smile. "So we'll just take a few pictures of you, and then when casting calls come up, we send your pictures to the agencies."

"I understand. This is a nice office," I said while looking around.

"I work too hard, so I needed to treat myself," Tako replied.

Ayuna laughed as he said this.

"I'm doing something in the office at the moment, but misses Moriako will take care of your pictures. I hope we will be doing work in the future together."

His statement sounded flat and practiced, but reasonably friendly. I looked at Ayuna, who was pulling a large camera from a black bag on her desk.

"So what we need are probably three basic photos," she said. "One of your face, one of you standing up and then another picture of you just being natural. Maybe at an angle."

She motioned for me to stand near a white wall. I stood up and faced the camera, as she snapped a few test shots.

"Hmm," she said. "Can you please remove your jacket?"

I took off the jacket and rested it on a chair to my left. She took a few more pictures and then explained to me the basics of the modeling industry.

"There are two important things to note," she said as she put the camera back into the bag. "The first is a 'keep'. Do you know what that is?"

"No," I replied.

"You have first keep and second keep. It just means how available you are. When agencies are trying to find models, they want to know the model will be available for the shoot. First keep means that you will definitely be available for a job. So if there is a fashion show tomorrow at seven p.m and you don't have any other obligations, that would be a first keep booking. Second keep is if you are not sure you can make the job. Sometimes different engagements overlap, and depending on how popular a model is, they might keep options open and have some jobs as second keep. Do you understand?"

"Yes," I replied.

"The other thing is a reserve. A big company, like Softbank if they do a campaign with you, they might want the exclusive rights to use your photos or videos for a certain period of time. The longer that time is, the more they pay you. So a reserve can be anywhere from six months to two years."

"So this is because they don't want people to model for anyone else?"

"In a manner of speaking. The company might use your images internationally on the internet, on television and in print, so they don't want the same model advertising for another company during that time."

"I see."

"So that's it, that's all you need to know. Do you think you will be busy in the near future?"

"I think everything will be first keep for me," I said with a smile.

"Okay," Ayuna said with a soft laugh. "I'll see you soon."

It wasn't long before I got my first e-mail about a casting call. Based on what I'd learned about the structure of things, it was a well-paying gig linked to Adidas, the clothing company. As I read the e-mail, I saw the directions to where the casting was being held and that Ayuna would be accompanying me. I also saw the gig would pay one hundred thousand yen over two days.

"Where we are going is near Odaiba. You should go there sometime," Ayuna said to me as we left the train station.

I'd heard of Odaiba. A beautiful, man-made island that had been the topic of countless documentaries. People had often told me to go there and see the giant Gundam they had erected there, but it was long since gone. We were going to a warehouse, and we first had to check in by an office housed in a shipping container at the entrance. As we approached, I saw two leggy blondes step out, all cheekbones and jaded faces. They strolled past us as if they were already at a runway show. Inside, a man asked Ayuna which agency she was with and she handed him a card. We went the same way the blonde girls had, through the rest of the parking lot and into a massive grey building. As I entered, I saw four people lined up by a door. The door opened as we walked past, and I saw a huge room, almost bare with the exception of some huge studio lights setup on a platform that directly faced a few chairs. A handsome guy was smiling at the camera, as someone snapped photos of him. The door closed with a hiss, and immediately I felt frightened. For all intents and purposes, it looked like they were doing the shoot already.

"You look very different today," Ayuna said to me. "When I met you, I thought you were handsome, but I can see more today."

It was interesting to hear this from Ayuna as I wasn't wearing anything fancy. Other than my usual pair of skinny jeans I wore a tight shirt that read "Shinjuku Surprise?"

In the next room, there were no less than one hundred models, mostly women of European descent. The room had the same dimensions as the photography room, with a few dozen rows of cheap metal chairs provided for seating. The women were all rail thin, with high cheekbones and piercing eyes. It was a sea of blondes and brunettes talking in a light chorus of different languages. There was a sprinkle of colour here and there, some girls who I could tell were half-Japanese or of full African descent. There few male models I saw guys who ran the gamut from handsome to very plain, and a few who resembled the touts I'd always see in Roppongi. As we walked in and took a seat near a group of young men, I felt the eyes of the room on me. Ayuna went to get a card with my face and number on it.

It was a long wait, and I spent most of the time looking at several of the female models. There were so many women, with such similar features. Many of them constantly smiled and laughed, with the offhand energy that said they did nothing else. Others looked brooding and pensive, eyes locked forward with focus. Many of the guys were eagerly chatting to the women around them, happily orchestrating future nights of easy outings by using their looks. In front of us, a man in tight jeans sitting near the door would occasionally call out a number, and the agency name. Some agencies had up to ten models in attendance. Of course, I had no idea which agencies were reputable, including mine, but I realized it didn't matter. Mick was right, if you had an office in Gaienmae, you had to be doing something right. A few seats away I saw a girl dressed in black shorts and a grey tank top. She was startlingly attractive despite her plain attire. As if feeling my eyes on her, she turned towards me, and gave a slightly tired, but friendly smile. This was a brave new world of skinny jeans and intense eyes. I snapped a picture of the casting area with my phone.

When I was called up, I went with Ayuna to the next room with the bright lights. Three people sat on the chairs facing the platform but one stood out to me; he wore head to toe Adidas and had the marginally contained energy of a very busy man. The other two people, a man and a woman, had pleasant faces and smiled as I came in, gesturing for me to go to the platform.

"Just be natural," the pleasant faced man said.

"Yes, we see that you are Jamaican, so act friendly!" the lady said.

The third man sat there, watching. Ayuna gave me a gentle smile and a nod, and I walked over to the platform. It wasn't a platform *per se*, just a large grey box about four inches off the ground. But standing there, I was on the edge of a skyscraper, with only these three people to catch me. The photographer came over and began snapping pictures.

"Relax, smile and do some poses," the pleasant man said again.

I tried some standard poses, and pointed at the camera, arched my shoulders and smiled a few times. My upper lip trembled rapidly. The clicks of the photographer's camera sounded like thunder.

"Give him the jacket," came a gruff voice. It was the man wearing the full Adidas outfit.

I slipped on the jacket, cool and black. It felt great against my arms. The photographer motioned for me to zip it up and I did, and he snapped some more pictures.

"Thank you so much!" the lady said as I walked off the platform after removing the jacket. The pleasant faced man said the same and the gruff-voiced man nodded at me. My heart was pounding as I exited the room. That had been both frightening and thrilling. A few moments later, Ayuna came out.

"One of the directors likes your look, so maybe they will call you back," she said.

"That would be great," I replied.

We walked back to the station and Ayuna wished me a good day, and I stood there for a little while. Where we were, you could smell the nearby sea, and I took in the scent of sea-water and fish around me. The streets here were also relatively quiet, and I was beginning to see that Tokyo wasn't just three districts with blurry nights and days where you woke up at three o' clock. That mix of nervousness and intrigue from the casting lingered within me. It was an interesting world, that world of beauty and those who market it. No one chooses how they look, but I saw at the casting that hidden behind most of those attractive faces was uncertainty. Sure there were a few standouts who probably got a lot of work, but many of those women looked so similar I'm not sure how well they generally fared.

I had no idea where I fit either. This was ironic, since I'd always operated with this philosophy of being between the lines, not too obvious and careful. But under those lights, with the people staring at me, my intention would have to be obvi-ous. I'd have to shed my day self and be reborn in the image of what worked if I was to do this. This was something I learned quickly, because I wasn't selected for the campaign.

Chapter 18

My next casting call was near Harajuku, in a building two streets away from Omotesando. I went unaccompanied this time, in line with a set of models who were mostly Japanese and European men. This job paid twenty thousand yen for a runway show that was happening next week. All of us stood in close proximity in the cramped lobby of the building for thirty minutes before being sent a few streets away to an office above a café. A lady in front of me spoke frankly about the industry. She was pretty but aging, definitely in her late thirties. She was part of a small selection of women who were trying to be cast for a skit that led into the opening of the show. Her voice was high but her eyes were flat as she spoke. She was married to a Japanese man whom she had met shortly after coming to Japan years before to model. It was at a runway show, in the days when she was getting so much work she had an apartment in Daikanyama and partied like there was no tomorrow. Beauty, she said is a delicate blend of actual beauty and personality, and she felt that she was able to convey that well.

"I'm not the most beautiful girl out there, I know," she said to me. "I am *pretty,* and I can say that, or else I wouldn't have been doing this for so long. People like people who can relax, who can help them relax, when they have sixteen hour days and pissy supermodels to work with."

There were one or two of those types in the line. Guys with such good looks it was hard for them not to be arrogant. There was also a girl who seemed angry to be there, her beautiful eyes heavy with mysterious concern. I still didn't have an opinion on this world of beauty. I wore my nice Jacket that Zeus had given me, and my nice jeans and the special shoes from my other suitcase, but all I thought about was the near future, and if I'd have to leave the city. This wasn't about being a model, it was just about survival. I didn't feel very prepared. Many of the men in line had portfolios with them. One person in particular, a fellow named Marc, got "loads of work" as told to me by the same woman. To me, Marc looked pretty normal.

He wasn't very tall and was reasonably handsome. However, he had done several major campaigns and doubled doing swimwear and runway. For now, I had no folder, just the knowledge that my agency e-mailed these people, they saw my photo and contacted them. I heard my name, and I went inside.

Three people sat behind a small desk. Before I could face them, a man in a very tight green shirt said "No! Too big!"

I paused as he said this and the other casting members nodded. "Thank you for your time," one of them said. I had been waiting for almost two hours to see these people, and I was in the room for less than ten seconds.

Days later, Ayuna called me personally to tell me about a Puma show. She excitedly told me that the casting director was doing a "Jamaican themed" show and loved the fact that I was Jamaican. This casting was also in Harajuku, but some distance from where I was previously. It was in the evening, around seven p.m. I slipped on the nice jacket again, wore another pair of my nice jeans and went out into the night. The scenario became routine, where on my way to the casting I'd see a few fellows that looked like me, tall and well dressed.

At this casting I had to walk for the casting director. An assistant gave me some Puma gear. I was upbeat and friendly when I met him initially, but there was no enthusiasm in his face as I walked down the short stretch of a small hallway for him. Earlier, I thought I'd definitely get the job, because I knew there weren't many Jamaicans in Tokyo. But, I didn't get the call.

The next casting gig was in a room the size of my room at the guesthouse. A line of young men stretched out the door.

"These Japanese girls are so easy to fuck," a tattooed guy from Europe said. "Especially when I tell them I model, it's like they want to just leave wherever we are and go fuck."

"Definitely, but I get these chicks to buy me stuff," said another guy, very suave in a Richard Gere sort of way. "I can't tell you how many hostess girls think I'm an actor or something. You know hostess girls earn crazy money, and before I know it I'm getting a new phone, an iPad or expensive dinners night after night."

The guys laughed as they kept talking. I didn't say anything to anyone, because the nature of what I was doing was already getting to me. I felt silly in the jacket and my jeans and the nice shoes. Normally when I looked in the mirror, I didn't have much of an opinion on what I saw. Lately I'd been scrutinizing myself more; the slope of my nose, the shape of my lips and the way my face looked. It was a fool's errand, because everything was ultimately up to the casting agent, but I was falling into that illogical place anyone who must question themself relative to something they can't control does.

I stepped away from the line for a little while, going to a backstreet. The conversation the guys were having was becoming annoying as they shared explicit details of recent sexual exploits. I tried to get into state, to feel like I wanted it. I needed to *intend* it. When I went inside, a broad-chested man with one eyebrow slightly raised handed me a shiny peach coloured jacket.

"Walk for us please," he said.

I took a few steps forward in the small space.

"Relax, relax," he said.

"I am relaxed," I replied.

"Walk more… natural," he said.

I turned around and went to the front of the room, this time walking back down more slowly.

"No, your shoulders are very tense. You need to be natural in this industry," the man said.

I wanted to slap him, even though I knew I was inexperienced. For someone who'd been walking his entire life, it was bizarre to have someone tell me I wasn't walking properly. The casting ended quickly, and I gave the man the jacket and stepped outside.

"Went well?" said the guy who looked liked Richard Gere.

"I don't think so," I replied.

"Too bad bro, hope you get the next one."

I left the area quickly. Those guys had that cool, relaxed energy I needed. Or did they? What had I done that first night in Tokyo to catch the eye of Tako?

The castings were a blur of people and places. There were storefronts in Ginza, a club in Aoyama and sometimes Shinjuku. I forgot about myself as I walked in front of many casting agents, being judged simply at a glance. A part of me truly wanted to believe I had a presence that meant something, that what Tako saw was real, but so far I had no confirmation. It was also expensive traveling around, since the agency didn't reimburse train fees. Plus, the constant moving around and eating cheap food had left me with something else; a cough that had been nagging me for the last week. After leaving another casting without feeling positive, I knew I was being reduced to a shell, as I reached and grasped for what, I didn't know.

Back at home after the casting, I coughed into my hand a few times as I chopped up my usual medley of vegetables and ground meat. The taste of the meal had become predictable, but after spending so much money on lunches recently, I needed to conserve. When the food was ready, I went to the entertainment room, where Mick, Dubz and Barbara were sitting. I hadn't spoken to Barbara in quite some time, not since our conversation about Japanese superiority.

I said a quick hello to the group as I sat down with my food. It seemed she was continuing this dialogue about superiority, since the topic was about all her ex-boyfriends and their large man parts. The contention for Mick and Dubz was the fact that all her ex-boyfriends were Japanese.

"You are so lying, the world knows Asian men don't have big ones. Just toss in any old Japanese porn DVD and you'll get your confirmation," Mick said.

Barbara replied quickly.

"I'm not lying," she replied. "I could barely fit my fingers around it." As she said this, she made a hand-cupping gesture.

I immediately got the image of an Ape in my mind, a gigantic, gargantuan man-thing with enough endowment to squire a nation of primates. But this wasn't a man-thing we were talking about here. It was a man. Dubz wasn't convinced. He took a sip of a beer he'd been holding while watching Barbara and Mick speak.

"Are you sure he wasn't of mixed ethnicity?" Dubz asked.

"No he wasn't, but he was pretty tall, if that counts," Barbara said.

"Well at least you had a good time in bed," Mick said, apparently pleased to acquiesce to this image of a super hung, tall Japanese man.

"It wasn't that great," Barbara said, looking up at the ceiling. "We were always going to love hotels and I didn't like that."

"Why didn't you bring him here?" Dubz asked. "You live on the nice floor."

Barbara sighed. "I know, but I'm always super busy with work and so is he. We tended to meet up in the city somewhere, for dinner, and he doesn't live close by so it was always a love hotel or nothing at all."

I smirked as I ate my dinner. If I was this mysterious porn star in waiting, I'd probably be going to love hotels all the time. My massive organ would mean it was my domain and the woman I was with must submit to my will or else. Possibly, I would echo this sentiment to her, then quickly drop my pants, listening for the gasp of surprise I'd have heard in so many bedrooms, public showers and doctor's offices.

"So how long were you guys together?" Mick asked.

"Just a few months."

"Ah, I guess it's not all about the dick then," Dubz replied.

Barbara laughed, then told Dubz it was the same with the next guy she met.

"Wait, this *other* guy had a massive one too?"

"Yeah it was pretty big," Barbara replied.

Barbara spoke without a hint of nervousness or embarrassment, as if dating men with giant penises and discussing this was as normal as eating Bento.

"Well, I'm sure he didn't give it to you good," Dubz said. "He had the tool but probably didn't know how to use it."

"The sex wasn't bad," Barbara said. "But it wasn't that good either. We didn't see each other much because he was really busy."

Mick sat up straight, completely intrigued by Barbara's accounts. He gave her a quiet stare.

"So what happened next, you know, with another guy?" he asked.

Barbara sipped on her beer. "The next guy I met was pretty nice, but we only went out for a month."

"Was he Japanese?" Dubz asked.

"Yes," Barbara replied.

"Ah hah! Let me guess it didn't work out because he had a small dick right?"

"No, his was pretty big too, but I didn't like his personality."

Mick and Dubz began laughing uncontrollably, while Barbara smiled at them, drinking her beer. While they were speaking, I'd sat quietly listening, coughing into my hand. Like many conversations I'd had with people in this room, this one was entertaining, but I had no further interest in it once I'd finished eating. I left the group and went back to my room. I sipped on a Chu-Hi in between coughing. Things were taking me close to my exit strategy, my last resort. My last one hundred and fifty thousand yen was to buy a plane ticket if I needed to leave the country.

Ayuna called me a day later. There was a commercial coming up and she said the casting agent had specifically asked for me. It was a four-day shoot for a large phone company, Docomo. The job had a one-year reserve, and paid one hundred thousand yen per day. When she told me this, I could see the future unveiling itself with me in it. Four hundred thousand yen could put me into next year. But just a few days before doing the job, I had to e-mail Ayuna and tell her I couldn't do it.

Chapter 19

The cold had gotten much worse. I lay in my bed, hardly able to move, my eyes the heaviest they'd ever been. Breathing in was a chore, and with each inhalation there was a chance I'd break into a fit of coughing that wouldn't stop for several minutes. With each expansion of my ribcage, I felt little needles stabbing the entire area around my torso. I slowly got up off the bed, trying my best to breathe shallow. It didn't matter. Any breath I took caused significant pain. I felt something jerk in my throat, and another fit of coughing started. I coughed up a green yellow mess of mucus, which I spat into an empty beer can. Hobbling over to the sink, I leaned on it heavily and opened my nearby micro fridge. It greeted me with a blank stare, empty save the moldy remains of half an onion. My knees hurt with each step I took, and my room felt like a winter's day. I tried going for the door before another fit of coughing hit me, and I had to pause as my chest constantly heaved on its own, the expulsion of air stronger and more insistent. My insides felt ragged, and as I spit out another wad of mucus, I saw that it was tinged with a hint of blood. I opened the door and stumbled to one of the bathrooms to relieve myself, forgetting to close the door as I walked in. I could barely stand straight, but managed to urinate without messing up the toilet. The house was deathly quiet. At this time of the day, there would be no one here. I went back to my room slowly, and reached into my pouch. I took out a few thousand yen, gasping as another wave of pain shot from my stomach up through my throat as I breathed. I had to get to a hospital.

I fumbled for a while as I changed what I was wearing, falling into another coughing spasm as I was crouched over, my jeans half pulled up. I waited for it to pass, and finished putting on my clothes. The light outside was blinding, and I cursed as I went back into my room, and fished in my suitcase for an old pair of dark glasses. I slipped them on and went out into the day, coughing, wheezing and spitting all the way to the main street. Because I didn't want to alarm whichever driver I would take a cab with, I stepped into a convenience store and bought a facemask, shivering in the artificially refrigerated atmosphere.

Back on the road, I managed to wave down a taxi. The back seat was pristinely comfortable. In fact, I'd never experienced such a sense of relief from the act of sitting down. I wanted a pillow and a sheet to lie down and curl up in that backseat as it drove around town in circles forever.

"Hospital," I croaked.

"Excuse me? Could you please say that again?" the driver asked.

"A hospital nearby," I croaked a little louder, sending me into an explosive fit of coughing.

The driver nodded with a certain urgency and drove me down through Shinjuku and the crowded streets of Shibuya. It was all a blur. The pain in my chest was everything and breathing had become even harder. *I'm slipping away,* my mind said. The driver was listening to something on the radio as we drove. The voice of an excited young man was announcing a huge AKB48 concert that would be held at the Tokyo Dome next week. I knew about the super popular, nigh ubiquitous girl group, but I'd never listened to any of their music. I clenched my teeth as a sharp turn from the taxi forced me to draw in a deep breath. The agony I felt now was a far cry from the anxiety pains I had experienced before; this was a hot knife dipped in pepper, dancing away in my lungs.

Through my now teary eyes, I got blurry glimpses of the people outside. The men in their shiny suits walking on the roadside, an occasional set of thirty-something year old mothers riding their *mamacharis* around, punk kids with spiky hair in loose baggy pants and women holding huge shopping bags with obviously nothing else to do. I hated these people, and their functionality. They were out there, breathing normally while my body was racked in pain, and the man on the radio enthusiastically kept talking about a concert I'd never see. We reached the hospital, and I paid the driver the four thousand yen for the cab fare, stumbling into the light. I stood there for a little while. The act of getting out of the cab had caused the most powerful coughing fit yet, stinging my tongue with the bittersweet taste of bile and blood. A dark hand was reaching for me. I followed the signs to the emergency section, almost too weak to properly explain to those around me how I was feeling.

Several hospital staff told me to sit and wait in various areas, while I froze, my hands tightly wrapped around my arms, my face mask slowly becoming dotted with red stains from the coughing. More time passed as I coughed and heaved. In a chair directly facing me, was an old man, who seemed to be asleep, his mouth half open and his head craned back. A growing, stress-filled panic now accompanied the pain. This would be a terrible place to die, I thought. Sitting in a hallway, across from an old man who was probably dead. Shivering and coughing, I felt completely isolated. I fought the tears that were coming. *No!* my mind said. I would not give the hospital staff the pleasure of being open witnesses to my weakness. But they came anyway, and the unceasing pain in my chest kept growing, and I feared that I was being ignored because I was a foreigner on my little plastic chair that could barely hold my buttocks. One concerned person who I assumed was a medical student took pity on me. I could barely see him, with my eyes filled with tears and snot running down my nose behind my mask. He asked me about how I was feeling, and it was difficult to describe. As well as I spoke Japanese, I'd never used much medical terminology. Through more fits of coughing I managed to tell him, I was feeling severe pain in my chest and felt cold. He nodded after hearing this, and trotted quickly down the hallway.

I couldn't sit up anymore, and lay on the chair beside me. My breath sounded like a saw running slowly over tough wood. I also had to pee again. Soon, I felt some strong arms hold me under my armpits, and lift me into a wheelchair. Under a quiet breath, I mentioned I had to get to the bathroom. My bladder was on fire. As the medical assistant pushed me into the bathroom, I stood up. I would have definitely fallen if he hadn't grabbed me.

"It's okay," he said to me as I fumbled with my pants.

It wasn't okay. My hands barely listened to me as I moved them, and only a few feet away from the urinal, I peed my pants. The urine felt warm against my legs, and again, I found tears running down my face, as the assistant held me, patting me softly on the shoulder.

The next few hours were a blur of faces and people. I went to an x-ray room, they took blood samples, and I had to pee into a cup. My jeans and underwear were gone, and I spent this time in an ill-fitting hospital gown with my backside mostly out for the world to see. I remember the cold feeling of the x-ray device on my chest, and the man operating it saying "Breathe in deeply". That action created such a paroxysm of pain it was a wonder I didn't fall to the ground. I was eventually given a bed but unable to sleep, the pain still coming brightly in the pulsing shocks of a waking dream. A few attendants buzzed around me, as I drifted in and out of consciousness. Then someone spoke to me when my eyes were closed and my face was trembling with pain.

"Hello, I am Dr. Junichi Kaneda," the voice said.

I croaked a response and lifted my arm slightly, for the first time noticing a thin clear tube attached to my arm, covered by a piece of gauze. My face felt odd, and it was then I detected the straps behind my ears and felt textured rubber against my cheeks.

"You had a severe case of, ah, "Pneumonia" and it was good that you came in when you did. We are giving you some medication through a vein in your arms to help, and also some oxygen to help with your breathing."

"How... long?" I whispered.

The doctor, obviously used to people speaking at my volume immediately responded.

"A few days, maybe more, it depends on how your body reacts. For now, please rest and I will follow up with you tomorrow."

I ended up staying in the hospital for a little over two weeks. On the first night I woke up, frightened. Someone had lifted up my gown, and I could feel the coldness of the hospital air on my genitals and thighs, and the touch of a glove covered hand on my ankle. Barely able to move my head, I glanced down, to see a solidly muscular woman taking a diaper out of a sealed plastic bag. She had nimble, gentle movements despite her imposing frame. As she slipped on the diaper, I also noticed that a curtain had been pulled around my bed. When she finished, she opened the curtain and left the room. I wasn't awake for long, and soon fell asleep to the pleasant humming of a machine somewhere beside me.

For the next few days I could barely move. On day one I was pristinely embarrassed when the same lady returned to change my diaper. She took slips of thick white towels pungent with the smell of disinfectant and wiped me up and down. The sensation was strange, and I felt loneliness shroud me as I lay there, freshly cleaned. The routine became less embarrassing as time passed, and eventually, I was able to hobble to the nearby bathroom and relieve myself. There were two other beds in my room, one empty, and one occupied by an older woman, with a pleasant face. Most of the time I saw her reading a Natsuo Kirino novel.

"You know my daughter told me to read this quite some time ago," she said to me one day.

I was sitting up eating my lunch, a tasteless bento with a side helping of lukewarm orange juice. The lady slipped a small pink bookmark between the leaves, and close the book.

"At the time I said to her, why? I mean, I'm older, so I'm used to more traditional novelists and I wasn't really into all these sort of new, "out there" writers. But that was before I got sick and before I came here."

She looked at me while I chewed my food.

"I saw the lady come in to clean you. What a sensation! You spend all that time in your life cleaning yourself, paying the bills and one day you are in a room with a person you don't know, and they are wiping your ass!"

I smiled broadly, trying not to laugh.

"You know what? The first day I was angry when the lady came. See, I have a serious problem with my leg. Exactly what isn't so important anymore, but I was having some severe pains and the first night I came here I could hardly move. So the lady gave me the diaper and I was so angry when she did this. I mean I raised two children and have a husband of thirty years. Who was she? Then she came back and cleaned me, and even though I was upset about it, I thanked her. Then she told me something quite interesting."

"What was that?" I said in a slight squeak.

"She said that she'd originally been a pretty good athlete and she wanted to be an Olympic level discus thrower. You can tell by her body that she was strong. So she took it seriously, doing part-time jobs at night and working out during the day. She often visited her grandfather who lived in Setagaya when she had free time. She had a key to his apartment, and one day when she went to visit him she found him dead in his bathroom. He had been doing number two, had a heart attack, and had fallen to the floor.

"She was devastated of course, and sat there for a long time, weeping. She called the hospital, and soon an ambulance was on its way. But before they came, she made sure to clean him up, because she didn't want them to see him in his own mess. She said that when she held his body with her powerful hands, hands she had trained for years to get strong, they felt weak. Her grandfather who had bathed her as a child and smiled at her as she graduated from high school, was in her arms, naked as the day he was born."

The woman paused, taking a sip of juice from a similar container on a tray beside her.

"After that, she decided to use her strength to help people, and that's why she's here. But what I liked about her story was the part about being naked. I tell you young man, the day I felt that woman holding me and wiping me, it was as if you put me in the middle of the Shibuya crossing with no clothes on and told me to sprint from left to right."

Now I couldn't help letting out a little laugh, which caused me a mild fit of coughing. The lady waited until I'd started breathing normally again before she continued.

"So I said, when you are exposed like this, what's the point of walls and opinions? So, I called my daughter and told her I was going to read the book she'd always pestered me to read. Maybe we all need to get our asses wiped as adults, not just when you are my age, but to remind you of how you were once helpless, and everything you've done up to this point is to get away from that helplessness."

The woman's word's stayed with me. In another few days she had left the hospital, being greeted once or twice by a young woman I assumed was her daughter. As the days passed and I slowly regained my strength, I found the quiet of the hospital unnerving. A slow, gradual anger built within me. My phone had not rung once the entire time I was in the hospital. It seemed, I was correct about being a phantom in Tokyo, able to disappear without a trace, to the worry and regret of no one. This wasn't anger from an annoyance with the people I met, it was an anger reflected by my choices, and all the decisions that had led me to this situation.

The day I was discharged, I was told I was recovering well even though I had lost ten pounds. My legs still felt a bit wobbly as I walked back down the hallways that I'd barely navigated upon my entry there two weeks prior. I sorted out the particulars of my discharge, and felt numb when I was told my hospital bill was three hundred and fifty thousand yen. With a shaking hand, I took the bill from the receptionist and thanked her. It was good to be outside, looking at the sun overhead. I felt as if the jaws of the city had opened for a while, luring me in with a fake promise, and I'd darted out of the way, just as it was about to catch me. I would not be consumed.

Chapter 20

The crow was tinkering with a clock. He sat on a stool, with his toolkit spread out before him, with a watchmaker's visor over his eyes. I approached slowly and cautiously. There was nothing around us except a black void. The only source of light was a bulb hanging above the crow's workbench. It was a hanging bulb, and the electric line it was attached to stretched up into the blackness, impossibly long and high.

"Fixing watches are a bitch," the crow said, picking up a tiny screwdriver with its wing. "When you have so many moving parts, something's bound to go wrong. I mean, it could be this gear here, a bent piece of metal over there, the possibilities are endless."

The crow turned to me, smiling eerily. "But y'know, like my good wife says, sometimes fixing broken things helps us fix ourselves."

As if noticing my puzzled expression, the crow laughed in a series of soft caws.

"Ah, you think I didn't have a wife? Well, us crows gotta get laid too you know."

I stepped a bit closer to see what he was working on. So far, it had been obscured by his left wing. He gleefully whistled the opening song from the *Sound of Music*, while he poked and prodded at the mystery item on his work desk. I got closer, but the crow was getting bigger now, his back muscles rippling and growing with each step closer I took. The visor barely fit on its head, and the little workshop vest it was wearing began to tear. I took another step, and heard the vest rip and watched it fall, emitting a thunderous clatter as an assortment of tools in the various pockets hit the ground. The crow laughed again, but this time it wasn't a soft caw, but a growling caw like iron poles grating against one another. The left wing was getting impossibly large, and yet I still approached, wondering what was behind it.

The crow stood up and spread its wings in a rush, and momentarily a gust of wind caused me to close my eyes. I opened them to see the crow gone. On the table was me. A strange plastic looking version of myself, with the chest open, and the innards strewn about the worktable. Above me, I heard the crow flapping its wings, so loudly, I feared to imagine its present size. The deep, cawing laugh echoed from the void above and I ran into the darkness, away from the workbench and the lifeless eyes of my plastic clone. The cawing became a shrill scream, and then I was awake, reaching into the darkness at nothing. The sound of the air conditioner was all that greeted me, blended in with the rapid pace of my heart's pounding.

The day I had returned to the house, I'd walked straight to my room. If anyone was in the entertainment room or cooking in the kitchen I didn't know. All I saw was the white hallway through the lobby, with the promise of my bed in my suite. Then I had fallen immediately asleep, with the lights on, fully clothed. The next day, in the bathroom, I could see the difference in my features. My cheeks, though never plump by any stretch of the imagination, were mostly devoid of any roundness. My shoulders and ribs were somewhat thinner, and my jeans were looser on my thighs. I had become a more angular version of myself. As I took a bath, relishing the warm water spraying onto my body, I realized there was no anger inside me about the timing of this bout of pneumonia. Sure I had lost out on a good bit of money, but sitting in that hospital day after day, unable to do anything was more frightening than losing potential income. The steady beeping of the hospital machines around me and the occasional farts I would hear then smell from the lady sharing the room with me were the most daunting things I'd faced. That was the reality of complete immobility; a state where everything existed mostly in your mind, and the world out there was something you dreamed about but couldn't access. As I scrubbed myself, I thought of the woman with her powerful hands that had tended to me, remembering the vulnerability I'd experienced in that moment. But more than all of that, I thought of my phone, which had been placed in a little tray near my bed. The phone that never rang, the phone that never questioned what had happened to me. That was the real message. Life wasn't waiting on me with a happy smile and white-gloved hands and neither were the people around me. I was lucky the city hadn't swallowed me whole, leaving me lying in a morgue somewhere. The cold focus I'd felt after doing auditions around town had now become an emotionless brand of cold intention, that I always felt right under the surface of my skin. But I wasn't angry with anyone around me. They all had what I'd been lacking from the start; that kick in the balls will to go out and make it happen. They faced the day with their smiles and their anecdotes, their long working days and nights filled with chase and intrigue. Of course they had worries like me, but they acted differently towards making things happen while I had lain immobile without being unencumbered by disease or illness. I couldn't lie silent any longer, and neither could I keep looking on myself in the same way. My phone needed to ring. I wanted to be known and to be seen. Screw the day I fall on the street and no one knows I'm not there. That isn't a life.

This house and its odd characters provided access to one thing: information. Everyone had a story on how they survived, and how they evolved during their time here. This more than anything, would be what I planned to leech. Expert opinion is always better than learning through rough bumps in the road. I finished taking my shower and walked back to my suite. My phone was flashing a red light, indicating a message. It was from Ayuna, about another casting call, for a small show at the Armani Exchange store.

The store was another one of those I'd only seen in Tokyo in terms of the décor. There was elaborate velvet carpeting on the walls, with moody ambient lighting and clothing that I'd never seen people wear in the daytime. Hanging with the other models downstairs, I stood patiently by a wall, listening to music on my iPod. A girl walked into the area very quickly, holding a handbag as large as a backpack. She wore black tights, white heels and a white top with frills on the shoulders that moved slightly with each movement she made. Her hair was short, and I could see that the sides had previously been shaved and were growing out. She turned in my direction smiled, and waved. Then, the features and the body language came back to me. It was Mari, from the night I met her in F-Bar, my first night in Tokyo.

"How are you sir?" she said with a smile.

She slipped her glasses upwards to the top of her head and looked directly at me. I was stunned by her looks. This couldn't be Mari, I told myself, remembering our initial meeting. But there, in front of me she stood almost my height, with her chiseled face, small pouty lips and the eyes that she said were destined to put her in modeling. She was right. In the light of the day, her eyes held me strongly, despite her casual smirk with her glasses perched atop her head.

"Long time no see," I said.

She stepped forward and gave me a hug of pure strength.

"Yes! *Somebody* didn't call me!" she said, punching me in the shoulder.

Yes, I remembered, I was supposed to call her. It felt like eons ago, the night with the cab ride and the strange hotel party.

Beaming a smile, she stepped back and folded her arms while looking at me. "I'm glad to see you. It look's like you decided to use your gift."

"I guess so," I replied. "But I haven't gotten any gigs yet."

"You will, trust me," she responded. "Listen, I have to go and see my agent, so don't be a stranger okay? Let's grab a drink sometime."

"Definitely."

"The skinny look fits you!" she said, turning around when another model called her name behind us.

I'd gotten used to the scenario of people and judges now, and I strolled in coolly when I was called, did my walk, answered a few simple questions and left. The usual banter of the guys and girls around me didn't hold much interest, so I went home.

The first time I met up with Mari, we had drinks at an Irish bar in Roppongi and ended up at the nearby Gas Panic. She had laughed at me when I suggested the place, because it had a reputation for being seedy. I shrugged my shoulders at this statement. Gas Panic was free, and I could buy myself at least one drink without getting stressed. Without any insistence from me, Mari bought me several drinks, and pulled me into the throng. It was mostly young Japanese men jumping around excitedly to the ear splitting sounds of pop music around us. In the middle of this, we kissed. Her lips were as soft as my mind had imagined, and with the bodies hitting into me as I held her, the moment consumed me. Afterward, when we left the club she was quiet. I didn't say much either, and walked her back to the train station and gave her a hug goodbye. Something about the night resounded in me more than just the kiss. The pounding, visceral music that had raked at my ears while I kissed her mirrored a building internal dialogue, something darker that I couldn't explain to myself.

We decided to meet soon after, at a small restaurant in Ebisu. It was on the second floor of a three-story building. I sat by a table on a small balcony, looking out at the growing blackness of the evening sky. Mari walked into my field of vision. I looked at my phone, then her.

"Your ten minutes are more like thirty. You are super late," I said to her.

She walked over with a smile on her face. I stood up and gave her a hug. A fragrant smell like a bed of roses wafted from her.

"Your smell compensates for your lateness," I said.

"Really? Thank you," she replied.

She gave me another smile, and I wondered what I had thought that first night when we met. I hadn't seen the power in her eyes, or the delicate femininity she now exuded in a rippling wave. A waiter brought us two glasses of water and lit a small candle resting in a black tray on the table. Mari sat down and lit up a cigarette, and we ordered some food from the menu. The meals were prepared quickly, and as we ate, she asked me intermittently about modeling.

"Well, nothing's happened for me yet, so I don't have the strongest opinion of the whole thing," I noted.

"That makes sense," she said. "But there is something different about you, not just the weight loss. Your eyes were brighter when I met you the first time."

I didn't feel like talking about my experience at the hospital or the possibility I'd be leaving Tokyo, but I mentioned Briggs and what he was doing, and how I had begun dabbling in taking photos around the city.

"A good photographer can do well here," Mari said, slurping on some noodles.

True, I responded to her. But I explained that it takes time to build a reputation and clients and I wasn't sure how to do all of that. Mari paused, and then leaned back in her chair.

"Remember when I told you about my decision to become a model and why? Well, it wasn't easy, because like I said, I was a really ordinary girl who loved eating onions on my grandfather's farm in the summer. Coming into this fashion world you meet a lot of strange people and people with different agendas. It didn't take me long to understand I needed a way to cope with things. So, I have my business self and then my regular self.

"The girls I saw that fell hard and fast, were always girls who put too much of their real personality into their work. Youth and innocence are easily exploited. So you have to figure out how to be this person that people can like and relate to, but also someone people can't push over super easy. If you can do that, things might improve."

I believed her, but she was a lovely young woman with *those eyes,* and me, well, I still didn't see what Mari and Tako saw, not yet. Mari had a nice sense of an inner self, I could see that. There was work for me to do yet.

"When I was walking over here, I thought I had something to tell you," Mari said. "But maybe I think, I don't need to talk about it."

"If that's what you want," I replied.

She let out a sigh.

"Okay, well, there was the kiss we shared the other day, and it was very good so… I was a little curious. I want to know what you think."

"I thought it was good too," I replied.

She looked at me for a few moments while the light of the candle danced in her eyes.

"Is that all?" she said.

"What do you mean?" I asked.

"I mean, are you curious about anything else," she replied.

"I want to kiss you again, and probably more," I said to her.

She smiled a different kind of smile and took a sip of her water.

"That sounds fine."

We left the restaurant soon after. Because it was early, she suggested that we take a walk through Shibuya. I agreed, and we walked the streets I'd now become quite familiar with. Mari showed me some of her favourite albums in a nearby Hard-Off store, and I showed her some old video games I used to play on Super Nintendo. She told me about a possible party at Trump Room later, and whipped out her phone to text the promoter about it. She took me to a restaurant I'd never been to, somewhere near Camelot. Gripping my hand tightly as we went up the elevator to the eatery, she said I *had to* try the cheesecake. It was good, and our next stop was a video arcade across the street from a two story McDonald's that I remembered falling asleep in on one of my previous Tokyo trips. We played mostly air hockey, and I found Mari's energy exciting. There was something about women who modeled that always create an extra layer of perception around them. From walking on the runway to playing air hockey, when models do it, it seems more fun.

Later, we went to Trump Room. We walked inside, going up two flights of stairs.

"You have to do this!" she said.

She darted over to a Moose's head hanging on the wall, and gave it a delicate peck on the cheek. I cringed, thinking of all the germs on that monstrosity of taxidermy, but Mari waved at me excitedly and I walked over and pretended to kiss the moose.

"Got it!" she said, looking at her phone.

I chuckled at the picture when she showed it to me, immediately noticing my more sunken cheeks and sharper jaw line.

"Drinks?" she asked.

I nodded, and she bought a Campari with soda, while I drank a beer. It was a light crowd, and we stood listening to music and people watching before heading to the next dance floor. A man wearing a witches' hat constantly doing the Macarena was our joke for the rest of the night.

She lived in an apartment a few stops away in Shinagawa. In a similar fashion to the last time we'd went out, we had a lot of drinks and laughs, but as I held her hand walking down her quiet neighbourhood street, I didn't feel the same tension I did after we had left Gas Panic. Her apartment was small and clean.

"Your bed reminds me of this hotel I went to when I first came to Japan," I said.

"Really? That is interesting. What about it?"

"I'm not sure. I think it's just, the way it looks and how close it is to the wall," I said.

I took off my shoes as we spoke for a few minutes, and then kissed her.

The softness of her lips extended to her entire body. As I kissed her neck, her shoulders and the soft area above her breasts, I was surprised at how womanly she felt to me despite her slender frame. The silky skin felt smooth and welcoming for the happy passenger that was my tongue. I kissed her nipples slowly, feeling her tremble at my touch. Kissing her hands, shoulders and fingers produced the same effect; trembles in her thighs, sharp moans from her mouth and slight squirming. By the time my hands found the soft wetness between her thighs, the room was filled with her ecstatic sighs. She looked gentle in this way, because her eyes were closed, hiding their usual intensity. In the dim light of her bedroom, I could see the milky complexion of her skin, and the small, taut shape of her ass. Her insides felt welcoming to my fingers. I took off my clothes and slipped on a condom. Kissing her gently, I entered her slowly.

"Oh, oh my god," Mari said.

"Are you okay?" I asked.

"It's so big!" she said, laughing.

She felt heavenly, as I could feel the muscles of her vagina occasionally clamp on my shaft, raising gooseflesh on my arms. She scratched my back and asked me to slap her ass where my thighs connected with it as her voice grew louder and louder. After just a few minutes, she moaned.

"I'm coming, oh god, I'm coming!"

She came solidly, clutching me in a vice as her body shook. Her panting was heavy, and she looked at me, her eyes blazing with surprise and intrigue. She would come three times as I did my work, with me eventually getting lost in her little mound, erupting as her slim body held mine. In the morning, I took her from behind as she watched us going at it in the mirror. At the edge of the bed she straddled me, moaning from our coitus. She came several times again and fell on the bed, spent. My chest shook as I also came, trembling as I felt the stirrings of a secondary male orgasm. Mari gave me a rapturous smile as we lay beside each other.

"You are amazing," she said.

"*Arigato,*" I replied.

On the way back to the station, I kept seeing her on top of me and the way her eyes looked when she had orgasm after orgasm. Something about that made me feel excited as a man. Her softness, her glow. In a day she was heading to Hong Kong for a week and a half to do some work. Would she carry this glow with her there? Or would she shift into her other personality, balancing it all while having memories of me in her mind?

The next day or two were difficult. I started spiraling, realizing that my situations with Yumi and Mari were just flashes in the pan of this strange existence. I probably wouldn't even be here much longer. This thought began to overwhelm me in little increments, each day when I woke up, every time I went to the market for my routine meal, and when I bought beers at the convenience store. The universe was teasing me with the promise of what could be, while I was careening down a chasm, unable to stop myself. The stirrings of a major panic were coming on, and I wished I could talk to Carmen, but the nine thousand yen sessions were costly now, and I found myself walking at night through parks and streets, with drinks in my hand, looking at everyone and no one, wishing I could scream at the night.

Chapter 21

I'd crawled into a shell, avoiding people in the house and politely declining requests to join the guys out on the road. If I was going to fail and leave the country, it would be in a puff of smoke, so no one would be left the wiser. Damned if they were going to know what was happening with me. I found myself regularly back in my room again, laying there in a semi-comatose state, ignoring the frequent pangs of hunger in my stomach, trying to visualize some kind of new reality. I glanced at my camera often, knowing it was filled with thousands of images, but what could I do with them?

I crawled out of bed and took a shower. Ayuna had called me for another casting. I felt extremely tired on the train and I took slow steps towards the casting area, which was some-where in Harajuku. My body felt thinner and lighter, and I had forgone wearing Zeus' nice jacket and opted for a light t-shirt and my usual skinny jeans. I said hello to the people organizing the casting and took my number, waiting in a chair in the lobby of some kind of office building. There was nothing more I wanted to do than sleep and return to my room and forget the day.

"You're here?" a familiar voice said.

I turned to see Mari behind me. She looked great as usual, in tight black jeans and a sleeveless black top that matched her handbag.

"I can't believe you didn't contact me once since the last time I saw you," Mari said, her voice low and tempered.

"I'm sorry—"

"You think it didn't mean anything? Nothing?"

Her voice was getting louder.

"Things have been weird," I said, very awake now.

"Things? What things? I thought you were different you know, but you are just another asshole."

My lips trembled with anger.

"Hey I'm not an ass—"

"You couldn't even send me a message or a text? Nothing? Fuck you!" Mari shouted, walking to the front of the room and sitting with her back turned to me.

A few heads turned in the room, and some of the smug faced guys chuckled and pointed at me. I sat there, burning with anger, as I gritted my teeth. The fatigue was gone, and in its place was a barely contained fury. *What did she know?* Her and her little expensive bag and sexy face, what the *fuck* did she know about me? I thought of the hospital and my phone in its little tray and how it never rang, and I wasn't sure, but I swore I could hear the bubbles popping in my vein as my blood boiled. If I was some A-class model, I'd probably just leave, but the job potentially paid forty thousand yen, so I had to deal.

They called my number.

I let out a hiss, and walked to the viewing room. Sitting behind a table, were three people, two dressed casually with one man in a loud pink shirt riddled with holes.

"For this show we are looking for edgy people," the man in the pink shirt said.

"I can give you edgy," I replied, surprised at how normal my voice sounded.

"That's good," the man said.

An assistant came over to me and helped me change into a tattered leather jacket that resembled the style of the shirt the man was wearing. I had taken off my shirt, so I was wearing the jacket alone, exposing my chest and abdominals.

"Okay, now walk for us. Remember, edgy!" the man said, his eyes glinting with a strange excitement.

The walkway was roughly eight feet long, and as I stepped forward, I didn't see anything around me. All I heard was the man mumble something about "good physique" and I kept hearing Mari's voice shouting curses and the idiot guys in the line laughing at me. The trembling I'd been experiencing in the chair had shifted into a subdued rage that made everything sharper and clearer.

"Can you do something stylistic for us?" the man said.

I nodded and turned back and walked again, this time, removing the jacket in a swift motion, slinging it over my left shoulder. I leaned forward a little bit and clenched my jaws, pausing for effect, then stood straight. The man in the pink shirt clapped excitedly.

"Yes! yes! Good intensity!" he said.

He leaned over and said something to the people beside him, who nodded as he spoke.

"Thank you for your time, we will contact your agency," the man said.

I thanked him and put on my shirt quickly, happy to get out of there. I didn't see Mari on my way out, and hurried towards the door to avoid any further confrontation.

"Hey man," the voice of a guy came.

The face was familiar. I'd seen him on a casting before.

"I'm Marc," he said, extending a hand.

"Yes, I think I remember you from the Shibuya casting."

He smiled his multi-campaign smile and laughed.

"I remember you too. I was surprised they didn't want you for the show, guess those guys were being picky."

"Oh?"

"Yeah, I thought you had it, most of the guys in the line were pretty lame," he said maintaining his smile the entire time.

I could feel my anger subsiding standing around him. Like Briggs, he projected a very casual warmth. Beside him, a cute Japanese woman kept looking at her phone, then him, in that order repeatedly.

"I saw what happened with Mari, that's a bum rap," Marc said.

"I guess," I replied, looking reflexively at the floor.

"Well man, me and some folks are heading to Velours tonight, you should come through and blow off some steam," he said.

"Velours?" I asked.

His eyes widened in surprise "You've never been there? Wow you have to come through! Don't worry, I have a list, so just drop my name and you are good to go, cool man?"

I nodded and told him goodbye, unsure of why he had invited me out in the first place. Stepping out into the day, I felt a painful embarrassment. The contempt I saw in Mari's face and the way her lips had trembled as she spoke gave me a sick feeling in my gut. The anger came back when I thought of how I'd reacted, sitting there complacently as the room had filled with chuckles and murmurs. The thoughts became a dull ache in my head for the rest of the day.

Later, before heading out, I did some research on the establishment. I saw that it was a reasonably upscale place, and dressed fashionably, in fitted slacks, nice shoes and a vest buttoned over a dress shirt.

"You look like you are ready to party!" Dubz said to me as I was leaving.

A slight nod in reply was all I could muster as I went outside and headed to the train station. The club was in Aoyama-itchome. It was a good walk from the station to get there, behind some buildings a short distance from the sidewalk. The bouncer at the door was dressed pretty sharply, and ushered me towards a woman at the entryway. I told her Marc's name, and she nodded, asking me if it was only me.

"Yes," I replied.

"You can go in," she said with a slight bow.

The first thing I thought of was that the place looked like somewhere a wealthy gangster would take his girlfriend for a drink. A semi-transparent glass floor with various objects embedded beneath ran from the front to the back of the club. All the décor was dark and upscale, from large black couches in the shadowy V.I.P areas to the counter tops and staff attire, which were black suits. The staff had a very intense look to them as they ran around with glasses of wine and mixed drinks to various clients. It was a pretty full house, even though it was a Thursday night. I walked down the walkway to see a DJ with an ornately styled head of braids playing house music from a laptop on an elevated platform. A lot of people were on the dance floor, including two girls who smiled at me as I appeared. A firm hand tapped me on the back.

"Hey man! You drinking?"

It was Marc, dressed in a sharp purple suit complimented with a black dress shirt, and luminous silver cufflinks.

"We are over here," he said, pointing to the middle V.I.P area. There were about twelve people in there, a few guys and several sharply dressed young women. "But first, let's get you a drink. I have a tab here, so get whatever you want."

"A tab?"

"It's cool man, the promoters here love me because I always bring cute foreign girls to the club. I helped a few of them hookup with chicks too, so now I have a tab."

He laughed, and it stung my ears over the noise of the music in the club. I ordered a Bacardi and coke, and he had the same.

"I appreciate the gesture Marc, this place is nice. But why'd you invite me here?" I asked.

Marc took a heavy swig of his drink.

"I saw what happened to you today at the casting. Pretty fucked up scenario if you ask me. Maybe you and Mari had something going on, maybe not. Whatever it was, she blew up on you in front of everyone but you kept your cool. You didn't even react man, and then you went and did your casting. All business."

I hadn't thought of it exactly that way, but I kept listening while I sipped on my drink.

"But just looking on your face I can tell you are searching for something. Living in Japan man, there are people who are good with whatever they are doing, and then there are people searching, and you can just smell it on them, like they just fucked in a tiny hotel room with no air conditioning on."

He laughed a bit hard at this, and took another gulp of his drink. He looked directly at me as he spoke, his gaze hypnotic and penetrating.

"So I saw you today, and I was reminded of myself when I just started out. Like most people, I came here just to get away, with no real plan. I just bounced around guesthouses for a month or two, until someone suggested I try modeling. I can't even remember what the guy's name was. He was some guy from Australia. Now yeah, you might hear that I've had a good run, but before coming here no one had *ever* mentioned that to me, not once in my life."

"But you had good relationships with women?"

"I had a few girlfriends here and there, but listen it isn't about that," he said with a sigh.

I was surprised by the sheer emotion his face projected.

"It's about the slightest observation changing your entire reality. A person offhandedly mentioned that to me, and I found an agency, and my first campaign was for a Softbank commercial that paid me almost six thousand dollars. Suddenly I had money in my pocket, and for a while I was *famous* dude. Women were throwing themselves at me, people said hi all the time and took pictures, it was crazy.

"But every now and then, I wondered what if that guy hadn't mentioned that to me? What if I'd never acted on it? The statement was entirely his. It wasn't my idea, goal or dream, but his little observation ended up changing my entire life here."

He turned around and waved at the bartender to get us two more drinks.

"So what does that have to do with me?" I asked.

"I can see you're the kind of guy who's never been told that little observation. You probably stumbled upon this modeling thing randomly or as some kind of last resort yeah?"

"Yeah," I replied.

"Yeah? DUDE! I don't care what happened between you and Mari, but don't you realize she's one of the most booked models in Tokyo?"

"I didn't know that," I replied.

"A man in this industry should know these things. To see her blow up on you like that isn't some bitch behaviour either. Trust me there are crazy bitches running around town that I could talk to you for days about. When I saw the way Mari acted today, it was like she was trying to keep cool, and she's *always* cool. I've never seen her get angry at a casting."

I paused, taking in his words, looking at the ice in my drink make slow turns around one another.

"You seem to me like a guy who doesn't know what he has," Marc said.

"What do you mean? You don't even know me," I replied.

"It doesn't matter man. You know why I came to Japan? I was tired of living in my tiny little state in the U.S. I was depressed, I even thought I wanted to kill myself. Something kept telling me to leave, and I'd always been curious about Japan, so I worked for a few months, saved up some money, and came here. I don't need to know you to see that you were pushed here by something, to Tokyo. Weren't you?"

I couldn't reply.

"Exactly. Stuff is more obvious in this kind of deal, modeling, because it is very superficial. Models are always surface first, and then you learn more about them afterwards. But I've found this to be so similar with other people I've met. So many things we do; going to school, chasing girls, getting wasted or whatever, we are just looking for some kind of purpose. Some of us are unlucky, we find out late in life what that is, and we spend the rest of our days chasing that down. But sometimes a person tells you how it is, or gives you and idea of where you could go. A normal guy can't get a girl like Mari, or just waltz into F-Bar without being signed to an agency."

"You heard about that."

Marc laughed again, threatening to deafen me.

"I felt like I'd just pass along an insight. Even the way you are reacting to this says something. I've tried to tell people with potential this before, and most of them get pissed or can't handle what I say because of ego. You are listening, and listening is the first step."

At that moment, one of the most attractive women I'd ever seen walked over. She was tall, with dark brown skin and explosively attractive features.

"Marc, Marc, Marc," she said with a smile.

Marc gave me a smile. "Duty calls my man, but remember what I said. I'm done talking about this stuff tonight! Let's have some fun! Bartender, two more drinks"

The girl glared at Marc.

"Sorry, three more drinks!"

I followed them back to their section. Marc gave me a hearty introduction to the group and then spent the rest of the evening chatting to his friends, or walking around the club mingling with different people. I had fun with the group, taking tons of pictures with them via their cell phones. A leggy blonde from France who also modeled had my attention as we shared drinks and light conversation. There was a subdued insistence in the way she looked at me with an occasional smile, and how she shifted her feet if I complimented her. I could see the layers of our interaction clearly, though she never touched me or made any overt displays of affection. I felt a touch of déjà vu, and remembered the artsy girl I'd gone to the improv show in Shibuya with. She'd had a similar energy. True statements didn't always need to come directly like Marc's impromptu intervention. I could tell what she wanted, and this time, I didn't hesitate. When we left the club together and took a cab back to Yotsuya, I thought that Marc was right. Telling me that Mari was a top model in Tokyo put things into a different context. I hadn't been on a specific quest to be with her, but I had liked her. These memories got stronger as the blonde took off my shirt and pants in my room, and started kissing me all over with the whirring of the air conditioner playing it's usual symphony in the background. The sex was cold and brutal. I took it all out on the blonde, only too happy to be pounded mercilessly as she moaned loudly in the tiny space of the room. I slapped her ass, I grabbed her hair and propped her on the wall. My arms were like steel and I raged with an unending tumescence long into the night, all the while seeing Mari's eyes in my mind.

In the morning, after she had left, I received a text on my phone from Ayuna. I'd been selected for the show, which she noted, was for super popular underground designer, Kaoru Tetsuya.

Chapter 22

Rip Fuck.

This was the title of my first show, where we'd be wearing ripped clothing and suggestive accessories. For the last three days, I'd been doing light rehearsals at a space in Shinjuku, a small room that could seat about forty people tightly. The excited man in the pink shirt the day of the casting had been Kaoru Tetsuya. When I went to the rehearsal area on the first day, he had smiled and patted me on the shoulder, saying, "Mr. Intensity!" He was above average height, almost as tall as I was, with a very long and slim face. His eyes blazed with radiance. I heard from one of the guys in the show that he became famous after dressing models like cyborgs and exposing their genitals on the runway. A part of me hoped I wouldn't need to do anything like that for this show, even though I desperately needed the money.

After today's rehearsal, I went to the house, lounging in front of the television, eating my usual gruel. Briggs walked into the entertainment room. He wore a shirt that read 'I'M BRIGG IN JAPAN.'

"You know Marc Reynolds?" he asked.

"Marc who?"

"Marc Reynolds, the model," Briggs replied.

"Oh… yeah, I met him the other day," I said.

Briggs sat down and opened up a thin laptop.

"He is super famous in Tokyo man, and I saw you all over his website recently, check this out."

I looked through a gallery of images, many of me with several handsome men, the French model and her friends. Her friends were quite attractive, even more so in the pictures. Under the images, were several captions, including "Next top model!" in a picture of Marc with his arm around my neck as I was laughing at something off-screen. There were comments too, with a few girls with attractive profile pictures leaving smiley faces. A few asked who I was.

"This is gold right here, when you hang with celebrities like this," Briggs said, taking back the laptop. "You can use this to propel a lot of your personal agendas forward."

He spoke in the same tone he had when he was explaining web analytics and things like SEO to me. I'd thought a lot about what Marc had said, and the subsequent frolic with the French girl had also boosted my energy. I could use a personal agenda.

"I've been taking some pictures," I said to Briggs.

I went to get my camera and showed him what I'd been doing around town.

"These are great," Briggs said. "But do you have anything lifestyle oriented? Not just temples and trees?"

I took out my phone.

"I've been going to castings for an agency I got signed to and I've been taking photos."

Saying this surprised me. I couldn't imagine myself only weeks earlier saying that without feeling awkward. Briggs nodded and scanned through the pictures I had on the phone.

"These are good, really good," he said. "You could do a kind of insider blog on the life of models here and mix that with your other photographs then with the right kind of SEO you could probably do some stuff with brands."

"Brands? How?"

"Through my site I get approached by brands every now and then to plug a product because of my high traffic. Sometimes they send me watches or shoes, things like that."

Briggs explained a few points about public relations and how 'new media' was changing the way companies interacted with consumers. It was no longer just blanket marketing to cold customers, they had departments devoted to infiltrating the audiences of people who had a high viewership rate and website traffic. This information came from him in a stream again, but this time my head didn't hurt. There was sense in his words and I saw a possible plan in the works.

"You can earn income through web traffic as well, and affiliate marketing if you partner with some people. If you do PR for companies... they can pay you do to work."

"I'm going to ask you about the structure," I said to Briggs.

He smiled a little too broadly, only too happy to bring someone into his world of numbers and spreadsheet data. The Kaoru Tetsuya show would help me somewhat, but it wasn't enough to make me survive for a significant length of time. Tokyo city still had its jaws wide open; ready to clamp shut once my bank account was empty. I'd never been an internet aficionado, but there was nothing stopping me now.

We sat and spoke for some time, tossing out ideas about the site, what kind of content it would have and how I could market it. I started seeing the potential in brand building, in the manner that he had, I just hoped it would send some things my way over the next two months. After we took a short break from discussing the site, and me getting up to speed on different social media networks, I told him about the Kaoru Tetsuya show.

"Are you shitting me!" he shouted. "Do you know how famous this guy is?"

"Not really," I replied. "But I'm doing a show with him in a few days."

"You saw him today?" Briggs asked.

"Yes, I've seen him almost everyday for the rehearsal."

"Wow. This guy has been featured in Vogue, Rolling Stone and tons of magazines here," Briggs said.

One thing I realized about Briggs, was that he was current. If I wanted to be a brand, I needed to be current as well. "You just need an RSS feed that sends you information on your interests, and you spend twenty minutes a day reading the articles that get sent to your e-mail inbox. That is usually all I need to stay up to speed with things," Briggs told me.

After he gave me a list of tasks to complete, I spent the rest of the evening learning as much as I could about the current scene. I watched videos of hot clubs, checked out video blogs from other foreigners like Briggs in Japan, and subscribed to many RSS feeds focused on Japanese fashion as well as international fashion. When it was twelve a.m, my eyes burned and my head was bursting with information. It wasn't just the information about fashion I'd scanned through, but articles on blogging and personal branding. I fell asleep with a YouTube video playing on screen, where a man was talking about how to use what you like, to make money.

The day of the show, I felt nervous. It wasn't the people dressed in all sort of high fashion who waited patiently outside the doors of the building. Neither was it the company I shared, of no less than twelve other models, slim and attractive with youthful aloofness. The nervousness wasn't a result of the atmosphere either, which was now completely transformed from the mostly empty room I'd been practicing in to a heavily decorated atmosphere. There was angry rock music blaring through two large speakers on either side of the stage. Photographers ran to take pictures of a few people walking in who I assumed were celebrities. There was a palpable energy in the air, a fusion of cool and hype, but that wasn't why I was nervous. The crow wasn't bothering me either, flying around somewhere hissing and laughing. Nor was the sad little voice from my sleepy town singing in my ear, when everywhere I went I was followed by Carmen's ghost. What I worried about had everything to do with the last day I had finished practice.

The aggressive walk I'd done that day at the casting in Harajuku had been molded by one of Kaoru's assistants into a more controlled gait. I learned to project attitude without being overblown, and to keep my mind clear as they played the same heavy rock riffs over and over. He showed me how to do turns and pause for the camera.

"Remember, always give them a few seconds to take the picture. Sometimes a model gets nervous and turns around quickly, and it really pisses off the designer. The show isn't about you, it is only about the clothing."

I absorbed everything he had said. The other models with experience had all relatively good ways of walking, some natural, some odd, but it tended to fit their look and style. We walked over and over until the routine became commonplace, and I could feel a readiness inside me. It wouldn't matter who was in front of me. There would be just me and the stage, the roaring rock music and my cool clothes. But on that last day, Kaoru Tetsuya came to me and told me he wanted me to open the show. Even with my limited experience, I knew this was a big deal. From the snippets of conversation I'd been privy to, or chatting with Tako at the agency, I'd learned that people who open and close shows are viewed as "strong" which is good for more exposure. When Kaoru told me that, I felt a sudden shock of fright. This created *pressure,* and like my first day walking into a Japanese junior high school, I could feel eyes on me. But not the eyes of distant teachers or curious students. These would be the eyes of the sort of people that skated down the ramp of a fast, superficial world, soaring over the regular folk, stomping on small egos. Kaoru's eyes would also be watching me, and that was enough to make me nervous. After hearing Briggs talk about his fame, I'd done some light research on him. He was a big deal. At thirty-three years old, people were calling him the new face of young Japanese fashion. I saw dozens of articles in both English and Japanese, including many showing famous celebrities wearing his clothing. This was the long-faced man I didn't have a second thought about when I stormed down the carpet in a small room. Now I was preparing to storm down a runway that possibly, the world would see.

Thankfully, I had no chest pains to accompany this nervousness. There was some time before the show started, and I took a look at the stage. 'RIP FUCK' was hung in a crudely assembled sheet metal sign over the runway, which had been extended. It was about three feet wide and covered in a weighty transparent plastic. Under the plastic were knives, chainsaw blades and dozens of other sharp objects. These were laid in no real order over another sheet of plastic, this being white. Bright lights underneath the sheet perfectly displayed the contours of the objects and their sharp silhouettes. Bordering the sitting area facing the stage was a small fence made from real barbed wire. Directly behind these fences were two small squares. I smiled, knowing what they meant.

Because of the nature of this event plus the things I'd been learning from Briggs, I knew this was an exquisite opportunity to get my personal brand going. I'd worked out getting him access to the event, with the condition he snap some photos of me while I was onstage. He'd agreed with a giddy smile, only too happy to be schmoozing with Japan's elite. I busied myself chatting with some of the other models and taking pictures of us backstage. I hadn't seen Kaoru at all since we were preparing to start but I heard he was inside the building. We did make up and got prepped for the show. In the room with the models, I could hear the din of voices outside amidst the music.

The air in the room was cold, keeping us all alert. Kaoru's assistant, Yoshi, looked tired but excited. With a wireless headset on, he stood by the racks of clothing for our outfits, ready to engage in the madness of changing people every sixty seconds or so. I'd been advised to lose any shame in changing naked around the other models, if there were any last minute changes that needed to be made. The rock music quieted, and I heard the voice of an announcer make some introductory comments.

"Let's get ready," Yoshi said.

I took a few breaths to get myself mentally organized. My outfit consisted of a thin yellow jacket with what appeared to be claw marks across the surface. Visible on the fabric between the spaces the tears made, the words "I weep, I cry" were visible in tiny print on a dark material interwoven with the jacket. I had no shirt on, and my torso had been painted red. The jeans I wore had a similar look to the jacket, ripped with little words visible under the tears. These read "I scream, You scream". A shoe sponsor had given us boots to wear for the show, and mine were spray painted gold. I wore a necklace of plastic grey razorblades and yellow glasses with blood-red lenses. Another man came into the back area, one of the original men at the casting, and ushered us forward. I stepped out into the darkness of the rear hallway, which arched towards a doorway that led to the stage. My heart pounded as I heard the announcer speak.

"And now....," the voice said. "Kaoru Tetsuya presents.... RIP FUCK!"

The man nodded at me to step forward and I went towards the stage, waiting for the cue of music. The music came in a thunderclap to my ears; a screeching chorus of tremolo picks and heavy bass riffs. When I walked out, and stood at the back, I posed in the manner I'd practiced, and I heard the crowd murmur. All I saw were the bright lights around me, huge circles in my red vision. Each step felt like a long, slow walk, and in the moment, my nervousness became controlled excitement. This was nothing like anything I'd ever experienced. Photographers lining the end of the stage were snapping photos unendingly, and if Briggs was there, I didn't know. When I reached the end of the stage, as I'd been directed to, I clutched the razor necklace and pretended to lick it. The ensuing cheers from some members of the crowd made me almost smile as I paused for photos, turned around and walked back behind the stage. The next model, a polish guy named Alfred, was going on, in an ensemble consisting of tattered leather shorts, high boots and a leather bandana filled with holes. He walked with a knife in his mouth.

"Let's go!" Yoshi said urgently, as I ran back to the room.

Inside, I saw Kaoru looking at me as Yoshi helped me dress, his face a mask of complete seriousness. For the next outfit, I'd be wearing a leather tank top and tight black jeans with more slash marks across them. Complimenting this was a complicated set of armbands with several silk buckles along their breadth that ran up to my elbow. The shirt read "I WEEP" in bloody red letters, and I slipped on a gaudy gold belt to compliment my boots. Behind me, Kaoru pulled up my jeans and adjusted the tank top a few times, as I stood there with my arms wide, feeling quite like the human mannequin.

The second time on stage was just like the first, with my blood raging as the music raged, feeling drowned in the prestige and attention. The lights of the cameras flashed from every angle, yet they didn't bother me. Something the chaos kept me level. The modeling room was packed with guys, half naked or hurriedly taking of their pants to put on another one. It was busy, with Yoshi, Kaoru and the third man chatting rapidly to one another. After I did my fourth round on the runway, I heard the announcer's voice again as I walked quickly back to the changing room.

"Quick!" Kaoru hissed, "The First outfit! Now! We don't have much time!"

Frightened, I took off all my clothes quickly, temporarily naked as I put on my original ensemble. The other guys were rushing as well, putting on their first selected outfits. The rock music seemed louder to me, and I felt my heart pounding again. Things were moving so fast I had no idea if the show was running on time or not.

"Ladies and gentlemen, Kaoru Tetsuya!"

Kaoru stood close to me, wearing a black version of his pink ripped shirt from the casting, with an exact pair of the tight black jeans with the scratches I'd previously worn. Behind me, the other models were ready.

"Let's go guys!" he said.

We walked behind him as he came out, to a resounding chorus from the audience. I saw him smile and wave to people as I clapped. Now I saw the crowd clearly for the first time, and it wasn't what I had imagined. There were people crammed tightly into the space, dressed in their best outfits. Fanning out behind the special seating for special guests were at least forty other people. I had seen none of these persons while I was walking down the runway. There were elegant women in dresses, kids with wild punk hair, and men in sharp suits. Without knowing who many of them were, I could feel the tingle of their various histories; musicians, actors and well to do persons. Two men with chainsaws stepped on the red squares on opposite sides of the stage and turned them on. The crowd became ecstatic at this display, and the flashing lights tripled in number. The men shut off the machines, Kaoru bowed and waved one more time, and we exited the stage, going back to the changing room.

"We are having a small after party in a studio behind the stage area," Yoshi said. " Please wear your outfits to that if you are going to stay."

I felt powerful in my outfit as the thrill of doing the show still washed over me in little bursts of energy. I quickly headed into the main area to find Briggs. The crowd had already grown smaller, as many people were already heading into the studio. One of the fellows with punk hair grabbed me, exclaiming, "Cool guy!" and then snapped a picture of us with his phone. The other guys who were with him had a similar look; wild heads of hair with similarly styled outfits of sharp vests and fitted black pants. Their faces were filled with a casual arrogance that I hadn't seen with any of the other models during all the time I'd been at castings. Whoever they were, they were truly famous. One gave me a thumbs up and whispered something to his friend, who starting laughing uproariously. A few more people complimented me on the show, and the outfit I wore. I smiled and shook hands, lightly chit-chatting with some of them as I scanned the room for Briggs.

To the far rear of the room, I saw him with his camera out, talking to Kaoru Tetsuya. He was wearing an even more outrageous outfit, this time a black jumpsuit patterned with vertical glowing lights. I approached cautiously; worried he might go overboard with his antics. This concern was unwarranted as I saw that he was very relaxed as he spoke to Kaoru, who laughed a few times as he asked him questions on camera. He made a few comments about the show and nodded right after saying "Hello everyone, this is Kaoru Tetsuya and the Tokyo Rover." Kaoru saw me and walked over, giving me a strong one-armed hug around the shoulders.

"Mr. Intensity!" he said with a laugh. "Thank you for your participation. Maybe we can work again in the future baby."

I thanked him as well, as he started walking towards the studio, immediately chased by a few persons with cameras. Briggs was grinning behind me. Whatever excitement I'd seen in him before couldn't compare to this moment. His eyes were wide open, exposing the whites more than normal, and a broad smile was etched firmly into his face, not going away, even as he spoke.

"This was an incredible opportunity, thanks so much," he said. "Here's your camera, I'm going to see if I can chat with a few other people here."

I saw him walk to one of the elegant looking women (whom I'd later find out was a super famous actress) and begin speaking with her. I took a look at the pictures. With the runway glowing under my feet and the bright lights everywhere, I looked more like a performer than a model. Briggs had taken some good shots; showing the size of the audience, and also photos of the other models. But the last picture was the true gold. It was the moment Kaoru had hugged me around the shoulder and spoken to me. Briggs had captured the photo in a way that gave us the look of old friends; Kaoru looking at me with a smile, my face slightly tilted down as I took in our joke, a seemingly private one.

I did a few quick rounds at the after party, taking pictures of people in attendance, including shots with Kaoru and a few friends. Mari was there, very chummy with a tall handsome blonde guy. I froze in place, feeling the residual energy from the night I went to her place come to the surface. We locked eyes for a while, and I couldn't feel anything from her, not the slightest movement in the stagnant pond between us. She kept staring at me without expression and I did the same, as we battled with our eyes. The tall guy walked over to me. I could see he was one of those big, dumb guys with personality problems.

"You troubling my girl?" he said.

I turned my gaze to him, staring into his eyes with the coldness of who I was now, unafraid of his additional height. The man inside him retreated, and his mouth remained half open, but he said nothing. Then Mari slipped her arm around his waist and pulled him away slowly.

"Who is that guy?" the man said to Mari.

She gave me a backwards look as they drifted into the crowd.

"Nobody. He's just one of the models."

I left the studio and went to the dressing room, and dropped my camera into its case. I walked quickly to the bathroom. It was hard to breathe again, and I closed my eyes and gripped the edge of the sink until my fingertips were pale. There was so much happening here, in this rapid-fire world of exchangeable people. I felt like trash, ugly and abused, but in the mirror, still painted with my jacket on with makeup on my face, I looked sharp. Was it only months ago that I had been prowling the streets of my little town, half drunk and bored, wishing for something to change? Everything felt unreal, and I stood there until my heart stopped beating as quickly, and I could collect myself. There were two versions of myself looking back at me in the mirror. One was the weak, broken teacher, and the second the man who had just done a Kaoru Tetsuya show. *Screw her,* I thought, and went outside. I went back to the changing room, and felt a quick panic.

The camera was gone.

I frantically looked through the closet, tossing a few people's leather jackets to the floor, and shifted a few boxes around, but I didn't see it. In front of me, the hallway was empty and there was no indication anyone had been in there. The camera in this moment was irreplaceable. I stormed outside, nearly running into one of the models walking into the changing room. I went into the show area first, seeing nothing there. I passed through the lounge and to the bar, where the after party was being held. Many of the male models were happily entertaining a few girls who had come to see the show, and a busy waiter was running around with a drink tray, trying to serve them as quickly as people were drinking them. I perked up as I saw a flash in the middle of the crowd and saw a short, balding man with a heavy camera around his neck, bruised and abused with use. I walked to the bar and took one of the complimentary drinks. It was an extremely sweet straw-berry cocktail. After gulping it down, I looked towards the front of the crowd, near the entrance to the bar. There I saw a girl in a white dress, holding a camera, laughing and taking pictures of some people sitting on a black couch. She laughed as she snapped away. I saw the strap of the camera, noticing the colours were red, gold and green. I walked over and tapped the girl on the shoulder, barely able to contain myself.

"That's my camera," I said under a heavy breath.

The girl wore huge Dior glasses and a pearl necklace. When I touched her, she turned and smiled at me, as if to say it didn't matter she had stolen my property.

"It's a nice camera," she said. "Isn't it guys!"

She turned back to the group, and pressed the shutter button again. Whoever the group was—some typically hand-some guy in a sharp suit sitting with two well-dressed women—I didn't care. I tapped her more firmly on the shoul-der.

"I'd like it back," I said to the girl.

"Okay, okay, don't get your panties in a twist," she replied.

She turned to me and pushed out her hand with the camera in it, then pulled it back. I let out a sigh.

"You didn't say please," the girl said.

Please? After she stole my camera? What if I'd never found her out here?

"I'm not saying please, you can't just take people's thing like that."

I held her in an angry glare for a few moments. Her group became quiet. The bright smirk on her lips wavered, then she handed me the camera without a word. I turned around and walked off without saying anything else to her, going immedi-ately to the changing room. Someone called to me, but I didn't respond. *The nerve*, I thought, of that silly girl and her bug-eyed glasses. It made me angry again, seeing how she had reacted when I came over, as if what she did wasn't anything. What was she doing in the men's changing room in the first place? That plus Mari and her idiot new beau. I needed to get out of here. Behind me, I heard someone come into the room. It was Tako.

"Good show today, good presence," he said with a smile.

"Thanks," I replied, still feeling the twitch of residual anger in my fingers.

"So in a week you'll get the money for today deposited into your account, like I said, I take care of my guys."

"I appreciate it, Mr. Suou," I replied.

"No, no, I'm always Tako," he said with a slight nod, then walked out the door.

I turned on the camera and looked through the pictures. Whoever the girl was, she had been busy. There were numerous photos of her with several people of the people I'd seen in the audience, including Briggs. In each she had a pouty smile, or a wide laugh. I disconnected the lens and covered the mirror on the camera, and slipped the components into the camera case. I didn't care who she was, I just wanted to get paid.

Chapter 23

When I exited the Roppongi station, it was a repeat image of the last few nights; the overhead lights dim as I approached the escalator, the train attendant waiting patiently to cut off access to the escalator soon after I got off, and my company; men heading home on the last train or thrill seekers ready to conquer the night. Tonight I was hitting the streets with Dubz and Mick. A girl who worked part-time at a club had invited me out and told me to bring friends.

My stomach growled with the need for food, and I walked down the strip. I spent the next twenty minutes in front of a family mart eating horrible tasting chicken bento and sipping on two Suntory drinks. As the cold meat squished in my mouth, I thought about the new blog. Briggs was right about his world of data and brand building. The scene I had stepped into with dry feet not too long ago was changing the way I interacted with people. I recently landed a gig that paid five thousand yen for a music video with a supermodel turned singer. It was fun even though I was only in one scene, where I stood reading a newspaper as I watched her walk by. The woman was beautiful, tall and slim, with hair like a raven's wing. I met the director of the video shoot and the assistant who cast me, both people with the casually busy energy behind the scenes people have. With each gig or casting I did, I made sure to take pictures of the settings and the surroundings (if the casting people allowed it) keeping the slowly growing numbers of people following my blog abreast of my activities. It wasn't very difficult to populate it with content. Often I recycled images from the Kaoru Tetsuya show, as well some from the night I went to Velours. With most castings were some sort of after activity of drinking at an Izakaya with the other models, or meeting up in the city if the people were reasonably friendly. We constantly exchanged numbers and took photos of our slim angular faces, sometimes over exposed from the flash or the angle of the sun. But as I uploaded the images and dropped little notes about what was happening with my life, I could see the marked growth in my lifestyle. I played around with fashion comparison photos, using clothes I already owned to make short articles on "Tokyo Style". This was easy to do, and created a slight boost in user interaction. Sometimes I proposed random photo shoots in Omotesando and Harajuku, and put all the pictures on the blog. A slow shift in perspective was happening internally; a slow cross into new territory from the old me to whatever I was about to become.

Halfway through one of my drinks, my phone buzzed with a message from Dubz.

Look forward!

I looked up and smiled, seeing him wave at me from twenty feet away. He walked quickly over to where I was, glancing at my drink.

"That's a good idea right there," he said, going inside.

Soon afterwards, he came out with a can of his own. I asked him about Mick, whom he said was working late. My phone said the time was near twelve a.m.

"This late?" I asked.

"Maybe he's doing extra *curric lick her* activities," he said.

I laughed.

Mick appeared soon afterward, looking unusually tall in a pair of boots.

"Fendi," he said with a smirk.

As we walked up the strip, Dubz and Mick did their usual antics, chatting to girls along the way with comic gestures and big smiles. There were many people out tonight; the sidewalk was filled with bodies. A short man of African descent approached us, turning and walking in tandem.

"You guys like strippas yes? You want to see some titties tonight?"

"No thanks," Mick replied.

The man caught my eye, and smiled. "Three thousand yen, all you can drink and touching is okay,"

"Touch okay?" Dubz asked. "This man is serious!"

We kept walking, as the man immediately approached another set of foreigners and said the same thing, this time in French. I had always liked Roppongi. It was easy to feed off the energy on the strip; watching language savvy foreigners use pickup lines to pull girls, spotting the charged energy of people new to Tokyo, buffered by the shouts of the touts who rose from the ground like the asphalt, and the girls everywhere; a mix of jaded faces and those tinted with the bristling excitement of making a night happen where anything goes. The first time I had come here, Tokyo's beat had hit my head like a bell in a belfry, but not now. I didn't walk with the frantic steps of a guy raging through bars looking for skanks. My steps were sure and comfortable in the swarm.

Dubz said hello to another girl, who smiled and laughed as she walked away, her sweet smell rapidly replaced by the stale Roppongi aroma of cigarettes and spilt beer. She had a million clones like her, with the same red hair, faces caked with makeup and finger painted cartoon eyes. I would meet her again, in some way, somewhere.

A hand touched my shoulder. I turned, half expecting to see another tout, but it was Zeus, dressed in a casual brown suit standing beside a remarkably attractive girl.

"What's good man!" he bellowed.

"Long time no see," I replied.

"I'm probably going out tomorrow night, hit me up," he said, giving me a final pat on the shoulder. He walked away with the girl, swallowed quickly by the throng.

We enjoyed the strip for a little while, popping in and out of alternating bars, doing shots drinks with girls we didn't know, passing idly through the Don Quijote store, and making alternating trips back to the Family Mart for drinks. Eventually, we were under a sufficient buzz and ready for the club. Katsumi was the name of the girl I knew, and I sent her a text message to tell her we were nearby.

Once we reached there, Katsumi greeted us outside and waved us in. I thought her outfit was nice; fitted pink shorts over black leggings, with a shiny silver top. Inside, the club was filled almost entirely with men of African descent, many in slightly exaggerated hip-hop garb. She introduced me to a guy at the bar who worked in the Navy, who I decided to call Navy Boy. Everyone had a few more drinks, and soon enough, interpersonal relationships became the hot topic.

"Man, Japan is tough," Navy Boy said. "It's like the women are beautiful right? But all they want to do is get married."

He explained to me that whenever he hooked up with Japanese women, they'd immediately start pestering him about getting married. In relative terms I could see why. He had casual all-American looks; low cropped hair, slightly above average height and blue eyes. He would be the perfect candidate to bring home to mommy. Japan was candy land for fellows like him, with its obvious regard for Eurocentric ideology. Mick was by the bar, sipping on his drink. He walked over.

"Hey man I heard about this place where all the hot girls go after they finish working. I think it's called the White Door."

I nodded, wondering how many bars in Tokyo had these ambiguous names. I hadn't chatted to any girls. The last two hours were spent listening to music and coasting on my buzz. Katsumi was talking to a basketball player sized guy, and I figured she wasn't that interested in me. I was open to going elsewhere. The group of us decided to find the White Door, with our new member, Navy Boy. We didn't know exactly where it was, except the vague directions Mick got from someone inside the club that it was "Behind the Softbank Store somewhere". Navy Boy was excited, and immediately comfortable in our company.

"Come on man," he said. "Let's see some ladies!"

A tall, Tokyo-savvy looking foreigner was walking past. I asked him where the spot was. He pointed to a building fifty feet away.

"But I'm going to Laguna Café man, that's where *all* the hot girls are at this time."

He strutted off and I told the guys I had found the place. When we reached the building, we walked up a flight of three steps, stopping at a door watched by a Vietnamese bouncer. I asked him if there were people inside and he didn't understand what I was saying. I switched to Japanese and told him my friends and I wanted to look inside.

"People are there," he replied without any expression.

He let me walk in and I saw a typical bar space, dark and filled with mostly men. I told the guys the bad news, but mentioned Laguna Café.

"That's it!" Navy Boy said. "We got two Jamaicans and two Americans, I mean, sorry buddy where are you from?"

"Canada," Mick replied.

"We've got the Olympics right here! Let's go!"

The allusion was lost to me, but Mick and Dubz laughed as we went forward, in the direction I'd seen the young man take. The building was quite plain, and would have been easy to miss. On the third floor, there was no sign indicating the café, just a simple black door with an opaque glass.

"One thousand yen," a short man on a chair by the door said.

We paid and went inside, each of us stopping in our tracks. From wall to wall there were models and hostesses, in a far greater number than the men in attendance. A woman a full two inches taller than me danced up a storm in the middle, her skin glowing under the orange lights. The girls were of all varieties; thin blondes, mocha-skinned girls with large hair, a couple brunettes with cold eyes and some gorgeous Japanese girls. Some of them, I recognized from castings. I began walking to the bar but the guys stood in the same place as if waiting on a cue. I motioned for them to follow me, as I said hello to the tall girl who had been dancing in the center of the room.

"I know where you are from," I said.

"Really?" she replied.

"Yes. You are from Eastern Europe, but not Germany or France, so it has to be Sweden or Slovakia."

She froze in amazement and clutched my shoulder. Her exceptional beauty seemed to pause as well, as she tried to figure out how I knew where she was from. The look of puzzlement vanished, and the smile was back.

"Yes, I am from Sweden," she said. "How did you know?"

"I can read minds," I replied.

It wasn't rocket science, what I'd done. She didn't have a French accent, or a German one, and I'd met far more Swedes than Poles when I made my rounds to castings. This deduction of mine was paying off, as she laughed and rubbed my arm. Dubz, Mick and Navy Boy were standing by the bar with drinks in their hands, staring at the women. I told Dubz about a girl I recognized from F-Bar, the Brazilian with completely European features. Dubz went over to say hello, and a friend of the girl immediately pulled her away to another section of the room. Mick struck out three times in a row, first trying to talk to some icy Russians, one of the mocha-skinned girls, and then a brunette.

"These girls are too hot man," Navy Boy said.

Previously I'd have probably thought the same thing, but I saw women like these often, and felt no intimidation. The usually animated Dubz and Mick were now relegated to awkward hellos and desperate attempts to get in with the girls by buying them drinks. Watching their awkwardness aroused no sympathy in me. I had mostly lurked in the background when out with them before, but not this time.

The tall girl from Sweden (Her name was Febe) pulled me into the middle of the dance floor, writhing and grinding on me. I laughed as she did this, and two of her friends, smoky-eyed brunettes, did the same. Dubz looked on me in shock. I brought the ladies over and introduced everyone, while chatting to the tall Swede about my blog. She *ooohed* when I showed her a few pictures on my phone of the Kaoru Tetsuya show.

"I heard that show was amazing, I can't believe you opened it!"

She squeezed my arm playfully. One of the girls chatting to Mick stepped away from him and interrupted the conversation Febe and I were having.

"His friends are strange," the girl said in a heavy accent.

"They just aren't used to the scene," I said with a smile.

"His website is very cool," Febe said.

The new girl immediately looked me in the eyes.

"Do you have Facebook?"

Navy Boy seemed to be doing well with one of the pretty Japanese girls, who giggled a lot as he spoke. Mick's face looked stressed as he worked the brunette, who sipped her drink and made no eye contact as he spoke to her. Dubz had spoken to one of the brown-skinned girls, excited to learn she was Jamaican, but she wasn't friendly.

"This is a good scene man, a good scene," Dubz said, more to himself than to me.

I patted him on the shoulder, and chatted to a pretty girl from America. Within minutes, she had asked me the same question: "Do you have Facebook?"

Navy Boy was ready to leave, and Mick and Dubz were by the door, faces marked with the shadow of failure. I decided to leave. The few remaining girls danced oddly in the middle with wild eyes, strung out on something. I said hello to the Brazilian girl, but she didn't recognize me and didn't respond to my greeting. Navy Boy came over and leaned into my ear.

"My girl wants to grab some ramen, and we know what that means," he said with a sly smile.

"Let's just hope she doesn't want to marry you," I replied.

Navy Boy let out a long, whooping laugh, and gave me a hearty handshake. If the girl knew we were doing a victory dance, she didn't care. She stood there, dripping with perfection, waiting patiently to leave with him.

We all stepped outside into the subtle darkness of early dawn. My phone vibrated and I saw that I had a message from Katsumi. She wanted to meet me by the McDonald's on the main strip. Downstairs, Febe and her friend were idling by a lamppost, smoking cigarettes. She was a vision.

"Where do you guys go after this?" she asked.

"After this, anywhere you like," Dubz replied.

I teased the brunette about being mean to Mick, and we all walked towards the strip, skipping on waves of uncertainty. By the time we reached the McDonald's, everyone was laughing comfortably.

Katsumi smiled at me when I came in, her eyes mysterious under the stylish bangs of her hair. As we ordered our food, Dubz told the girls how awesome our place was, and everyone decided to head there. We were a gang of noise as we entered the train station. During the wait, I chatted to Katsumi about idle things, noticing that similar energy I'd detected in the French model from a few weeks before. It was her casual proximity to me, the way she'd touch my hands every now and then when I said something normal and the little jabs I'd get from her eyes when she thought I wasn't looking. When we were on the train, Febe sat across from me, being thoroughly entertained by Dubz, but her face turned to me often, sharing smiles. Mick seemed to be doing well now. The formerly icy brunette was chatting away, telling him something about Europe and the nature of women there. I took in the entire scene thinking how we'd started with a blank canvas of a night that was slowly turning into a beautiful painting.

We got off the train and stopped by the convenience store near the house, getting a bottle of vodka and some soda. As we all walked back, seven strong with lukewarm McDonald's in our hands, I remembered something. Yumi had messaged me sometime recently on a day I'd either been at a casting or a shoot, telling me she was going to be in Tokyo, hoping to have lunch. That day was tomorrow, or more correctly, today. *Crap,* I said to myself. I felt some regret, but it was fleeting. As we turned onto the small street leading to the house, I caught Febe smiling at me, and as Katsumi to my left pinched the small of my back I knew I wouldn't be seeing Yumi this time.

Chapter 24

Things were echoing around me with a different timber. There was growing interest in the blog now, and I looked through the e-mails of my virtual confidants, who were intrigued by the pictures I posted on the website with models and well to do people. I'd made sure to capture the moments around town and share them without shame, which resulted in increased traffic, but also the first profitable actualization since I had started the blog. A promoter liked the style of my photography, and offered me a job shooting pictures for his latest event. Unaware of what photographers regularly charged, I said fifteen thousand yen, to which he agreed. The ringing endorsement of the last few weeks felt pyrrhic, because I couldn't see myself here for much longer.

The Kaoru Tetsuya gig had given me a slight reprieve, but only slightly. The sum total of my funds was dangerously low after my stint in the hospital. I'd reconsidered teaching, even going by the former offices of my company to see if the dark determination inside me had overridden my previous anxieties. It didn't. The despair I felt standing out there wasn't the drowning sensation I'd experienced the first time, but there was despair, real and tangible, represented by the tension in my chest and a brief spark of pain, like a match going out in the dark. I'd gone home that day and looked into my room, clean as ever with one barely unpacked suitcase lingering near the bed. There were no posters on the wall, no memorabilia resting on the tapered edges of the sink, and not even a forgotten article of clothing from a friend. So far the memories of Tokyo were the same they'd always been; a spotty collection sauntering across the walkways of a cloudy night sprinkled with alcohol.

The event was tonight and I'd given Zeus an invite to tag along. We met by the Hachiko exit at the Shibuya station. Tonight he looked casual, in jeans and a black v-neck shirt. It was a ten-minute walk to the place where the event was being held, at a building like many around us, decorated with bright neon lights, and the memories of a thousand hookups. I met Seth outside. He was a short, sinewy man, with spiked black hair and a face filled with piercings.

"Glad you could make it," he said while looking at me and shaking Zeus' hand at the same time.

We walked upstairs into the ever-familiar atmosphere of places like this. I liked the interior, cleanly designed with the sharp contrast of black and white. The first floor was sparsely occupied, and I took a few pictures of the layout. The people milling about were smiling and laughing; on a set playing in front was a DJ with yellow dreadlocks. Zeus and I held our ground for some time, idling at the bar as we observed the slow dribble of folks coming in.

"Ah, now the crowd is starting to look good," Zeus said to me, as three tall, attractive women came in.

"Yes sir," I said in agreement.

Zeus ordered us several beers. Seth came over to me with a young woman beside him. I felt a tense recognition. This was the woman who had temporarily stolen my camera after the fashion show.

"Hey guys this is Kitty, one of our deejays tonight," he said. "*Some* people consider her a big deal, but she's the only girl I keep telling to leave me alone because I'm taken."

Kitty laughed, then looked on me for a few seconds.

"I know you," she said.

"Yes, you do," I replied.

Seth looked at us both and smiled.

"Guess famous people tend to know each other eh?" he said.

Kitty walked quickly between us to the bar, picked up my beer and took a heavy drink. She pinched the material of Zeus' shirt between her left thumb and forefinger and rolled it.

"Hermés," she said.

Taking another deep drink of my beer, she walked with it in her hand back towards Seth, pinching him on the buttocks as they left the room and went upstairs together.

"Interesting choice in women you have," Zeus said with a smile.

I sighed, thinking of the beer she had stolen, but Zeus thrust a fresh one in my hand within seconds. Seth had told us

The DJ downstairs was from South Africa, and the music was good. For a few minutes, Zeus and I laughed about his latest Tokyo shenanigans. Then a friend of his started a conversation with him, and I took a walk.

Seth hadn't told me this was a costume party, and he wasn't wearing a costume, but there were several men dressed like hip versions of count Dracula, and also a few women in witches hats. A tall man with broad shoulders came into the room in a stream of black makeup wearing a boa and fake fur jacket. He wore a pink, deep V-neck shirt that revealed the forest of hair on his chest, tight silver pants and black stiletto heels. I took several pictures of him. On the staircase leading to the upper floor, stood three Japanese girls wearing blue outfits. They were in 'selfie' mode, taking picture after picture of each other with their faces pressed tightly together. I said I liked their outfits, surprised when they replied in crisp, clear English.

"We go to an American University here," two of them said in unison.

"I see," I replied softly.

They were very cute, particularly one with braces that reminded me of a shorter, younger Yumi. We spoke for some time in between taking photos. The one with the braces was an artist, working to become a master painter. She extolled passionate statements about her career path and she namedropped several classic Japanese painters she said had influenced her. In the middle of this brief art education the crowd to my left parted, and I saw Zeus looking at me. He towered over two girls on either side of him and raised his beer in salute to me. *You've got gravity now*, the expression said.

The floor upstairs had white tiles, white walls and a similar DJ setup. I took pictures of the people dancing and those who requested personal photos, including a man who continuously high-fived me as often as time permitted afterward. Kitty was playing up here, and as I took pictures of her, I looked at her face. She smiled slightly as she did a slow, rhythmic rock to the music. It was the kind of smile a woman has when a man just starts kissing her in the right places, and the first jets of erotic energy start flying through her body's bloodstream. I liked it; how the light fell on her face, and the incandescent smile that belayed her focus on the complex equipment before her. There

was also her style, with her hair in a slight pouf, the Sennhesi-
ers large and obvious hanging off her slim neck, and the glitter
I saw on her shoulders, visible under the low wings of her
designer top. There she rocked and swayed, not once looking
at me as I took the pictures.

Time passed until I saw the clear signals of the party's impending end, with couples openly kissing against walls, a
wasted Dracula asleep by the stairs and the incomprehensible
parroting of those remaining in the air. Seth was nowhere to be
seen. I went back down to where Zeus had been the entire
time, maintaining his position at the bar. A man approached
me. He was also dressed like Dracula, but in a drab, functional
way. He handed me an envelope that had "photographer"
written on it, bowed and went upstairs. I thanked him and
walked over to Zeus, who was still chatting to one of the girls
I'd seen him with earlier. Sadly, the three girls in blue outfits
had already left.

"Excuse me one second," Zeus said to the girl, turning to
me. "So where is the next stop, it's damn early."

I looked at my phone. Two forty-five a.m was pretty early
in a town where people partied until six.

"Not sure," I said, thinking about the money I'd just
earned that I didn't really want to spend.

From the stairway, Kitty walked over. She came over to me
and took the camera out of my hands.

"Stand beside him," she said, pointing to Zeus.

I did as commanded, as she cajoled the girl with him to
take a picture with us. Then she requested a picture with me,
and I took it with her, liking the scent of whatever perfume she
was wearing. Not done, she roamed with the camera some
more, taking uncomfortably close facial pictures of drunk guys
and girls and a man with devil horns packing boxes. Then she
walked over, handed me the camera without looking at me, and
drank the rest of Zeus' last beer.

Seth suddenly appeared on the dance floor, with his eyes
red and his hair slightly mussed.

"Hey guys, let's go somewhere man, it's still early," he said.

"That's what I told him," Zeus replied, turning to the girl
beside him. "I'll catch up with you later."

We all went outside. There was a group of stragglers trying their last hand at picking up the weakest links in varying groups of drunk women sitting on the sidewalk. Walking quickly past the spectacle, we all went into a cab. Seth wanted to go to Muse, but Kitty said she was tired of Muse and demanded we go to Womb. Seth nodded and spoke to the cab driver, telling him the address, only a few streets away.

Within moments we were inside, walking through security with no problems. After we reached upstairs, I could see there was a good reason why this was considered one of the top ten clubs on the planet. Impossible to hear from the outside, it was a feat of engineering that carefully cocooned the club's atmosphere of raging decadence. It was dark, and the flashing strobe lights and dancing lasers showed glimpses of the tightly packed audience, sweaty and amped up on god knows what, facing the DJ; screaming and dancing. I remembered the first time I'd come here, with a girl whose name I can't remember, that had kept smiling at me as she paid for us both to go in. Then in the depths of those arms and dancing bodies, had kissed me. We were lost in the womb of Womb that night, spinning around in a pool of arpeggios and reverbs, needing nothing but our tongues and free-roaming arms.

Many people had said hello to Kitty on the way in. She had smiled and waved, hugging a few people here and taking a quick picture there.

"Your friend seems like a big deal," Zeus said.

"She's not my friend, and I have no idea," I replied.

"Come on man, we are all friends tonight," Zeus said.

"I guess so."

Seth and Kitty went in separate directions as Zeus and I hit the bar. I felt pristinely tuned in to the roar of the rhythms, as if I was listening to God's hour of power on a mystical frequency modulation. Zeus seemed unaffected by the spectacle around him, as he stood straight with his drink in his hand, staring at the mob in front of him.

"There is no way I'm getting fucking laid in this place," he said. "Music is good though."

We had a few more drinks as the music rose in a crescendo that pulled me out of my buzz. My camera was safely checked into a locker at the front, and I had no problems dancing for a little while, jumping with the crowd, cheering and screaming. Tonight, I didn't care about the crow, circling the skies watching me, or the jaws of the city, ready to bite me in half with its teeth of broken buildings and cracked highways. I just felt beads of sweat on my face, the excited pats on the shoulders from some young men around me, and the blinding visuals of the lasers. I took a break and walked past a section where a dozen people lay in a state of exhaustion, unmoving as a muscular bouncer walked around them, tapping them firmly on the face.

"Let's go somewhere else," Zeus said.

I nodded, but not before a small hand held onto my wrist. It was Kitty, who had pulled her hair out of the pouf, revealing a long set of multi-coloured locks that fell below her shoulders.

"You guys leaving?" she asked.

"Yeah I think so," I replied.

"Let's take a picture here," she said.

I smiled with her as she took the picture with her phone. The shot was great. Our faces were clear, and luckily the club lights had illuminated the dense outline of the crowd behind us.

"Good picture," I said.

"Of course, I always take good pictures. But hey, some of my friends are at Vanity, we should go there," she said.

Zeus, standing nearby nodded.

"Vanity is a good bet," he said.

Zeus had spoken.

We walked outside. Kitty took Zeus' phone from his hand and dialed a number, walking away from us in long steps as she spoke into his phone. He shrugged, smiled and grabbed me playfully around the shoulder as we followed her. Further up the road, we hailed a cab and were on our way to Roppongi. It was past three in the morning, and I felt zero fatigue.

Kitty's friends had a private booth at Vanity, a place I'd never been to. I liked the décor, with its abysmally long couches in the middle, and the large windows like eyes to the city outside. It was filled with the noise and energy of people who never sleep. In the booth were three people. One was an older gentleman from England who spoke in quick bursts, as if he couldn't catch his breath properly. The second was a sultry, heavily tanned woman who said she was from Okinawa. She had the softest hands I'd ever felt when she shook mine. Kitty's energy mirrored the man's youthful attitude, and I wondered what their connection was; a man from England that spoke like a wheezing asthmatic and a tanned woman who might have been a professional surfer. The third person was a dark beauty with full lips singing Sinatra's *My Way* when we walked in. Zeus had taken up residence on one of the couches directly across from her, not speaking, just looking at her. As she sang, she looked at him and smiled, and so did he, as they communicated telepathically. The older man, whose name was Andrew looked at me and winked, then sang an early 2000's hip-hop song. I nearly died with laughter. They had a few bottles of premium liquor and chasers on the table, and invited us to drink. I barely took a sip of my drink before Kitty forced me to accompany her in singing 'Summer Nights' from the movie *Grease*. As I botched the song horribly, Zeus and the girl he'd been eyeing laughed at me. Kitty had transformed into someone else, singing the song in the style of Betty Boop, with perfect body language and key, gestures and lip pouting. The man from England and his lady friend laughed too, his laugh like his speaking; a series of barked, sucked in breaths. They seemed not to care that Zeus had immediately zeroed in on the girl that was with them, nor did it matter who I was, or how I knew Kitty. We sat and drank some more, singing songs until our voices were a little sore, and outside the club was almost empty.

Zeus lived nearby, and left walking arm in arm with the girl from the booth, while I hopped into a cab with Kitty and her two friends. The Englishman told the driver to drop them off first, then myself and Kitty afterwards. After being dropped off somewhere near Gaienmae, he handed the driver a ten thousand yen bill, waved goodnight, and left. Kitty held my arm.

"Tonight was so much fun! Do you like tea?"

"Actually, I do," I said.

"Good, I just got some fresh tea and I'd like you to try some."

Kitty lived in nearby Aoyama. Her building was modern and elaborately designed, with a dark grey finish, and tall, tinted picture windows along the breadth of each apartment. The lobby was impressive; with a mixture of wood paneling and tiles on the floor, accompanied by three sets of leather couches that faced small marble tables. Everything was clean and angular, lit by chandeliers and lights that wrapped around a series of ten columns facing clear windows twenty feet high.

She didn't say much going inside, as she did something on her phone and we walked into an elevator with black doors. The floors went by in a quiet hiss, her pretty face slightly yellowed by the elevator lights. There was something fragile about her, but not in the way Mari had felt in my arms the first time I hugged her. Kitty's fragility had less to do with her slim, exotic frame and more to do with her overbearing intrusiveness; as if one stone thrown at the right point could shatter it all. The elevator pinged loudly when we reached the fifteenth floor, and got out.

Her apartment made Zeus' dull by comparison. The floors were a dark marble, and the strong smell of luxury goods filled the air. Kitty shambled through its expanse and nonchalantly tossed her bag onto a couch, the kind of which I'd never seen. It was white, filled with a repeating pattern of stars in various colours. The couch looked as if it could easily seat ten people, but was small in the looming sprawl of the spacious abode. Facing it was a heavy, dark table, covered with fashion magazines and a few empty soda bottles.

Many works of art dotted the walls, ranging from the bizarre to the exquisite. One painting, about three feet by three feet in size, had an image of three men engaging each other sexually, smeared with splashes of red paint. Another image was of an African woman painted with skin so dark it had a blue tint, while her sensuous eyes stared hauntingly forward. There were Andy Warhol composites, intricate mosaics created with *kawaii* characters, and framed vintage t-shirts. A few of the art pieces were framed in cast iron, ornamented plastic, or spray painted pipes. Adjacent to a television that was bigger than the one at the Greenleaf house, was a wall covered with pictures. In it Kitty posed with people I assumed where high in the upper echelons of Japan, as well as dozens of foreign celebrities.

Whoever had helped with the interior decoration had a delicate touch. Despite the high number of works of art, vases and upscale furniture items in the apartment, nothing felt gaudy or out of place, except a rhinestone studded Doraemon bust that sat atop its own private column in a far corner. I took in all the details under a state of complete intrigue; I'd never been in such a lair. Kitty had been bustling about behind me, in the kitchen for the last several minutes.

"It's ready," she said.

She poured the light green tea into a large black mug that had 'EPIC' written in bold gold letters on its outer surface. She handed me a cup of a similar make with 'FAIL' written on it.

"This is Gyokuro. Very good tea," she said, taking a delicate sip.

I agreed, the flavour was unlike anything I'd had before. She went down a large hallway and through an open doorway. In her room, the first thing I noticed were a set of handbags hanging on hooks from the wall. These were the sort of hangers I'd only seen in a department store, but never someone's house. I could make out a few brands; Gucci and Kate Spade but I didn't know what many of the others were. The area was spacious, accommodating a freshly made sultan bed, a black standing mirror in the left corner, and a walk-in closet the size of my room. Everywhere there were boxes of shoes and accessories. The smell of chemical preservatives, expensive perfume and high-end leather made her room feel more store than sleeping place. She lay on the bed, without taking the sheet off.

"Ah, I'm so tired! I'm glad my bed is so soft. The first one like this I had, it was very firm, I gave my friend that mattress and got another one. Now I'm so happy!"

She laughed, and in the middle of the bags and clothes, I saw her as a little girl, swimming in pool of her own making. I was starting to feel tired now, and lay beside her on the bed. Kitty stood up and went toward her closet, looking through a drawer.

"I like the shape of your legs," she said. "They have character."

"My legs?" I asked.

"Yes, your legs are long, but they have character like my father's legs. He was a good runner, and he had legs like yours. People would never say he was the fastest or the best, but if you saw him running, you'd have to watch, because he not only had good form, but nice legs. I always thought it would be better to look good while running, instead of running really good."

I laughed at this.

"Don't laugh at me!" she said with a smile, " It is *not* weird that I like observing little convenient things about people."

"My legs are a convenience?"

"Of course, I can't possibly be the only woman to tell you that they liked your legs."

"Sadly, you are."

"Well screw them. Your legs are nice looking which is convenient, like my pubic hair."

"What?"

"Yes, my pubic hair. I know a lot of guys are into the fuzzy jungle thing, but I didn't like the idea of it growing every which way. But when I hit puberty and when it started to grow, it grew perfectly. Here I'll show you."

I gestured for her to stop, but she'd already pulled a clip at the back of her skirt. It fell, revealing her slim legs. She wore dark purple underwear, which she pulled down quickly. The thin fuzz of her pubic hair grew into a faint V above her barely visible labia. She pointed with her fingers.

"It doesn't grow outside these regions, so I never have to shave. I can wear sexy underwear, swimsuits and tiny shorts without any worry, and if I meet a forest lover he's good to go."

She turned back to the drawer, pulled out a small pair of shorts and came back into the bedroom.

"You make me feel comfortable," Kitty whispered into my ear.

I fell asleep with her holding me, as an automatic curtain slowly closed the bedroom window, hiding the city outside. When I woke up, I saw her sitting on the far side of the bed, typing on a silver laptop. She wore my shirt from the night before and also my socks, sipping from a steaming cup of tea on a tray beside her. The cup was labeled 'FAIL', the one I'd been drinking from hours before. As steam rose from it and vaporized into the air, I smiled.

Chapter 25

Spending time with Kitty was a look into a different state of being. She was quite busy, DJ-ing at product launches special events and clubs, while occasionally doing a photo shoot for a magazine or making an appearance in a music video. Many of her connections came from her work doing campaigns over the last several years, from large brands to promotions for emerging designers. She told me about her infrequent appearances on TV game shows, and her obsession with Winterfresh bubblegum. Apparently, her habit of taking people's things was well known within certain circles. Not only was she often caught with people's cameras and phones, but also occasionally scarves and other accessories left idly around.

"If they didn't want it, why would they leave it there?" she said to me one day, when we were having coffee at Starbucks.

"Kitty, has there ever been a time that someone reprimanded you for taking their stuff?"

"Maybe once or twice, but you were the only one that looked angry, silly boy. Did you think I was really going to steal your camera?"

"Well how would I know?"

"One look at me and everyone knows I'm harmless, plus I return everything once I find out who it belongs to."

I shrugged my shoulders.

"So what if you take something from someone, they don't know its lost or they don't know where to look. What then?"

"Well that's their fault," she replied with a laugh. "You shouldn't leave things lying around."

Her intrusiveness had grown on me. While I slowly worked on getting more gigs doing photography and shows around town, Kitty had become a relative presence in my life. She'd pop up at the house sometimes, often calling me on someone else's phone. This, made me realize, she had remarkable memory. When she came over she'd invade the kitchen, order people in the house around and steal several of my shirts. Once or twice she slept over, and used my toothbrush and towel, also taking a pair of my boxers back home to sleep in. We'd talk about her days and mine, and she'd tell me about the guy she was dating, some kind of asshole K-pop idol, and how she'd seen him on a TV show as a kid, and now he was this big thing and when he came to Japan they'd met at an event and they'd started dating. She was also on everyone's lists or had lists of her own, so going out with Kitty was partying at a much higher polynomial. Pretty much everything she did was mostly free, and high end. We hung out in booths more than once at Vanity, popped into exclusive events in Ginza and Kichioji and watched fireworks on the roof of a small luxury liner that held an annual electronic music party she played at. She'd occasionally receive giveaways from product launches by big brands, one or two of which she invited me to. Sometimes we'd just hang at her place and drink tea. I'd work on my blog while she watched TV or read, and it didn't matter how long I stayed. Sometimes she left when I was still there, not telling me when she'd be back, and I'd leave later on, after wrapping up my work. She was actually quite responsible in her own matters, despite her somewhat kleptomaniac proclivities. As I spent time with her and her friends, roaming around town in cab after cab, taking the occasional picture and chatting at length about simple things, I felt a growing sense of comfort. Her random phone calls in the evening asking me esoteric questions about pop culture, or checking to see if I'd tried some new flavour of tea gave me things to look forward to. The pleasant side effect of our friendship was tons of content for my blog, but I hadn't started seriously monetizing yet. I'd taken some of the product at the launches and done reviews of them, which got a lot of feedback, and occasionally I'd post pictures from the booth of an upscale club or an event somewhere, but the requests for photography didn't come often, and in the last six weeks I'd done two shows, which still wasn't enough to keep me solvent.

One night, she called me crying, and told me to take a cab to see her. I did so immediately, leaving the middle of a heated discussion with Mick and Dubz about international politics, chugging the beer I'd been drinking and went into a cab up the road, anxious to know what it was all about. She met me outside of her building, pulling me inside after tossing too much money into the taxi driver's hands. Her eyes were red and her face was stained with makeup. I could tell she had recently left an event, because she wore an elegant black frock with thin silver shoulder straps. We went upstairs and she told me the guy she'd been seeing had cheated on her with an up and coming model. I held her on the huge white couch and she cried into my chest, eventually moving her head up to kiss me on the neck. She was wild and insistent with her lips, but I eased her off slowly, hugging her and telling her it would be okay. We sat together for some time after that, watching TV and drinking from the same big cups. She'd changed into one of my pilfered shirts and my boxer shorts. I knew she wore them on purpose, but she wasn't all smiles just yet. Her face was still puffy and her large enticing eyes were slit with worry. But she brought a blanket from her room and wrapped it around both of us, as the huge TV played in the background and I felt her slim legs between mine, her head on my chest, her fingers playfully touching my neck.

If she was my emotional companion until I left, then so be it. Maybe she was the city's last gift to me, a tease before its jaws settled on my ribs and tore me asunder. Kitty had broken into the dark pockets of space I'd been used to traveling alone. The people I'd met thus far were mostly transients, excited by where they were but not always by who they were. Kitty was flawed of course, but seeing her running around in my t-shirt and underwear, or watching her tell off a bouncer twice her size outside a club did something to me. I didn't need to be drunk to enjoy time with her, I just needed time. All my actions to this point had been predicated on the idea I'd been leaving, a fuck it all reaction to impending inevitability. But now, with this girl in my arms I hadn't even slept with, I felt the most calm and clear.

The vast scope of her daily life was inversely proportional to the increasingly narrow vacuum of mine. Maybe the gravity Zeus spoke about and the gift Mari said I had were the same things. Forces pulling in specific directions, bound to eventually meet and interact, creating something unpredictable from the wells of chaotic uncertainty.

We went to a party soon after, which I heard was the kind that happened once in a blue moon, the sort that people try everything to get access to. It was at the residence of a very wealthy man, a man with a penthouse on the top floor of a famous building. On the way there, with Kitty in the cab beside me, I felt complete in this delicate step into the elite's belly. She wore a well-tailored white dress with matching white heels.

The man who threw the party wore a smoking jacket and a large diamond necklace, with dark purple glasses. He walked with a dog in his arm most of the time, laughing heartily with everyone in attendance. From him I received a hard slap on the back and a hello as I took one of the endless drinks being served to everyone. The room we were in had was massive, with bay windows on either side of a balcony exposing the city's bosom. The people were a mixture of those who belonged and those who had worked their way in; which created a mood layered with a nervous, wanting energy blended with the bourgeoisie mannerisms that make every action look like an afterthought. Kitty did the rounds, laughing and chatting. I received a hearty hello from Andrew, the man I'd met at Vanity, and the woman with the dark tan, who I learned was named Yumi. I saw one of the kid's with the spiked hair from the Kaoru Tetsuya show, and Kitty pointed out some *uber* celebrities to me, people with their faces currently on billboards in Shibuya, silently hawking products or films. I was lost in the intrigue of this atmosphere, as people drank Remy Martin like water, and spilled Johnny Walker Green on their arms during playful banter. Many people were dressed like the host, in elaborate, uncharitable outfits, running around like little Liberaces. I also glimpsed Mr. Oba, in a turquoise striped suit and hat, his unwrinkled skin glistening from the chandeliers' lights.

The energy grew in a cascade of talking and laughing, as a band played relatively up-tempo music on a platform near the room's entrance. I took a walk to find the bathroom, marveling at the high ceilings in the hallway, and artwork on the walls I was afraid to touch. I passed by the bathroom entrance and kept walking to the end of the hall. A large window showed me Tokyo in all its glory, with the tops of buildings flashing their red lights, the feathery snakes of distant traffic hidden within the dark folds of the night's obscuration. There was no one around, and the social hurricane in the large room down the hall was a faint trickle from where I stood. I took a light walk down another massive hallway, mostly dark and quiet. From a cracked door I could hear the unmistakable sounds of passion, and I peeked in, seeing the smooth buttocks of a man with his pants down to his knees, and the long, supple legs of a woman clamped around his waist. He thrust into her with a frantic insistence lacking closeness or comfort, but she seemed to be enjoying herself as she moaned and pulled his hair. She arched her head back, her eyes closed, and I could see who it was.

It was Melodie, in a silver dress that must have hung below her knees based on how far the cloth was pulled up to her hips. She and the man were leaning on a large bookcase, so lost in their motions they didn't know I was there. Melodie, my mysterious and nigh invisible roommate, up here of all places. For a few heartbeats, she looked directly at me, as the man declared he was close to orgasm, and she smiled. It was the first smile I had seen on her face, filled with contempt and equal parts pleasure. Then, she closed her eyes again, as the man kept moving his hips, faster and faster. I walked away before they were done, back past the window with the view, and into the bathroom.

When I returned to the party, I was surprised to see the new swell of individuals. Stunning women of various ethnicities were everywhere, clinging to the arms of short men with confident, casual swagger. The atmosphere was warm, broken only the intermittent flash of lights from phone cameras. I had a few cups of punch sitting in a crystal bowl, as Kitty came over to me and squeezed my hand. Eventually I saw Melodie again with the man from the room. Her body language was similar to that of the other women. She smiled and laughed with him, keeping close proximity as he chatted with men that looked like him; men in their forties in dark suits, used to a world of acquisition in one form or another. Kitty and I went to the balcony where about ten people were, and she slipped her arm in mine.

"Beautiful isn't it?" Kitty said, gesturing at the landscape.

Yes, I said. Like the view from the window by the bathroom, it was man-made perfection. The moment swept over me, cool and fresh. Kitty by my arm and Tokyo in front of me, mired in a lake of ambivalent outcome. I turned to her, wanting her lips on mine, ready to feel them press against me and remind me what was real. We stared into each other's eyes, easing forward till we were pressed closely together. Nothing was said, but the knowledge was there. My face got closer to hers, hers to mine, and then I froze, in both fear and amazement. Standing behind her, was my grandfather.

I stepped back roughly, hitting the arm of a man near me. His drink glass fell an shattered on the balcony floor.

"What is it?" Kitty said, her face pale with fright.

The most I could do was point a shaky hand at my grandfather, standing in a cool dark suit, with a glass in his hand.

"It-it-it's my grandfather," I said.

"What?" Kitty asked

"There!" I shouted.

He waved at me with a relaxed smile, and swallowed his drink quickly. Coming over he whispered into my ear: "Let's get out of here."

I found myself outside with no memory of leaving the party. I took a look up at the high building, imagining Kitty on the balcony in her pretty dress.

"Let's goooo buddy!" my grandfather said, his voice higher than normal. "Where can we get a drink around here?"

I didn't know where I was. The streets looked warped and oddly iridescent. He touched my shoulder with a *whack* and in seconds we were in a bar manned by a sole female bartender.

"Two shots of your best," he said to the woman in perfect Japanese.

Rubbing my fingers on my temple, I tried to slow my breathing as the woman put the shots down in front of us.

"Okay, we drinking? You not gonna pussy out on me are you grandson?"

I shook my head in a nervous no.

"All right! Bottoms up!"

The shot was ghastly, and I saw my grandfather fish some money out of his jacket, which was now lime green, and hand it to the woman. Then in a flash, we were back on the street, him now in a yellow suit, waving his arms excitedly. His features had changed. His complexion had become darker and his suit had a foul odour.

We walked up a street or two, when he stopped me, holding me with a hand on each shoulder.

"Let's take the train buddy, I've always wanted to take a train in Japan."

The steps leading into the station curved upwards animatedly as I took each step, and descended them carefully, while my grandfather slid down the center pole, landing expertly at the bottom. I could hear the train arriving, and hurriedly bought a three hundred yen ticket. We entered the train and I winced as he came near to me. It was the smell; acrid and rotting, filtering through his sleeves each time he raised his arms beside me. He chuckled in a fetid breath as he pointed to a few girls on the train.

"These Japanese girls sure are cute," he said with a laugh.

The only grounding sense for me was the cold support pole on my arm, and a few drops of moisture on my neck and face. Hoping someone would explain what was happening, I saw that the people sitting on the train weren't even real; just frozen cardboard cutouts. Next to me, a man stood with one arm holding the standing pole and in the other, a cell phone. He was a completely flat image, moving slightly, like a weathervane, with the train's vibrations. I reached out to touch the man, when the train came to a screeching stop.

"Shibuya," the train operator's voice hissed.

Immediately an image of the train came to mind, without a front car that propelled us forward. Instead, I saw a huge mollusc-like creature, dripping with slime and sharp teeth.

"Shibuya!" the voice screamed.

I felt bony fingers prick my arm. My grandfather's face was slowly filling with holes as he laughed, gesturing to the now open train doors. The cutouts of people frozen in time were now gone, and the train idled, completely empty. I stepped onto the walkway, hearing everything around me fall quiet, as the sound of my rubber soles squelched on the pavement. I walked slowly, wondering where everyone had gone, as my dead grandfather gleefully skipped in front of me.

"You hear that? Listen!" he shouted, as the suit he wore shook dreadfully on his rapidly decaying form. He pointed a smelly hand to the exit, and skin fell off his hand, landing on the ground with a *plop*.

The sound I was hearing came from the station's speakers, and I recognized the music. A sleepy classical song wept into my ears, *Claire De Lune*.

"Isn't this perfect?" my grandfather said, turning towards me.

Now his face was showing bone and bits of grey flesh hanging in meaty patches. A large flap with bits of hair at the top of his head wiggled like jelly with his excited movements.

"Remember I bought you that Disney movie and you'd heard this song? You'd be at my house and run to me because you were afraid of the forest. Remember?"

As we exited the train station, I did remember. The dark blues and blacks of that fantastical forest, with its lone pink bird, roaming in complete isolation, with only music and a lake as its companion. The fear I'd had was imagining myself forever in that place, walking through endless days of itchy vines and pungent marshes lit under the permanence of a bloody red sun in the sky.

"Bet you can't remember the name of the composer, bet cha, bet cha, I bet cha!" my grandfather shouted.

I had no immediate answer for him, because I was lost in the image before me. The cardboard cutouts of people I'd seen on the train had become a pervasive phenomenon. A policeman stood by the officer's box with his hands on his waist, invisible from a certain angle. All the people, from those holding hands, smoking, laughing idly or frowning were all still and unmoving. It was hundreds of people as two-dimensional images moving slightly on invisible axes, like an ajar door rocking on a windy day. The stillness of it all accentuated the frantic motions of my grandfather.

"Hey! I'm talking to you!" he shouted, knocking over one of cutouts.

It was a young man in hip clothing. When the cutout hit the ground, it shattered into hundreds of pieces.

"No!" I said, reaching forward.

The pieces of the young man were rubbery and sharp, and I frantically tried to put him back together, when the stench of my grandfather became too close for comfort.

"Tough luck for him, yeah? So who was the composer kid? Hint, it rhymes with pussy."

He was crouched beside me like a school kid, with his hands on his knees and his shoulders arched high, the big flap of skin from his head hanging by threads of flesh near his neck.

"Debussy," I replied without feeling any sense of humour.

I held a fragment of the young man's eye in my hand.

"Yes, yes! I'm glad you learned something from that gift I gave you!"

He laughed in a screech of coughs, which resulted in a spray of rotting matter from his mouth. As I watched, he ran around, dropping people at random to the ground, watching them shatter while hooting maniacally. The palms of my hands were wet and I could feel my shirt clinging to the sweat on my back. I turned away from him, and ran up the street. More objects had this two dimensional look now; including a taxi parked near a designated smoking area, and a bus, with a person's foot visibly sticking out the door. The sky had become a deep purple, and the buildings swayed dangerously, moving in curves like a belly dancer's stomach. I could hear the song again, louder, coming from somewhere behind me. I squeezed my hands and slapped my face to see if it was all real. All I felt was the familiar texture of the hair on my forearms, and the sting of my wet palm on my cheek.

Stumbling into a public restroom I turned on the tap water, thankful that it wasn't frozen as well. I splashed the water hurriedly onto my face, getting more of it on my neck and shirt than I intended to. In the mirror, I saw myself, and like my grandfather, there were growing holes in my cheek and my nose was falling off.

A rolling whimper escaped my lips.

Outside, I ran through different streets, trying to get home. The silhouettes of the people weren't completely frozen now. Some of them vibrated slightly when I came nearby, and several would look at me without turning their heads. They were all curious living posters with moving eyes. Now the skin on my hands was also peeling, and I found myself in a park. It was near an elementary school, and in the dim atmosphere I saw an aging jungle gym and small children's swings. I sat on a nearby bench, choked with fear. I dared to touch my face, and felt my finger go directly through the flesh, and touch bone. With another *plop*, I heard some of my body matter fall on the metal rungs of the bench I was sitting on. All the while, that bloody song was in the air, somewhere, soaring over the psychedelic clouds in the sky, bouncing off the movements of the buildings still squirming like snakes. Shutting my eyes tightly didn't help. Whether I closed them or not, I could still see everything around me.

Down the road, under a lamp, I saw something. It was very tall, dressed in a trench coat and an old fedora, it's features lost in the shadow cast by the sharp contrast of the streetlight. I stood up and shuffled forward, the skin and flesh of my feet squishing audibly against the insoles of my shoes. Whatever the thing was, it was ten feet tall, and as wide as two men. I saw its arms, large and black, without fingers I could clearly discern. But they hung by its side as the fedora covered its face. It looked up, and I saw that it was the crow. Enormous and looming over me, it looked at me with lifeless black eyes.

We both stood there, under the sharp light of the street-lamp, as the world around us spun faster than normal, with the last trickles of *Claire De Lune* playing in the distance. Then it opened its beak and I could hear it scream, a scream that didn't come from its throat, but everywhere around me. The windows of all the buildings shattered and they writhed aggressively, as if hurt. Everywhere the scream echoed in a rolling moan. I stepped back as the crow, in its ridiculous trench coat outfit, kept opening its mouth wider, increasing the space between its lower mandible and upper beak. Its throat pulsed and it started to jerk, the wide bird shoulders moving frantically. The mouth was now open impossibly wide, at nearly one hundred and eighty degrees. It gurgled a sound like punching meat. Then, a hand pushed out of its throat, and it gurgled more violently, heaving and cawing. I took one last look at its eye before the head split open completely, bursting in a rain of blood and bone. The massive body fell backwards to the ground, and the noise in the sky stopped. The buildings stopped squirming and I could see the night sky again. The body was still jerking, and I could hear the frantic breaths of whatever was inside trying to get out. Things got quiet, and when the creature that came from inside the crow stood up, I could see the blood covered body of a young man. He turned around, and I felt ice in my veins. It was me, naked and covered in the crow's blood, a dark smile on my face. A black pair of wings burst from my back and I cawed like the crow, loud and towards the sky, and shooting up in the air with blinding speed. The force of this exit created a gust of wind that pushed me to the ground and I felt myself shatter like the frozen people I'd seen before. As the pieces of me spread out on the sidewalk, the last thing I saw was the dark silhouette of my crow self, flying in the sky, until everything became dark, and I couldn't see anymore.

Chapter 26

A man sweeping in front of a store was the first thing I saw. My face burned on one side from the hot ground. I was laying face forward. The man muttered to himself as he performed a ritual I'd seen in front of many stores. He threw cups of water on the sidewalk in front of the store, then began sweeping the liquid away in rapid, even strokes. Only a few feet away from this, I could understand his dismay as I lay there in my nice clothes looking like another casualty of the night. A brief pang of fear coursed through me as I remembered the night before, and I touched my hand. The skin gave slightly, but didn't fall off, and I breathed a sigh of relief. My mouth was uncomfortably dry and I could feel my tongue sticking to the roof of my mouth. I tried licking my chapped lips to no avail. Easing myself up off the ground, I could smell the strong odour of dry sweat through my clothes, and there was a mysterious four-inch cut along my left arm. Blinking in the midday sun and rubbing my sore cheek, I got a bottle of water from a vending machine and took a sip. The man was still sweeping with gusto, looking quite happy that I had moved away from his storefront. I looked at the signs around me, unfamiliar with the streets. There were some memories from the night before; flashes of dark images and lost time. Vaguely I thought of Shibuya, and the bizarre menagerie of frozen people I'd seen. Shibuya, yes, I was probably somewhere near there. I drank some more water and politely asked the man where I was. He grunted and kept sweeping, ignoring my enquiry.

I walked through a few more of these back streets, carbon copies of the one I'd left, little stores that sold stationery, discount clothing and snacks. My Jacket felt hot, and I took it off and slung it over my shoulder. Soon, I saw a metro sign for Gotanda Station.

Gotanda? How did I end up out here?

Fortunately I still had my wallet and keys in my pants pocket. I went to the station and boarded the train, half-expecting the slithery voice from last night to chant the names of the stations from a throat caked with phlegm. The voice spoke in the standard nasal intonations of whoever the train conductor was. But I pinched my skin again, my eyes stretched and wide open. The world had been warped. I had *seen* people shatter on the ground.

Things felt uncomfortably normal. People on the train stared forward nonchalantly, with blinking unfrozen faces devoid of concern. The trained hemmed and hawed with its regular yawn, rumbling on the tracks at a normal level of volume. As we went over a small overpass, the morning sky had no ulterior motive, flat and bright with a scattered set of clouds as its entourage.

This was the world I'd always known, a world that I took steps in where the ground was solid and I could feel the burn of food that was too hot on my tongue, the sensation of a woman's soft lips on my face, and the stink of a long bathroom session. It was here I could feel my chest moving under my shirt; hear the click of my teeth against each other if I was cold. Here, I could feel the muscles in my lips form into a smile when I enjoyed a familiar song or reveled in the beauty of an attractive night sky. Here I could feel the soft fabric of my jacket against my fingers, and the delicate pinch of my pants on my calves and the dry part of my ankles where my socks rubbed against the insides of my shoes. Then I remembered the sensation of my skin falling off, saw the holes in my face, and felt frightened again.

An attractive girl a few seats down from me in a short skirt with headphones rocked her head to whatever she was listening to. I stared at her for far too long, wondering if she was a construct, wondering if everyone was a construct. *Madness*, I thought to myself, it must be madness. The world couldn't be cracking. Is this where the dissolution of hope and despair met? In a colourful world of dark dreams and bloody monsters? A feeling rose from the depths of my consciousness, a dark thing, a wave resembling a hammer, ready to destroy the paradigms of my reality.

I had to talk to Carmen, I didn't care what it cost. When I came off the train in Harajuku, my vision was a deluge of people. I didn't trust what I was seeing in front of me; the plainly dressed man waiting idly on the sidewalk, the well-dressed woman casually waiting in a taxi, or the cute girls giggling near a vending machine. Their normalcy told me that everything could start rippling again, with the sky dark and buildings swerving overhead. Reality was clearer and sharper, with the people around me vomited in a spewing stream from buses, trains and cars. They were a cloudburst of skin and hair, rubber shoes and nylon bags, piquant body wash and spicy cologne. The chorused mesh of their voices projected outwards into the open air, lips clapping like fingertips at a poetry reading; the ruffle of their clothes a thousand men flapping carpets, their footfalls a low thunder like a Bison's stampede. These were people, yes, but they couldn't be people. They couldn't be normal. I resisted the urge to touch a man near to me, to feel the welcoming density of his shirt, and the slight warmth his skin would give to my palm through the fabric. But I couldn't, I couldn't handle seeing the man fall to pieces, stop moving or stare at me with those haunted eyes. All of them, they could all do this; freeze in step and leave me back in that world of the night before. I took a deep breath, refusing to acknowledge whatever was happening. The dark wave still sat within me, slowly rising.

I went to Omotesando, walking quickly through the clean streets, noticing the dance of light on the huge windows of the luxury stores, and the legion of women walking with their expensive purses clutched tightly to their bodies, mannequins with purpose.

I'm not crazy.

I jogged up the road and through a few of the back streets until I came to the familiar building of Carmen's office. Up the steps I went in quick jumps and to the door. It was locked, and I pounded it with my fists. It was locked, and I tried to open it, shaking the handle until my wrist hurt.

"Please! Open up!" I shouted, but no one came.

I turned around, leaned on the door and slid to the ground. The air was pregnant with the absence of people. *Dammit,* I thought. Today was Saturday. The office wouldn't be open. My mouth was dry again, and I felt my tongue starving. Then terror filled me. A woman standing on the sidewalk looked up at me, unmoving. There was no breeze to blow her dress, and no cars driving past as an object for reference. It was just her staring at me, for an eternity. I slid back and moaned, thinking it was happening to me again, that the world would shift into its grisly doppelganger, but then she looked away, moved forward, and continued walking down the street.

I panicked, with tight pains in my chest and my breaths escaping in a fluctuating rush. I went back to the train station and had another bottle of water. I felt very, very tired. On the way back home, I made sure to avoid eye contact with whomever was around me, should they turn into statues. I didn't want to return to that place of monsters and the massive crow, that place where I flew through the air, naked and covered in blood. Something inside my mind stretched. I could hear the *kek kek kek* of something buckling to pressure, a clay pot slowly being covered with hairline fractures. This couldn't be it; me falling apart as a result of another thing I couldn't touch. My mind.

Nothing mattered except solid ground. Nothing mattered except me. I had to hold on to that. Too many things had transpired in this city. Connected things, things of *intention*. Things with meaning should be the bulwark of the psyche, boosting and fortifying. My body shook internally as I waged this battle. I continuously touched my hands and my face, ensuring that nothing would shift or change. The tough plastic of the train seat's exterior felt good on my hands, and the stink of a salary man's smoky jacket was ambrosia. Yes, familiarity was what I needed, the grounding memories.

Walking back to the house, I stared down the road at the convenience stores and the supermarket. I walked through each of them once, running a finger along the breadth of a shelf filled with condiments, pulling out and replacing cans of cold beer in the fridge, and holding ice cream containers, relishing the icy burn in my palm. I stood in front of my favourite drink, the Chu-Hi. My hand trembled as I reached for it, wavering with indecision. The welcoming hiss of the can and the punch it would usually give to my tongue might not bring me back this time. My hand returned to its pocket, and I left the store. I walked slowly along the streets, my body dry of energy. I touched my hands once more, feeling the hairs along my forearms, clenching and opening my fists while rubbing the insides of my palms. For now, I was still whole.

The house was stunningly vacant. I went to my room, in a fog. I sat in a corner, staring at the bed. Sleep was frightfully close. When I awoke, where would I be? I fought my eyelids and their slow push to make things dark. My knees were up to my chin now, with my arms around my shins, as I rocked in the little space. I was no longer in Tokyo. I had gone back to my sleepy town, searching through my memory archives for everything that had given me resolve before, everything that had kept me together. I held on to the memories of myself standing on the school roof, waking up in the early mornings and using tricks to keep my mind occupied. I clutched the thoughts steadfastly, as the dark wave inside me became a tide, eating away the shoreline of my consciousness. Reason was also eroding.

My memories morphed into a battalion of men on this virtual beach, working hard and fast to build a wall to prevent the dark water from coming in. They heaved in unison, faces coated in a shiny slick of sweat as they worked, all the while the black mass swelled. I gritted my teeth, searching further and deeper inside myself for clearer reasons, stronger reasons to keep me from being swallowed. I saw Yumi's face and my Grandfather's face in these stream of images and all the faces of those who had come and gone, every person a sturdy new block in the hands of the men raising the wall. Every joke, laugh and smile fell from the air in solid form, slapped quickly onto the thin cement of my willpower. The tide had reached, and it surged and strained against the foundations of my being, blasting at the stone with the roar that only water can make. It tried again, rearing backwards and coming forward, as the men barked orders amongst themselves and fortified it more. The wall became thicker and stronger, higher and taller, till the dark water lost its resolve, and retreated backwards into the distance. Away it went, until the dark sea was a motionless mirror. My strength was gone. I lay down slowly, falling into sleep's welcoming bosom.

I woke to the sound of knocking on my door. It was Mick.

"Hey man, you need to check this out," he said.

I walked into the entertainment room, where Mick, Dubz and a few other people were watching the television screen. The image of a tall building somewhere in Tokyo was constantly being shown, intercut with clips of people hurriedly leaving a ground floor lobby, many of them chased by camera people. I recognized the location; it was the residence of the wealthy socialite whose party I had recently attended. A reporter with a face of steel was speaking.

"Reports are coming in that someone put some kind of drug in the drinks at the—"

I slumped into the chair, amazed at the display. There were images of people running wildly around the street, a man whimpering to himself on the ground and a lady in a couture dress screaming at nothing.

"Some of Tokyo's most prestigious celebrities were taken to local hospital to receive—"

There were no words in me. Just an image of myself a brief spell of time before, in the corner of my room, almost broken. Almost a shattered thing.

"At this time there are no strong suspects believed to have caused the chaos that—"

For a brief second, I saw Kitty on screen, walking quickly with a set of people out of the lobby. Still dressed in the clothes from the party, I sat on the couch and watched the images over and over.

"Tokyo is so crazy," Mick said to himself.

It was drugs, I said to myself.

A man with a very rigid appearance was on screen now, talking to one of the reporters in the TV studio. He wore a plain, functional suit. The reporter introduced him as a chemical expert.

"Whatever was used had to be a very potent hallucinogen, possibly one called—"

This revelation barely gave me relief. No one could tell me battle I had waged internally wasn't real, that I hadn't stared in the face of my demons. I had gone far into the depths of myself and came back from the black.

"What kind of things do people see from such a drug?" the reporter asked.

"You cannot imagine," the stiff man replied. "The places the mind can take you—"

I went back to my room thinking about Kitty. My phone's battery had died sometime during the previous night and I hadn't charged it since my return. After plugging it in, I saw a dozen missed calls, all from Kitty's number.

I called her immediately.

"Kitty, are you all right?" I asked.

"Yes. Oh my, it was all so frightening," she replied.

"Let's meet."

It was late evening when we met at the nearby National Park. I'd been here only once before, and never while I was a resident of the city. The rolling stretch of green grass and the carefully manicured trees were pleasant to the eye. Kitty soon arrived, dressed casually in black jeans and a dark blue top. When she hugged me, her touch and her smell was the world. She held me for a long time, before looking up into my eyes.

"I didn't know what happened last night," she said. "At first, I had no idea what you were talking about when you said you saw your grandfather, and then you just left. I got so angry, but then a few people in the party started screaming or doing weird things, and I could see that something was very wrong."

"Why would someone do that at a party like that?"

"I don't know," Kitty said, looking at the ground. "This is one of the biggest scandals to happen in the city ever."

"And to think we were both there," I said, rubbing her hand softly.

We sat on a bench nearby, not talking for some time, staring at the people in the park, like dots in the distance on its verdant carpet. I put my hands in my lap and I told her I was leaving Tokyo soon.

"What do you mean you are leaving?"

Her voice was a delicate mixture of tension and surprise. I told her everything, about my issues in Shizuoka, the panic attack at the head office, my therapy sessions and then my subsequent foray into modeling and photography. I explained my situation at the hospital and its toll on me, and finally my exit strategy, which I was only a few days away from implementing. She listened to everything I said, without replying until I had finished.

"My family has money," she said. "I can help you."

"I can't take your money," I replied.

"Why? Don't you want to stay here?"

"I do."

"Maybe this is why you met me, so we could work something out. You ever thought about that?"

"Not in that way, no. Remember I didn't like you so much the first time I met you."

"I hated you the first time I met you," she said with a smile.

"There we go!"

We laughed and settled into a quiet moment.

"I'm hungry, I haven't eaten since yesterday."

"Let's get something to eat then," Kitty said, slipping her arm in mine, leaning her head on my shoulder.

I wanted to cave. The way she leaned on me felt so familiar, even though I'd only known her for a few weeks. We ate dinner at a curry restaurant in Shinjuku. As we ate and spoke, I saw that her eyes had that slit, anxious look. I thought of her on the couch the night I'd gone over to her place when she was crying. I had wanted to kiss her and submit to her advances, but I hadn't. That night I'd stepped back into the margins, and now Kitty was across from me at a table, and I could see the gulf growing, the same gulf that had kept Yumi at bay, and this new one, of my creation.

We left the restaurant going our separate ways. She wanted me to come over, but I didn't feel up to it. I was seeing her in a new light, more powerful than any I'd contemplated in recent history, and I didn't want that hanging over my head days before planning to leave. But I had no choice, because she was already in there, stealing parts of my brain and using them without my permission. I laughed at this thought on the train back home, watching the blurred flash of opposite trains thundering by. In total, I just had a little over two hundred thousand yen left, and it was time to make a serious decision. I opened my laptop and started looking for flights to Kingston. Many of the flights were around the price I had thought, between one hundred and twenty thousand up to two hundred thousand yen. I picked a flight and left the computer on, with the ticket purchase window still open. I took a walk up the road and to the convenience store, ready to drink a few Chu-His and escape things, but at the entrance I paused. There shouldn't be a need for me to drink. There were people I could call and reach out to. I could escape in hilarious conversations with Dubz and Mick, or rally up a few people and go out on the town. But then I thought of Kitty and my true mental comfort. Her atop me, small and soft, listening to my heart.

I bought the drinks and returned home, drinking them slowly as I looked at the prices listed on the computer screen. Eventually the drinks had their desired effect, and I lied down. My phone rang and I answered it without opening my eyes. It was Kitty.

"I think I have an opportunity for you," she said.

* * * *

The building stood high in front of me, glaring in its significance of design and form, the sun's rays riding across its lambent plains of exquisite windows. Inside was possible resolution or nothing at all. Kitty had called many of her contacts with a determinate purpose, which lead to this meeting. A large clothing company would be casting for a major campaign soon. It would be lucrative, because of its demand for models to be in both photo shoots and television commercials. The office was on the thirtieth floor. I rose into the sky, looking down on everything around me, wondering if those I'd be meeting today would be like the building, grandiose in their worldview, unencumbered by my forgettable ennui. I waited in a neat lobby, with my portfolio in hand. In it, I had images that gave me depth, images of not just myself but my brand. It was complete summary of all I was in an envelope less than an inch thick. Right there, I began channeling all the power within me. If I had to walk for these people, I would strut like the gods coasting on clouds, my eyes would shoot out iridescent beams of significance from the depths of my soul. Should I be asked to smile, it would be a smile to save the world. The receptionist called my name, and I walked inside.

* * * *

I'd paid my rent.

This meant I was now hanging on a rung of uncertainty, wavering on a tightrope of chance. No more was there the option of an escape from the city by air. I'd told Kitty my choice, and she smiled and hugged me when I met up with her a day afterward. The outcome of the casting wouldn't be decided for now, but she wanted to celebrate the possibility of my success by going out. We had a light tasty dinner and red wine, in the calm climate of a midtown restaurant. Whatever our words were didn't matter, because it was an occasion for the forgetting of things. After we had the food, she took me a to a karaoke bar with a skylight, in a glittery building in Shinjuku. She stood in the booth with her head leaning slightly to the left, swaying as she sang along with the words on the screen. The way the light danced on her face was alluring; it rippled in little blue multi-coloured squiggles, looking nothing like what was on screen. Her voice filled the chamber with its richness, the notes escaping her throat passionately. She turned and looked at me now, her lustrous eyes filled with messages about me, and only for me. I saw myself wading deeply into the rivers of her beauty and sprinting through the meadows of her mind, skipping and leaping over arroyos and little brooks, the sky aglow with her promise. The song wasn't playing anymore just for us; she was making a statement as she pointed her finger in my direction then stood between my legs and rubbed my shoulder with her free hand. There was comfort here, tickling the spaces between my fingers and blowing softly on the back of my neck. Outside, beyond the confines of our little booth was the city: proud, resplendent and as always, watching and waiting. With her, I saw more to the reality of red sky mornings and dark nights of warm and passionate encounters. There were the streets that had been a veritable maze, the unending blast of lights and sounds to the senses; the screeching brakes at the train tracks, hoarse-voiced workers with body signs screaming *irasshaimase*, the black cabs stuffed with men heavy with the scent of smoke and those ubiquitous malls, teetering on the edge of reality chock full of girls texting and taking selfies, burning money on luxury goods to impress guys with superbly coiffed salon hair. This wasn't just a stream of data hitting me, it was perspective and form; edges I hadn't seen before were now in front of me. If I looked west I knew what lay there or didn't. The boroughs and the possible bars, the seedy spots and the quiet streets, the empty parks or the crowded neighbourhood theatres; the gay clubs and the sex shops, and the after work pileups where for an entire stretch of a block men in matching suits ate Ramen and chatted to each other like penguins in concert. Looking at Kitty, this all fused together into the idea of something that could last more than just one song. The delicate contours of her body mirrored the contours of everything around me. As I got lost in the streets and deep cans of Chu-Hi, I could get lost in her taste and smell; those fierce eyes and her beauty, cast on me like the penumbra the early morning made on the city's highest buildings. Those lips that still sang in clear high notes, lips that felt like the softness of a dream itself, if a dream could imagine softness, falling on my mind like gossamer. Tokyo was a final word because now it was real, and she was real, her thighs soft against mine, the microphone on the ground now, her atop me with the screen flickering *New Song?* Her lips are pressed against my neck, and I sigh with release and relief, like a man who's found something interesting and exotic. Her tongue roams and so does mine, as we will no doubt roam through the streets to our next destination, or end up naked and adrift between this world and the ethereal one we create in a snort to the senses of erotic madness. Yes, she was real, and everything was real, powerful and pulsing like I wanted her. I wanted it all, to stay, to exist, to survive. I pulled her to me and kissed her warmly and deeply, acknowledging this contract, with our tongues signing on the dotted line. Then, we stumbled outside the building and kissed again, with the light warmth of the early morning on our faces, and the city behind us, winding and vacuous, filled with stark emptiness that streets have when everyone isn't up yet.

終わり

ABOUT THE AUTHOR

Marcus Bird was born in Jamaica and received his degree in Film Production from Howard University in Washington D.C. He has written for Comedy Central in New York, the Jamaica Observer, several online publications and had two short stories "Gaijin Girl" and "Sleep" published in the 2010 and 2012 editions of Japanese literary journal Yomimono. His first novel, "Sex, Drugs and Jerk Chicken" was published in early 2013. He loves traveling, dabbling in languages and having great conversations.

Questions for the author? E-mail him at:
marcusbird@gmail.com
Also, you can follow him on twitter:
www.twitter.com/marcusbird
For updates, his blog and other information, please visit:
www.marcuskbird.com

ALSO BY **MARCUS BIRD**

SEX, DRUGS and JERK CHICKEN

Three completely different young men find themselves in the sex-fueled, emotionally vacant backdrop of nighttime Washington D.C, as they search for meaning in a series of events that force them to deal with loss, love and question it all. Welcome to the social underbelly of Washington D.C, where we see shady parties in dark row houses with illicit sex happening in tiny rooms, statuesque model types snorting lines on marble side tables in million-dollar Georgetown condos and the occasional hookup in a grimy bathroom in one of many seedy bars on the Adams Morgan strip. Three young men—all coincidentally from Jamaica—find themselves together again in DC under different circumstances. Tony Edwards is dashingly handsome night owl who finds that his ability to attract women—and the subsequent circumstances that follow in a place like DC—expose him to more than just naked bodies and the occasional threesome. Winston is a hopeless romantic who finds his life spinning out of control after the re-emergence of an old girlfriend on the social scene. Bishop, an artist, tries to rationalize the death of someone close to him through a smattering of opiates, girls and his art. Sex, Drugs and Jerk Chicken takes us headfirst into a view of a version of American culture we don't always see but have probably heard about; sex with strangers, heiresses who like boy toys, insecurity eclipsed by alcohol, all through the lens of life in a big city.

Available on Amazon